A Litter of Bones

Also by JD Kirk

DCI Logan Crime Thrillers

JD KIRK

A LITTER OF BONES

© CANELO CRIME

First published in the United Kingdom in 2019 by Zertex Crime

This edition published in the United Kingdom in 2024 by

Canelo
Unit 9, 5th Floor
Cargo Works, 1-2 Hatfields
London SE1 9PG
United Kingdom

A CIP catalogue record for this book is available from the British Library.

Paperback ISBN 978 1 80436 814 5

Cover design by Tom Sanderson

Cover images © Shutterstock

Look for more great books at www.canelo.co

Printed and bound in Great Britain by Clays Ltd, Elcograf S.p.A.

I

MIX
Paper | Supporting
responsible forestry
FSC® C018072
www.fsc.org

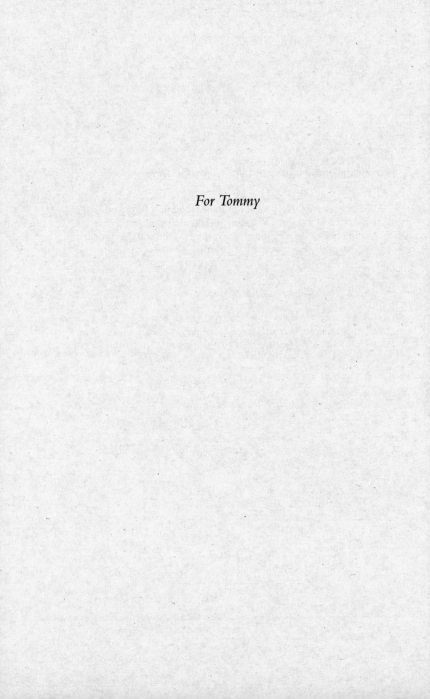

For Tommy

Chapter 1

The total collapse of Duncan Reid's life began with a gate in the arse-end of nowhere.

There was a trick to opening this particular gate, Duncan knew. The arm of the metal slider had been buckled for years, and if you tried hauling it in the direction the bend suggested it should go, you were doomed to failure. The trick was to twist and jiggle, creaking the slider loose of its mooring, allowing the whole thing to eventually swing free.

Or, if you were a seven-year-old with more energy than sense, you could clamber up the metal spars, jump down, and stand triumphantly on the other side waiting for your dad to get a move on.

'I win,' cheered Connor. He broke into a little dance. *The Floss*, he called it. All the rage, apparently.

Down at Duncan's feet, their Golden Retriever wriggled impatiently, the entirety of her copper-coloured backend wagging, her front feet pawing at the ground with barely contained excitement.

'All right, Meg. Give us a minute,' Duncan told the animal.

The slider clunked free. The gate had barely swung six inches towards him when Meg nosed it open and squeezed through. Connor dodged aside as the dog went haring past him. She bulleted ahead, running for no other reason than the sheer unbridled joy of being out of the car and off the lead.

'Someone's in a hurry,' Duncan remarked.

They watched as she detoured off into the trees that lined the track on the right, quickly vanishing from sight beneath the moss-covered trunks.

'Meg!' Connor called after her. 'Come back.'

'She'll be fine,' Duncan said. He pulled the gate closed behind them, wiggling the slider just enough to jam it shut, but not so far that he'd have to go through the whole process again when they left. 'She's been exploring round here since before you were born.'

Connor didn't look convinced but fell into step beside his dad as they set off along the track.

Living up here, they were spoiled for choice when it came to dog-walking routes. Granted, it was pretty much the only thing they were spoiled for choice for, but it was something. But, of all the routes available to them, this one stood out as a favourite.

The only downside was getting to it. The drive along the main Fort William to Spean Bridge road could be a nightmare in the summer. At this time of year, though, before the campervans piloted by overly cautious tourists had started to clog everything up, it flew by.

After that, it was just a turn up the Leanachan Forest road, a mile or so along a single-track lane with the fingers crossed that no-one was coming the other way, and then the usual wrestling match with the gate.

And then... bliss. Miles of forestry track, cracking views, and rarely another living soul in sight. In all the years that Duncan had been making the same walk, he'd met maybe twenty walkers, half a dozen cyclists, and one guy on stilts.

That one had caught him off guard and had sent Meg into a frenzy of panicked barking. It was a sponsored hike for charity, it turned out. Cancer, or something. Duncan had been too busy trying to get a hold of the dog and quieten her down to really pay too much attention.

Once he'd got her by the collar, he'd chucked a couple of quid into the collection tin and kept hold of Meg until the guy had teetered off around the corner, out of sight.

Today was looking like it'd be free of interruptions, and Duncan felt physically lighter as he let himself relax. Meg was a good dog, for the most part, but didn't handle strangers well, so the lack of life signs always came as a relief.

Sure, someone might come around one of the bends further down the track and set her off, but that was a problem for later. For now, the coast was clear.

Far off on the left, across a graveyard of tree stumps, the A82 curved ahead to the Commando Memorial, and onwards to Inverness. An irregular stream of traffic meandered up it, paintwork glinting in the uncharacteristically bright April sunshine.

At this distance, the traffic was whisper quiet. The only sounds to be heard were the chirping of the birds, and the faint crunch of the stony ground beneath Duncan's boots.

Up ahead, Meg exploded from within a crop of trees, ploughed through a mud puddle that painted her brown from halfway down her legs, then stopped in the middle of the path. She watched them for a while, tongue hanging out and chest heaving as she checked that they were still headed in the same direction.

When she was sure they weren't about to turn around and head for the car, she returned to the trees, getting back to whatever business she'd left unattended in there.

'See, told you she'd be fine,' Duncan said, giving his son a playful nudge. 'Filthy, I'll give you, but fine.'

'Did you see how much mud is on her?'

'I did.'

'She's *covered*!'

'She is. And guess who's cleaning her up when we get home,' Duncan said.

Connor grinned up at him. 'You!'

'Me? No way! You!' Duncan said.

'Nuh-uh!'

'Yuh-huh! I'll give you a scrubbing brush and a bucket,' Duncan said. He gave a little gasp as an idea hit him. 'You can do the car when you're at it. Two birds with one stone.'

Connor shook his head emphatically.

'Fine. You can hold her while I hose her down.'

Connor had no real objection to that, but it had become a game now, and so he continued to resist.

'Nope!'

Duncan stroked his chin, his finger and thumb rasping against his stubble. 'OK, she can hold you, and I'll hose *you* down.' He made a sound like skooshing water, and mimed blasting the boy with it. 'How about that?'

Connor giggled. 'I had a bath this morning.'

'You did? God, is it April already?' Duncan teased.

Connor didn't quite get the dig but giggled again, regardless.

They walked on for several minutes, rounding the gentle curve of the track, passing the little quarry on the left-hand side, where two diggers had sat mostly motionless for the past year or so. Rarely, when Duncan came up this way, they'd have moved a few feet, or the angle of the buckets would have shifted. He'd never seen any sign of anyone sat behind the controls, though, much less doing any actual digging.

It had been a while since Connor had said anything, and although Duncan was enjoying the peace and quiet, it wasn't normal. Friday was swimming day at school, and the boy would normally be full of stories about who was proving to be the best at backstroke, and which of his classmates had come closest to drowning.

Today, though, he'd barely spoken a word that Duncan hadn't teased out of him first.

'You all right, Con?'

'Yeah, fine,' Connor said, not looking up. He had found a stick that was almost the height of himself, and was walking with it like a wizard with a staff.

'If Meg sees you with that, she'll be away with it,' Duncan warned.

Connor nodded, but said nothing.

'How was swimming?'

'Good.'

'Everyone survive?'

Connor nodded. 'Yep.'

They continued on in silence for a while longer. A bird of prey circled in the air above them. A buzzard, Duncan guessed, although he had no idea. It might've been an eagle. It could've been a big pigeon. He'd lived his life in the Highlands, but the particulars of its wildlife were lost on him.

Similarly, the trees lining the tracks beside them. He had no idea what those were, either. Pine? Maybe. Beech? Very possibly. Oak? He didn't think so, but he had no idea what he was basing that on. They were trees. That was about as specific as he could get.

'Dad?' Connor said, after a few more steps. His eyes were still fixed on the ground, his voice quiet. 'You know Ed?'

Duncan ran through his mental checklist of the kids in Connor's class. He couldn't place an Ed.

'Which one is he? The one with the orange mum?'

Connor glanced up at him, brow furrowed in confusion. 'Next door Ed.'

'Oh, *next door* Ed. Yes. Sorry. I thought you meant someone in your class.'

'There's no-one in my class called Ed,' Connor replied.

'No, I know. I was…' Duncan gave his head a little shake. 'Next door Ed. Aye. What about him?'

Connor seemed to wrestle briefly with his next question. 'Do you like him?'

Duncan puffed out his cheeks. 'Do I like him? Next door Ed?' He shrugged. 'Suppose. I mean, I don't really know him. He seems nice enough. I think he's settling in all right. Why?'

Connor tapped the ground with the bottom of his stick as they walked, drumming out a little beat.

'Does Mum like him?'

Duncan stopped. 'I don't know. Why, what makes you ask that?'

Connor walked on a few paces, then he stopped, too. He stood there, chewing his lip, twisting the staff in his hand. 'Nothing. I was just wondering.'

Duncan cocked his head a little, regarding his son quizzically. 'That's a weird thing to just start wondering.'

Connor's cheeks blushed red.

'Con?'

'Where's Meg?' the boy suddenly asked, his eyes darting to the tree line.

'She's in there. She'll be fine,' Duncan said, shooting the forest the most fleeting of glances. 'She'll come back when we call her. Why were you asking about—?'

'Meg!' Connor shouted. 'Meg, where are you?'

He put his fingers in his mouth and attempted a whistle. All he managed was a blast of damp-sounding air.

Duncan sighed, then formed a C-shape with thumb and forefinger and jammed them in his mouth. His whistle was shrill and loud. It cut off the birdsong, instantly reducing it to an indignant sort of silence.

'Where is she?' Connor asked, scanning the trees. 'Why isn't she coming back?'

'She'll be fine,' Duncan assured him, but he gave another whistle and followed with a shout. 'Meg! Come on, Meg!'

Nothing moved in the trees. The canopy of leaves and branches cast the undergrowth into a gloomy darkness. There was still an hour or so until sunset, but the shadows were growing longer, and the breeze had gained a chillier edge.

'Stupid bloody dog,' Duncan muttered.

'What if she's hurt?' Connor fretted. 'What if something's happened to her?'

'Nothing will have happened to her. She's probably just rolling in something. You know what she's like.'

Duncan cupped his hands around his mouth and called the dog's name again.

'Me-eg!' he shouted, stretching it across two syllables.

They waited. The trees creaked. The wind whispered through the grass.

But beyond that, nothing.

'Bugger it,' Duncan muttered.

'Dad?' said Connor, his eyes wide with alarm. 'Why's she not coming?'

'She'll be fine. She's always fine,' Duncan said. 'But I'll go in and look for her, if it makes you feel better. You stay here and shout me when she comes back.'

Connor glanced both ways along the empty track, then nodded. 'But what if she doesn't?'

'She'll be back,' Duncan promised.

'But what if she's not?'

'She will.'

'But—'

'I won't stop looking. All right?' said Duncan, a little irritably. He forced a smile. 'She'll be fine. She's just being a pain. You wait here.'

Connor nodded again. 'OK. I'll wait here.'

'Good lad. And shout when she comes out. Nice and loud, all right?'

'I will, Dad.'

Duncan clapped a hand on the boy's shoulder. 'And don't worry. We'll get her. She won't have gone far.'

–

'Bastard,' Duncan hissed, clutching his cheek where a thin branch had whipped at him. There was no blood, but he could feel a welt forming, raising a thin red line across his skin.

The ground was moist and spongy beneath his feet, and a dampness crept up the legs of his jeans, sticking them, cold and clammy, to the tops of his ankles.

'Any sign, Con?' he called over his shoulder.

'Not yet!' his son shouted back, his voice muffled by the surrounding woodland.

Duncan cursed the dog a few times, then just cursed in general as he trudged onwards, his boots snagging in the undergrowth, the branches determined to have one of his eyes out.

Half a dozen shambling steps later, something moved suddenly on his right, rustling through the tangle of grasses. He turned, startled, almost losing his balance as he searched for the source of the sound.

A rabbit appeared briefly from a knot of weeds, realised its mistake, then vanished again just as quickly. Duncan didn't see it again, but heard it scamper off to some hiding place deeper into the forest.

'Bloody thing,' he grumbled, listening to the fading swish of the rabbit through the grass.

He was only a couple of minutes' walk into the trees, but light was already in short supply. Everything was painted in a gloominess that turned the shadows to pools of black and tinted everything else in shades of grey and blue.

'You got her, Connor?' Duncan shouted.

He waited for a response from his son.

'Connor?' he called again, when no answer came. 'You got Meg yet?'

Nothing.

'Con?'

The trees groaned around him. The breeze murmured through the undergrowth. Everything else had fallen silent.

Looking back, Duncan wouldn't be able to say for sure why he ran. Not really. There was nothing to suggest anything had happened. No one thing he could pinpoint as the reason for his sudden panic. Realistically, Connor simply hadn't heard him. That was all. It wasn't unusual for the boy to get distracted. His selective deafness was an ongoing family joke.

And yet, Duncan ran. He ran, fuelled by fear, pushing his way through the grasping undergrowth and the whipping branches, splashing through the soggy dips, and stumbling over the moss-covered rocks, something hot and urgent gnawing away at his insides.

'Connor!'

He hurtled out of the trees, slipped on an unexpected embankment, and slid down it on his arse. The puddle of mud at the bottom cushioned his fall, then schlopped forlornly as it lost its grip on him when he pulled himself free.

'Con? Connor?'

He'd emerged from the forest thirty feet or so from where he'd first entered it. He had a clear view of the spot where he'd told Connor to wait, but hurried over to it, anyway, in case he was somehow overlooking something.

In case he was somehow overlooking his son.

Where the boy had been was a long, crooked stick, lying on the ground. A staff, abandoned by its wizard.

'Connor?' Duncan bellowed. His voice echoed in both directions along the empty track, up into the forest, off across the graveyard of stumps, and on towards the distant road. 'Connor! Where are you? Con?'

And then, from behind him, came the sound of movement.

He sobbed, relief flooding him, lightening his head, slackening muscles he hadn't felt go tight.

'Connor, I thought I told you to—?'

He stopped when a muddy Golden Retriever padded out of the trees, tail wagging, tongue lolling happily.

Something deep in Duncan's gut twisted into a knot. He spiralled around, searching for his son. 'Connor!' he bellowed. 'Con, where are you?'

No answer came. Meg crept to Duncan's side, her head low, sensing his distress.

'This is your fault! Stupid bloody dog!' Duncan snapped.

Meg lowered her head, her eyes gazing uncomprehendingly up at him.

Duncan's voice softened. It took on a pleading edge. 'Go find him. Go find Connor,' he said. His fingers fumbled for the phone in his pocket as he stared at the dog, willing her to listen, willing her to understand.

He thumbed the phone awake. No signal. *No fucking signal*.

Duncan shot the dog a desperate, hopeless look. His voice cracked.

'Go find our boy.'

Chapter 2

Detective Chief Inspector Jack Logan waited for the door to buzz open, then continued through it and along another of the stark, unwelcoming corridors of Carstairs State Hospital.

He turned left at the bottom, through another set of doors, then up the wide staircase to the next floor. He could've taken the lift, but the stairs were usually quicker. Besides, you never knew who you might end up sharing the lift with, and what they might try to get up to in the confined space.

His feet led him through the hospital on auto-pilot, having made this journey too many times to count. There were plenty of places Logan wished he knew like the back of his hand. Venice. The South of France. The Bahamas, maybe.

But no. Instead, the place on Earth he was probably most familiar with was a maximum-security psychiatric hospital in South Lanarkshire, hoaching with rapists, murderers, and all manner of worse.

Once-upon-a-time, he would have struggled to believe the 'and worse' part, but twenty years on the job had soon leathered any such doubts out of him.

The beat days had been bad enough, giving him a wee taster menu of the sort of horrors he'd eventually be forced to gorge himself on.

It had gone from bad to worse when he'd moved up to CID, and since transferring to the Major Investigations Team he'd seen things that would make the average murdering rapist shake their heads in disgust.

Another door blocked his path, its two double-glazed square windows each encasing a mesh of thick wire. He stopped and fixed the camera mounted above it with an impatient look.

Logan caught sight of himself in the camera's wide lens and made a half-hearted attempt at smoothing down his hair. He ran a hand across his chin, as if he could wipe away the stubble that had been shading in his jawline for the past few days.

He had the look of someone who had been destined to find himself involved with the law, although not necessarily on the side he'd ended up on. He was tall and broad, but generally held himself a little stooped as if trying to keep his size a secret.

The door buzzed. Logan pulled it open, gave a nod to the camera, then continued through, grateful the delay had been a minor one.

They knew his face well here. Hardly surprising. He was more regular a fixture than some of the doctors.

There was a reception-style desk along the corridor behind the next door, a plexiglass shield protecting the staff member behind it. Logan stopped at the counter, set down the dog-eared folder he carried under his arm, then signed himself in.

'You're later today,' said the woman behind the shield. She was relatively new. He'd first seen her four, maybe five visits ago, so she was only a couple of months into the job. She was plump and soft-looking, and Logan doubted she'd last much longer. A quick glance at the newspaper open at the job section on the desk beside her confirmed his suspicions.

He didn't blame her.

'Crazy morning,' he replied, then briefly winced at his choice of words. 'Busy, I mean.'

His eyes flicked to the clock mounted on the wall behind reception. There was a little round cage over it, securing it in place. Logan knew it was there to stop any of the residents hauling the thing off the wall and quite literally clocking some poor bastard with it, but he liked to imagine that it was an inmate here, locked away like the rest of them.

He signed his name with a blip and a squiggle, then picked up his folder. 'Is he ready?'

The receptionist nodded. 'He's ready. Well, as he ever is. I wouldn't expect much.'

Logan grunted in response, then stepped away from the counter.

'Oh, but Chief Inspector?'

'Yes?'

The receptionist mustered a worried-looking smile. 'Dr Ramesh wants to see you before you go in.'

Logan stopped, turned. 'Who?'

'Mr Logan?'

A bearded Asian man in his mid-forties leaned out of a door a little way along the corridor and made a beckoning motion that Logan very much did not approve of.

'My office, please. I'd like a word.'

–

Ramesh was new, too. Newer than the receptionist, even. Unlike her, he had an efficient, by-the-book air to him

14

that came across as rude, but ensured he had a better chance of sticking the job than she had. He took a seat behind his desk as Logan closed the office door, then motioned to the chair opposite for the DCI to do the same.

'I'll stand, thanks.'

Ramesh tutted softly, took a moment to conclude that he didn't like having such a dramatic height disadvantage, and got to his feet.

The office was small, but fastidiously neat to the point it didn't look like a functioning workplace at all. Rather, it was like something IKEA might use as a showpiece for its new office range designed for the deeply unimaginative.

The desk was irritatingly uncluttered, aside from a vertical stack of six hefty-looking medical tomes all angled so their barely decipherable titles could be read by anyone sitting across from the doctor. Each spine was smooth and crease-free, and the carefully presented showpiece told Logan pretty much everything he needed to know about the office's current occupier.

'I'm not happy about this,' Ramesh said. He prodded the desktop with his index finger. 'I'm not happy about this at all.'

There was an accent there, but it had been smoothed over and filled in around the edges with Received Pronunciation. No doubt at some private boarding school down south somewhere, Logan guessed. This did not do his opinion of the man any favours.

'Not happy about what?'

'You. Him. This whole thing. You shouldn't be coming in like this. It's not fair.'

Logan shifted his weight, eliciting a groan from the carpeted floorboards beneath him.

'*Fair?*'

'Mr Petrie is a patient here,' said Ramesh. He was a few inches shorter than Logan but was doing an admirable job of pretending not to notice. He was also doing a better job of holding the DCI's gaze than most polis ever managed.

'Mr Petrie is a convicted killer who murdered three children,' Logan replied. 'He's also a key witness in an ongoing investigation.'

'Yes, but it isn't an ongoing investigation, is it, Inspector?' Ramesh asked, his accent bubbling up. 'You caught him. He stood trial.'

'*Detective Chief* Inspector,' Logan corrected. He raised his head and straightened his shoulders, forcing the doctor to lean back a fraction to maintain eye contact. 'And I'm well aware that we caught him, but he has continued to withhold vital information that will allow us to fully mark the case closed. Hence why I'm here.'

'Again,' said Ramesh. He pushed his high-backed leather chair in below his desk and rested his hands on it. 'I've looked back at the records. It seems you come here often.'

'Frequently,' said Logan.

'Some would call that harassment.'

'They can call it whatever they like,' Logan responded. 'Until he gives us the information we need, it's an ongoing investigation. After that, I will happily never give the bastard another thought.' He raised an index finger and leaned in a little closer. 'Although, I might spare a few minutes to dance on his grave.'

He turned his mouth into something that was designed to resemble a smile but wasn't quite there. 'How's that sound?'

Ramesh's fingers kneaded the back of his chair, as if massaging it. He inhaled slowly through his nose, either stalling for time or building up to saying something he thought might escalate the situation further.

The latter, it turned out.

'I know your Superintendent,' the doctor said. He left a pregnant pause there, giving that new nugget of information a moment to sink in. 'We're in the same golf club.'

Logan sniffed, shrugged, gave a shake of his head. 'I wouldn't know. Always struck me as an arsehole's game. I'm more of a darts man, myself.' He tilted his head forward, giving the doctor the briefest of nods. 'No offence.'

From the look on Ramesh's face, offence had clearly been taken. Logan wouldn't lose any sleep over it. God knew, he got little enough already.

'Well, I'm going to talk to him. To Gordon. About...' Ramesh gestured vaguely in Logan's direction. '...all this. It's not fair. It's not on. My predecessor may have tolerated it, but... it's not on. I'm not having it.'

'Aye, well, tell Gordie I said hello,' Logan replied. He held up the battered cardboard folder as if in salute. 'And I'll be out of your hair just as soon as Mr Petrie answers my questions. All right?'

The doctor's fingers tightened their grip on the chair as Logan turned and opened the door.

'And how is he supposed to do that, exactly?' Ramesh demanded. 'Hmm? How is he supposed to do that?'

Logan paused in the doorway, filling it. He narrowed his eyes, considering this, then clicked his tongue against the roof of his mouth.

'I'm sure we'll figure something out,' he said, then he slipped out into the corridor and closed the door behind him.

Chapter 3

Logan sat in a moulded plastic chair and gazed upon the face of evil. For its part, the face of evil smiled vaguely back at him, its eyes shimmering in confusion, never quite focusing all the way on the visitor.

Logan wasn't buying it. He had never bought it. No matter what the doctors said.

Owen Petrie. *Mister Whisper*, the papers had called him back in the day. Back when he'd abducted and murdered three wee boys and done his damnedest to snatch away two more.

It was statements from the two close-calls that had led to the nickname. They'd both mentioned his voice as he'd tried to talk them into his van—a soft, whispering rasp—and the tabloids had lapped it up.

He sat in an old-fashioned high-backed armchair now, cowed and shrunken by the size of it. Back when he'd been on the outside, he'd been a right Dapper Dan, suiting and booting it whenever he was out and about. Shirt. Tie. The works.

Now, he sat slouched in an old pair of grey joggies and an off-white t-shirt that was threatening to drown him. Food stains dotted the front of it, varying shades of orange blemishes suggesting curry was a regular staple on the hospital menu.

He hadn't shaved in days. Or been shaved, Logan supposed. His stubble was a salt and pepper lavvy brush, heavy on the salt. His hair had been trimmed on the left side of his head. The right side was mostly bald, the hair there never having grown back around the site of the injury that had put him in his current condition.

Supposedly put him in his current condition.

The room was a private one, and as drab as any of the others in the hospital. Aside from the chairs, there was a narrow bed, a narrower wardrobe, and a desk that never got used. The edges of all the furniture had been smoothed off, the corners chunky and rounded.

There was a good-sized window, divided into much smaller chunks by a crisscross of sturdy spars. The bleakness of the view—the window looked directly onto another even grimmer section of the hospital—pleased Logan immensely. Good enough for the bastard.

Too good.

The little rolling hospital table that was usually positioned by the bed had been set up like a barrier between both men. A plastic jug of room temperature water sat on it, untouched. Logan lifted the jug and placed it on the desk which, like everything else in the room, was within easy arm's reach.

'Owen,' Logan began, opening his folder. 'I'm told you've been bright these last few weeks. I'm hoping that means you're ready to help me.'

Petrie's brow knotted. Speaking was a struggle, like he was wrestling the words from his mouth one at a time, and they were putting up a bloody good fight. The voice still had the low throaty hiss that had earned him his nickname, and the sound of it made Logan's skin crawl.

'Help you? H-how?'

Logan held his gaze. 'You know how, Owen. We've been through this.'

He produced an A4 photograph from his folder and sat it on the table between them. It was a blown-up image, full colour but grainy, showing a smiling boy dressed as the Red Ranger from *Power Rangers*. The outfit was too big for him, the sleeves folded back to make it fit, but he didn't care. He looked proud as punch, his face upturned to the camera, his hands raised in a mock-karate pose.

Logan didn't need to see the picture to know any of this. It was long since burned in.

'Dylan Muir. Aged three.'

Petrie didn't look at the photograph. Not at first. It was only when Logan rapped his knuckles on the plastic table top that Petrie's eyes went to it. He smiled, not unkindly, and made a little 'Aw' noise that forced Logan to grip his chair to stop himself lunging for the bastard.

'He l-looks like a nice boy.' The words were slow, laborious.

Logan counted to five in his head, before continuing.

'Aye. He was nice, Owen. He was a good lad. Much loved by everyone. His pals. His sister. His parents. A great wee lad,' Logan said. 'And then, he died.'

A flicker of a frown crossed Petrie's face. He tapped the edge of the photograph with the tip of a finger, prodding at it as if to check if it were real.

'Oh,' he said, dragging his gaze up to meet Logan's. He continued to tap the bottom of the photograph as he battled with the next few words. 'What hap-p-pened to him?'

Logan leaned in, closing the gap between them. His voice became lower, his tone more menacing. 'That's why

I'm here, Owen. I was hoping that maybe you could tell me.'

Petrie didn't flinch or make any attempt to draw back. Nothing flickered behind his eyes. He was good, Logan would give him that.

'I d–don't know.'

'See, I think you do,' Logan told him. He shook his head. 'No. I *know* you do, Owen.'

He placed another three photographs down. Dylan Muir on the swings. Dylan Muir in at his mum's make-up, a line of lipstick smeared across his forehead. Dylan Muir with his hand buried up to the wrist in a bag of *Monster Munch*. Petrie watched them being set out with the concentration of a punter at a magic show, trying to figure out the trick and second-guess how it was done.

Logan gave him a few moments to take those images in before setting down the final photograph. This one was smaller than the rest, and the only one that wasn't in colour. It went on top of the others, slap bang in the middle.

Dylan Muir, tied to a chair, tears cutting tracks down his dirty cheeks. Logan could see the boy's expression without looking. Every line. Every crease. Every moment of suffering etched across his features. He knew it all.

Petrie lowered his head and peered at the final image, as if looking over the top of a pair of glasses. He studied it like this for a few seconds, then drew back suddenly, like he'd finally figured out what he was looking at.

'I d–don't like that one,' he said, his voice a slurred staccato.

'No, I don't like that one either,' Logan agreed. He fished in the folder and produced two more images. He set them down, one at a time. 'And I don't like that one of Lewis Briggs. Or this one of Matthew Dennison.'

Petrie's gaze was aimed squarely over Logan's shoulder now, out through the window at the grey building beyond. The DCI leaned to the right, interrupting the view.

'Look at them, Owen.'

Petrie shook his head.

'Look at the photos.'

'I d–don't w–want to.'

Logan snatched the photographs up, one in each hand, holding them in front of Petrie. 'We found Lewis. We found Matthew. Too late, aye. Far too late, but we found them. At least we could give their families that.'

He set the pictures down and picked up the black and white image of Dylan Muir, holding it with almost reverential care as he gazed into the boy's wide, trusting eyes.

For a while, Logan had imagined that they might find the boy alive. Somewhere. Somehow. Someday.

But then, in a rare moment of lucidity, Petrie had finally confessed to his murder, and shattered that dream.

Just like he'd shattered so many others.

'But we never found Dylan. You never let us give him back so we could give his family some sort of peace.'

Petrie's mouth flapped open and closed. His eyes were glazed, and he had a look of a goldfish about him, staring out at the world from behind a wall of glass.

'Cut that shite out,' Logan hissed. He clicked his fingers up close in the other man's face. Petrie's eyelids fluttered, but he was looking through Logan now, staring at empty space.

'Where is he, Petrie?' Logan demanded. 'Tell me what you did with him. Tell me where you left him. Tell me where to find him.'

Across the table, Petrie's frown deepened, the wrinkles on his forehead furrowing into shadowy grooves. He remained like that for a good ten seconds, then he blinked. Once. Twice. A hypnotist's patient coming out of a trance.

His face relaxed. He looked at Logan and smiled vaguely, as if seeing him for the first time but finding something familiar about him. Petrie's hand came up and idly traced the dent that had forever altered the shape of his skull, his fingertips following the line of his scar.

Finally, he looked down at the spread of photographs of the smiling three-year-old set out before him. 'H-he looks nice,' he mumbled. He ran his fingers across one of the photographs and raised his eyes to meet Logan's. 'Is he yours?'

Logan couldn't stop himself. He lunged across the table and caught Petrie by the food-stained t-shirt. Petrie's vacant, not-quite-there smile remained fixed on his face. He didn't flinch, not even when the DCI's other arm drew back, his fingers balling into a fist.

'Mr Logan!'

The voice snapped Logan out of it, brought him back to his senses. He released his grip but wasn't gentle about it. Petrie thudded back into the padding of the chair.

Turning, Logan saw Dr Ramesh holding the door open. 'I think you've outstayed your welcome for one day,' Ramesh said. 'Mr Petrie needs his rest.'

The door *squeaked* as he opened it wider.

'Don't make me ask you again.'

Petrie's vague smile twitched as he watched Logan gather up his photographs and replace them in the folder.

'I'll see you again soon, Owen,' the DCI said. A threat and a promise. 'Maybe we'll jog your memory next time.'

'I'm sure we can arrange something through the proper channels,' Ramesh said. 'But for now, I'm afraid I must ask you to leave.'

Tucking the folder under his arm, Logan made for the door. He stopped when he was level with the doctor, drawing himself up to his full height for maximum looming potential.

'I'll be reporting this,' Ramesh said.

'Good luck with that.'

He was about to leave when Petrie called to him. 'Sir? Excuse me, s-sir?'

Logan stopped, turned.

The smile crept higher on Petrie's face. His voice was a whisper, the words tumbling freely from his mouth. 'Say hello to that little boy for me.'

Chapter 4

Logan was halfway across the car park when his phone rang. He cursed out loud when he saw the name flash up.

Gordon Mackenzie.

Detective Superintendent Gordon Mackenzie.

The Gozer.

As nicknames went, it went around the houses a bit. From what Logan understood of it, 'Gordon the Gopher' had been an early draft, but it had been widely agreed by everyone at the time that it was far too obvious, and that should he overhear anyone referring to 'The Gopher' in conversation, the then-going-places DS wouldn't need to draw on much of his polis training to put two and two together.

And so, an alternative had been sought. Something that summed up his personality, maybe gave a wee nod to the Gopher thing, but wasn't as blatantly on-the-nose. One of the DCs in the department at the time had been a big fan of *Ghostbusters*. And, what with Mackenzie being a boggle-eyed bastard with a flat-top, he'd been named after the film's villain, an equally boggle-eyed bastard with a flat-top.

If you wanted to get technical about it, the handle didn't actually stand up to scrutiny. The boggle-eyed, flat-topped bastard in *Ghostbusters* was Zuul. Gozer was the unseen evil entity who eventually manifested as the *Stay*

Puft Marshmallow Man, but any attempt by anyone to raise this as an objection was quickly shouted down. *Gordon the Gozer* just worked, and the Strathclyde polis never let semantics get in the way of a solid nickname.

Logan's thumb hovered over the green phone icon on the screen, shifted to the red, then back again. That wee rat bastard of a doctor must've got straight onto the Gozer before Logan was even out of the building. It was barely after eleven on a Sunday morning. The DSup wouldn't be happy.

He decided to answer. Better to face his wrath now, than give it a chance to snowball into something worse.

'Sir?' he said. 'To what do I owe the pleasure?'

'Where are you?' the Gozer asked. His voice was clipped, efficient. Either Logan was in more trouble than he thought, or something else was going down.

'Just about at my car. Why?'

'We need you in at the office, ay-sap.'

Logan grimaced. *Ay-sap*. The first time he'd heard the Gozer say that, he'd assumed it was a wind-up. Surely no-one actually spoke like that? But, aye. Some folk did, it turned out, and the DSup was one of them.

What was wrong with 'now'? Or even just the standard one-letter-at-a-time pronunciation of ASAP?

Fucking *ay-sap*.

'Logan?'

'Sorry. Aye. Here, sir,' Logan replied. 'What's the score?'

'Best if I explain in person.'

In person? So, the Gozer was in the office on a Sunday morning? Jesus, it must be serious.

'I can be there in an hour.'

'An hour? What are you going to do, the Moonwalk?' the Gozer asked. 'Wait. Sunday. End of the month. You've been in seeing him again, haven't you?'

Logan made a non-committal *hmm* noise. At least Ramesh hadn't phoned his old golfing buddy to report him yet. That was something.

'We'll talk about this at a later date, Detective Chief Inspector,' said the Gozer, his tone suggesting it would not be an enjoyable chat for at least one of them. 'For now, just get yourself in here.'

'Will do, sir.'

'Oh, and if you're passing your house, you might want to grab some clothes and a toothbrush. Quickly, though.'

'How come?'

'You're being seconded. Up north. They've asked for you personally.'

Logan stopped walking in the middle of the car park. 'What? Why?'

'You wouldn't believe me if I told you,' said the Gozer. 'Just get in here. And don't spare the horses.'

Chapter 5

Under normal circumstances, Logan would've appreciated the view.

He wasn't that sort of guy, generally—a view sort of guy—but there was something about the landscape of the route between Glasgow and Fort William that could grab even the most ardent non-view guys by the collar and force them to sit up straight.

Most people thought it started at Rannoch Moor, and continued to improve during the twenty-mile build-up to Glencoe. To Logan, though, it started before that. The meandering road up Loch Lomond-side held its own charms, he'd always thought.

Granted, you didn't want to get caught behind a campervan. And the old stone bridges were so narrow they regularly brought traffic to a standstill as two buses jostled for position, their wing mirrors kissing as they inched past. But despite all that, there were few places on Earth quite like it.

It had been a while since Logan had been up this way, and the Crianlarich bypass was new to him. It shaved, by his reckoning, about nine seconds off the previous route, and he failed to see the point. Considering everything else that needed doing on the A82, it seemed like an odd choice.

From the new roundabout, it was a few minutes to Tyndrum, a quick stop at the Green Welly for a slash, then on up the hill into the great beyond.

It was round about that stage of the journey that he'd normally be forced to admit that actually, on reflection, Loch Lomond-side couldn't hold a candle to this. A couple of turns up the hill presented you with a view that almost went on forever, only interrupted by the conical snow-covered peak of Beinn Dorain, and its neighbour, Beinn an Dothaidh.

That was how his thought process usually went. Not today, though. Today was different.

The Gozer had been even more ashen-faced than usual when Logan had turned up at the office. The flat-top that had once helped crown him in both a literal and metaphorical sense was now a distant memory, along with eighty-percent of his hair in general. The boggly eyes were still a thing, though. Thyroid-related, apparently. Logan didn't like to ask.

The DSup had sat him down and offered him coffee. That was when the alarm bells had really started to ring. Logan had turned down the offer, keen by this point to crack on and find out what the hell was going on.

'A boy's gone missing up north, near Fort William. Connor Reid. Aged seven,' the Gozer had said, rattling off the details as if reading from a list. 'Last seen two days ago ten miles north of the town at…'

He consulted a notebook. 'Leanachan Forest.'

'So?' Logan had asked, then he'd immediately winced at how it sounded. 'I mean, aye, I saw something about it in the papers. Out with his old man, wasn't he?'

The DSup nodded the affirmative.

'That's CID though, surely?' Logan had asked. 'What's it got to do with MIT? Or with me, for that matter?'

Behind the wheel of his Ford Focus, Logan flexed his fingers, exhaled slowly, then tightened his grip as he replayed what had happened next. He didn't want to be replaying it. Not again. But it had been on a loop inside his head for the past hour and a half, and it didn't look like he was getting a lot of choice in the matter.

Time had wound itself into slow motion as the Gozer had produced an A5 print. The thick photo paper had made a definitive click when the DSup placed it on the desk in front of Logan.

The image was new, yet familiar.

Achingly, gut-wrenchingly familiar.

A boy. A chair. A rope.

Tears carving trenches down filthy cheeks.

'It arrived this morning.'

'Jesus. Where? Here?'

'At the house. That's a copy the local boys emailed down. We printed it off.'

'Delivered on a Sunday? Courier?'

'Couriers don't run weekends up there,' the Gozer had said.

'Hand-delivered, then,' Logan reasoned, still studying the picture. 'Anyone see anything?'

'Not that we know of.'

'How was it delivered? Through the letterbox?'

'Left on the step.'

The way the DSup said it had made Logan look up.

'On its own?'

The Gozer had shaken his head, just once. 'In an envelope. Attached to a soft toy.' He gave that a moment to sink in. 'Like before.'

Recalling the conversation again now made Logan's pulse quicken and his breath go short. He swung the car out into the right-hand lane and hammered the accelerator, sweeping past an old Clio that had been crawling along at under forty, the driver probably admiring the scenery.

It flashed its lights at him as he pulled back in. For a second, he considered hitting the blues and pulling the slow bastard over, but while he most definitely had the inclination, he was tight for time. He settled for raising a middle finger to the back windscreen, then continued on down the straight, widening the gap between them.

Even as he raced ahead, though, his mind went wandering back to Glasgow.

'A copycat,' he'd said. It hadn't been a question. Not really. A question implied doubt, of which he'd had none. Not then.

He'd been surprised when the Gozer had given another shake of his head. 'We don't know.'

'What do you mean, we don't know? We do know. Petrie's in Carstairs. I spoke to him myself this morning, so I reckon we can safely score him off the list of suspects. No' unless he's got a jetpack and a time machine.'

The Gozer hadn't looked amused.

'The envelope had the same message on the front. 'Surprise Inside. Open me.' Same typewritten text. Same spacing. Same three exclamation marks after both statements.' The DSup puffed out his cheeks. 'Same everything.'

Logan had fallen silent at that. The details of the other envelopes had been kept secret. They'd never been given to the press, or even shared outside those closest to the original investigation.

'Then it leaked,' he'd said. 'Someone leaked it.'

'Maybe.'

'*Maybe*?'

'Probably. I mean, aye. That must be it,' the Gozer had said. He'd sucked in his bottom lip, making his mouth go thin. 'The only alternative—'

'The only alternative is that we got the wrong man. That Petrie didn't do it. And we know he did.'

The Gozer had perched on the edge of the desk then. 'Do we?'

'What's that supposed to mean?' Logan had demanded, momentarily forgetting who he was speaking to. 'Aye. We know he did it. We got a solid conviction.'

The Detective Superintendent sighed wearily, but nodded. 'Aye. I suppose so.'

'It's a copycat, boss. That's all. The envelope stuff leaked, and some sick bastard is out there playing at being Petrie.'

Gozer said nothing at first. He picked up a stapler from the desk and fiddled with it, not making eye contact.

'And if it isn't?'

Logan stood. The face of the boy gazed imploringly up at him from the photograph.

'Then it'll be down to God to judge us, Sir.'

Chapter 6

Logan found the station after two false starts. It was situated across from a very loud, very active building site, and it was only as Logan pulled up that he spotted the BBC van tucked in behind a digger.

He muttered something uncomplimentary as he pulled the Focus into one of the many empty parking spaces. Then, he got out, blanked the five-strong pack of journalists who turned to study him as he approached, and pushed on through the station doors.

The building had been constructed recently, and still had that new smell to it. Logan had been to the old station a few times over the years, and while it had been in need of a lick of paint and a bit of tarting up, he'd have taken it over this one any day.

It was the remoteness he didn't like. The old station had been right in the middle of the town. Right in the heart of the action. The new one was out on an industrial estate three miles from Fort William town centre. How were you supposed to keep on top of things way out here?

It wasn't just that, though. The old station had felt like a proper nick. It had character and history baked into every one of its unappealing concrete blocks. This place was all plexiglass and curves, better suited to a call centre than a cop shop.

'You all right there?' asked a woman behind the screened-off front desk. She wasn't in uniform, but was instead dressed in a navy trouser-suit and frumpy hairstyle that made her look ten years older than she probably was.

'DCI Jack Logan. Major Investigations Team,' said Logan, producing his ID.

The woman opened a little hatch in the bottom of the plexiglass screen and motioned for him to slide the warrant card through. Fishing a pair of reading glasses from her pocket, she scrutinized the identification document.

'What did you say your name was?' she asked after a moment, as if to catch him out.

'Logan. I've been sent up from the Central Belt.'

'No one told me,' the woman said, still holding onto the card.

Logan gave her due consideration, then shrugged. 'I don't care.' He pointed to a heavy door off to the right of the desk. 'Can you buzz me in?'

'No one said anything about you coming,' the woman reiterated.

Logan sighed, ran his hand down his face, then tried to readjust his features into something friendlier.

'Look... sorry, what's your name?'

She peered at him over the top of her angular glasses. Like the rest of her get-up, they looked designed for someone in their sixties. 'Moira.'

'Moira? Moira what?'

'Corson.'

'Right. Nice to meet you,' Logan said. He leaned on the edge of the desk, his face close enough to the screen that his breath fogged the plexiglass. 'Listen, I'm sorry you weren't forewarned, but I've had a long day, Moira. And I suspect it's just getting started. So, how about you do us both a favour and buzz me through, eh? Can you do that for me?'

Moira held his gaze for a few seconds, then very slowly and deliberately placed his warrant card face down on the photocopier. She held his gaze as the machine whirred into life, scanning the document.

'You'll have to sign in,' she said, indicating two ledgers on the desk on Logan's right.

Wearily, Logan picked up a pen and began to write.

'Not that one.'

Logan drew her a fierce look, then tutted and signed himself in on the other book.

By the time he'd finished writing, Moira had slid his ID back through the hatch.

'Thank you,' he said, slipping it back into the inside pocket of his coat. He pointed to the door. 'Now, can—'

The door buzzed, and Logan hurried to push it open. The buzzing continued a while longer until Moira eventually removed her finger from the button and silence returned.

'Where did you say you'd come from, again?' she asked him.

'Glasgow.'

Moira looked him up and down, taking him all in and not approving of what she saw.

'Aye,' she said, smiling thinly. 'I should've guessed.'

–

'You found it all right, then?' asked DI Ben Forde, handing Logan half a cup of tea.

Technically, it was a full cup, but there wasn't a lot of cup to fill. Logan wasted a couple of seconds trying to fit a finger through the handle, then gave up and wrapped his hand around the cup instead.

'Eventually,' he said, taking a sip. He'd given up milk a few weeks back, and the tea tasted thin and disappointing. 'The sign at the roundabout said "superstore".'

'Oh, aye. That's the sign for the new Tesco,' said Forde.

He was older than Logan, although Logan had never figured out by how much. He'd been, 'No' a kick in the arse off retirement,' for at least a decade now, but showed no signs of making the leap.

For the most part, DI Forde was genial and soft-spoken. 'Gentle Ben' they called him, although Logan had once had the pleasure of seeing him take down a wee ned who'd been waggling a broken bottle around, and there had been hee-haw gentle about it.

He was a good few inches shorter than Logan, and lacked the girth that helped make the DCI so imposing. Still, he was a vicious wee bastard when he had to be, and while the arm of this particular lawman might not be all that long, you were in trouble if it got a hold of you.

Logan took another sip of tea. 'New Tesco? Is that what they're building across the road?'

'Hmm? Oh, no. That's the hospital.'

'So...' Logan glanced out through the window at the waste ground beyond. 'Where's the Tesco?'

'It's not happening.'

'It's what?'

'They're not building it. They changed their mind. They're building a hospital, instead.'

Logan blinked. 'Who is? Tesco?'

DI Forde gave a little chuckle. 'No. Tesco sold the land.'

'But...'

'But they'd already put up the "superstore" sign, so they just left it.'

Logan's eyebrows raised, then lowered. Forde beamed a big broad grin, then patted the DCI on the shoulder. 'Welcome to the Highlands, Jack,' he said, then he jabbed a thumb in the direction of the Incident Room. 'Shall we?'

Chapter 7

While Logan and DI Forde went back a fair few years, the other faces were completely new to him. No doubt he'd have seen one or two in passing at various events, but none of them were familiar to him now. Forde wasted no time getting stuck into the introductions.

'We'll start at the top and work our way down to the riff-raff,' Ben announced, shooting a look of mock contempt at a young Detective Constable who was perched with half an arse-cheek on an otherwise uncluttered desk.

Very few of the desks in the Incident Room were cluttered, in fact, which made Logan uneasy. He was used to rooms stacked high with documents—reports, witness statements, CCTV printouts, and all the other paperwork that piled up during an investigation. The fact that this one looked practically unused did not bode well for how things had been going thus far.

'You mean save the best for last, sir,' said the DC. He was late-twenties, Logan thought. Hair gelled, or waxed, or puttied, or whatever the hell they did with it these days, stubble carefully cultivated to make it look like he just hadn't got around to shaving for a while. Logan got the measure of him right away.

DI Forde gave a derisory snort. 'Aye, you tell yourself that if it helps, son,' he said, then he turned his attention to the only woman in the room.

'Detective Sergeant Caitlyn McQuarrie,' Ben said. 'Originally from Orkney, transferred to Northern MIT in... what? Two-thousand-and-sixteen?'

'Twenty-seventeen,' the DS said, and Logan detected just a bit of an island twang. Not the lilting teuchter of the Western Isles, but even in just those two words there was something that was unmistakably not of the mainland.

Her hair was flame-red, but cut short and tied back out of the way. She'd probably endured a lifetime of 'ginger' comments, and the hairstyle was 100 per cent about functionality, zero per cent about style.

She was closer to Logan's age than to DI Forde's. Eight or nine years younger than himself, Logan thought, which put her mid-to-late-thirties. She was short and slight—five-four, five-five—but had a presence about her that would doubtless add a few inches when required.

'Much as it pains me to say so, Caitlyn's one of the best detectives I've ever worked with,' continued Ben.

'Arguably *the* best,' the DS added, although the way she said it—light on the ego, heavy on the sarcasm—told Logan they were going to get along just fine.

'I suppose you could technically argue any old shite, if you put your mind to it,' Ben conceded.

He moved onto the only person in the room who hadn't opened his mouth yet—a well-presented, mid-thirties Asian man standing stiffly just a half-step removed from the rest of the group. He wore a new suit and a worried expression, and Logan would put money on him having recently transferred.

'DC Hamza Khaled. Recently joined us from CID,' said Ben, confirming Logan's suspicions. 'We haven't really got to know each other that well yet, but I've heard only good things,' Ben continued.

'We've obviously been talking to some very different people,' volunteered the as-yet-unnamed officer with the landscaped stubble. Khaled shot him an anxious look, then saw the guy's grin and clicked that he was joking.

'Where were you based before?' Logan asked, still trying to get the measure of the man.

'Aberdeen, sir,' Hamza replied, and Logan found himself surprised by the heavy Doric accent. *Aiberdeen.*

'Wait. Khaled,' said Logan, something stirring at the back of his mind. He clicked his fingers a couple of times, egging it on. 'Weren't you involved in that people trafficking thing with the fishing boats?'

'No' in the actual trafficking part, sir, but aye, I was one of the arresting officers,' DC Khaled said. He smiled, but warily, like he thought his jokey remark might land him in trouble.

'From what I heard you pretty much cracked the whole thing wide open.'

Hamza was quick to shake his head. 'Team effort, sir.'

'Aye, well, it was good work,' Logan told him. The DC seemed to relax a little then, the validation helping push away any thoughts of impostor syndrome.

'Last, and by every means least, Detective Constable Tyler Neish.'

The DC flashed his superior a grin, showing off his well-maintained teeth. 'You love me really, boss.'

Ben made a weighing motion with both hands. 'Meh.'

DC Neish held a hand out to Logan, but remained half-seated on the desk. Logan considered the younger man's offer, then extended his own hand, keeping his feet planted in a way that suggested he had no intention whatsoever of moving any closer. Ben smirked as he watched the power struggle unfold, knowing full well who was going to emerge victor.

After a half-second or so of internal struggle, Tyler stood, took the necessary step closer to Logan, then shook his hand just a little sheepishly. 'Nice to meet you, sir.'

'Aye,' Logan said. 'I know.'

Ben had to briefly turn away, his shoulders shaking with barely contained laughter.

Logan waited until DC Neish had returned to his perch, then addressed the lot of them. 'Thank you for the introductions, DI Forde. It's good to meet you all. Just a pity about the circumstances, but then I'm sure we're all used to that by now.'

Logan realised he was still wearing his coat, and began the process of shrugging it off as he continued.

'I'm sure Ben's already filled you in, but in case you need a refresher, I'm DCI Jack Logan. I was the arresting officer in the Mister Whisper case a few years back. I've been brought in to lead the charge on this one because of the similarities between both cases.'

He looked around for somewhere to put his coat, then tossed it over a chair, simultaneously disposing of the garment and staking his claim to that seat.

'Let me make one thing clear before we go any further,' Logan said, meeting everyone's eye in turn. 'Regardless of how similar aspects of these cases may be, Owen Petrie— Mister Whisper—is not behind them. We caught him. We put him away.'

Tyler raised a hand, but didn't wait to be asked. 'Didn't he fall or something during the arrest?'

Logan nodded. 'Off a car-park roof. Fell three floors, but lived to tell the tale. More or less.'

'How did that happen, sir?' asked Hamza.

There was a long, pregnant pause as Logan considered his answer. 'I cornered him. I guess the old "fight or flight" response kicked in. He elected to fly, which went about as well for him as you might imagine.'

'Sounds like an unfortunate business, sir,' said DS McQuarrie. There was an edge to her tone that wasn't accusing, exactly, but was certainly making an insinuation or two.

'Very much so,' Logan agreed. 'Although, on the bright side, it couldn't have happened to a nicer man. Regardless, we're 100 per cent certain that we have the right man locked up, and we know he can't have been behind this latest abduction. So, we need to figure out who is, find out where they are, and get that boy home.'

He let that settle for a moment. Then, when he was sure they were all on the same page, he looked to Ben. 'What's the latest?'

DI Forde cleared his throat. This seemed to be the trigger that switched him into polis mode, and his previously avuncular tone changed to a much more business-like one.

'We had the handover from CID this morning. I thought DCs Neish and Khaled could go over the report and look through the statements. Not that there's much in there. I've got uniform out doing door-to-doors around the abduction scene, but it's going to take a while.'

Logan raised an eyebrow. 'Lot of doors to knock?'

'No, opposite problem. Very few, but they're all a long way down dirt tracks. Almost certainly a waste of time, but you never know.'

'Has anyone spoken to the parents again this morning?' asked Caitlyn.

Ben shook his head. 'We've got a liaison there with them, and a couple of bigger lads to keep the press from making a nuisance of themselves, but no, we've still to get around there.'

'I'll do that,' Logan said. 'Unless any of you already have a relationship?'

The others confirmed that none of them had spoken to the family.

'Right. I'll speak to them, then. Be good to get a look at them. I want a look at the crime scene first, though,' Logan said. 'What about the stuff that arrived this morning?'

Ben gave a nod to DC Khaled. 'Hamza, could you…?'

Hamza sprang into life, crossing quickly to a desk in the corner, where a number of exhibits sat wrapped in plastic evidence bags. He retrieved three, placed them in a small cardboard box, and carried them back to the group.

Logan peered in as the box was placed on the desk beside him. 'This is the hand-delivered stuff,' Hamza said. He motioned back to the desk. 'CID took the cards and letters that arrived over the past couple of days, too. Nothing interesting, as far as we can tell.'

'Right. Good,' said Logan, absent-mindedly. He was staring down at the contents of the box, fighting the rising urge to vomit.

The bear was bad enough, with its faded grey fur and glassy eyes. It had been the first thing he'd seen, and the sight of it had stoked those initial fires of nausea.

The photo was several magnitudes worse, of course. Connor Reid looked nothing like the previous victims, and yet exactly like them. He shared the same look of raw terror that the other boys had, and the staging of the photograph was similar enough to be more than coincidence.

It was the envelope that tightened Logan's chest and set his guts churning, though. The Gozer hadn't been lying. It was identical—*identical*—to those that Petrie had sent. The second he'd clapped eyes on it through the plastic, Logan had been transported back almost fifteen years. Back to when he'd first joined the ongoing investigation. Back to when that bastard had been out there hunting wee boys.

Back to Dylan Muir. Back to Lewis Briggs. Back to Matthew Dennison, and to three families whose lives had been chewed up and spat out.

'You all right, boss?'

Logan blinked at the sound of Ben Forde's voice, whooshing back to the present. 'Aye. Fine. Have forensics looked at these?'

'Not yet,' Ben said. 'We need to get them up the road to Inverness for that.'

'Right. Aye, of course,' Logan said, irritating as news of the potential delay was. 'I'll take a look at them first, then one of the uniforms can horse them up there.'

He stole another look into the box. 'Do the press know about this yet?'

'Not that we know of,' said Ben.

'Thank Christ. We keep this to ourselves, all right? This does not get out into the wild until we say so. DS McQuarrie—'

'Caitlyn's fine, sir.'

Logan gave a brief nod. 'Get onto the liaison over at the house. Make sure the family understands the importance of keeping schtum about this. The vultures are circling out there, already. If this gets out, it'll be a bloody zoo.'

'Sir,' Caitlyn said, before reaching for her phone and heading for an empty desk in the corner.

He looked very deliberately to DC Neish. 'Where do I get a coffee around here?'

Tyler responded with a downturned mouth and a little shrug. 'Dunno, sir. First time here.'

'Right, then,' said Logan, picking up the box. He nodded to the door. 'In that case, let's make that your first line of enquiry. Black. Two sugars. Oh!'

Tyler hesitated halfway out of his seat.

'And make it to go.'

Chapter 8

Logan stood in a fine Highland drizzle, sipping lukewarm coffee through the narrow slot in a plastic lid and watching the SOC officers pack up their equipment. There had been a fresh surge of searching after the photo had arrived and the missing child case had been confirmed as an abduction, and Logan was hoping some new nugget of information might turn up.

No such luck. The second search hadn't turned up anything that wasn't already picked up first time round. And that wasn't much.

'We got a footprint,' said Ben, gesturing off the path and into the woods. 'Headed that way. Size nine or ten.'

'Male, then,' Logan mused.

'Or a real brute of a lassie, aye,' Ben agreed.

Logan sucked some more coffee through the plastic lid and cast his eye across their surroundings. There was a cordon of tape blocking the path ahead, and then another back where the path started, just on the other side of an open gate.

The little parking area beyond the gate was probably busier than it had ever been, thanks to the platoon of polis vehicles currently crammed into it. Logan hadn't been able to squeeze the Focus in, so had abandoned it with two wheels on a grassy verge, the other half clogging up the already too-narrow road.

A few uniforms were scattered around, heads tucked into the shoulders of their high-vis vests, feet stamping to drive out the cold. DS McQuarrie was over talking to some of the SOC lot. She had a notebook open, but didn't seem to have heard anything worth writing down as of yet.

The path—a gravel track probably wide enough for a forestry vehicle, provided the driver had his wits about him—stretched out for a third of a mile or more in both directions, before reaching the gate on one side and a bend at the other. That was almost a mile of visibility.

Off to one side of the path were a couple of acres of scrub, tree stumps, and not a whole lot else. Not a lot of hiding places, and none within easy reach.

Logan walked through it in his head. 'So, the dad goes into the trees after the dog. Our man is presumably waiting in the trees, grabs the boy, and heads back into the forest before the dad gets back.'

'That's about the size of it,' Ben confirmed.

'Dogs been in?'

Ben nodded. 'Tracked him headed northwest through the forest. There's a little car park—well, a bit of waste ground, really, but it gets used as a car park. Trail goes dead there.'

'Anyone see anything parked there?'

Ben shook his head. 'Sadly not. But an old boy at one of the cottages reckons he heard a motorbike roughly around the timeframe we're looking at.'

Logan tried to visualize this. 'Struggling kid on a motorbike. How would that work?'

'With difficulty,' said Ben. 'We're checking it out, but it's worth noting that the fella who told us about it is ninety-three, has two hearing aids, and reckons he invented Roger the Dodger, so we're not putting a lot of stock in it.'

'Sounds sensible, but worth checking.'

'I'm sure it won't come as a surprise, but we have no CCTV.'

'CCTV?' Logan looked around at the rugged Highland landscape. 'I'd imagine *colour* TV is stretching it. What else do we have?'

Ben consulted his notebook, flipped a page, then flipped back. 'Right now? That's about your lot. The Scene of Crime lot took a cast of the print, so we're trying to find out what kind of shoe it is. Walking boot of some kind, they reckon, but then that's pretty much par for the course up here.'

'What about the trees?' Logan asked. 'Have the forensics guys searched the route the dogs followed?'

'To an extent, aye.'

'What do you mean "to an extent"?'

Ben shrugged. 'It's a big forest. And CID organised a search the day the boy went missing. Public got involved and trampled right through it.'

'Jesus Christ,' Logan sighed. 'So, for all we know the footprint belongs to one of them?'

'No. That was spotted before the search. Dogs went through before anyone else went in,' Ben said. 'We don't know much, but we're pretty sure on what we have.'

Logan grunted begrudgingly. 'That's something.'

A movement along the road leading to the gate caught his attention. A *Sky News* van drew to a halt behind Logan's car, unable to get past. The driver gave a couple of short blasts on the horn.

'Did he…?' Logan shifted his gaze from the van to Ben and back again. 'Did he just toot at me?'

'He did,' Ben confirmed. 'Twice.'

Logan jabbed a finger in the direction of the van. 'Do me a favour. Get over there and get rid. I'd do it, but I'll only end up strangling someone.'

Ben was well aware of the DCI's feelings on the media, and touched a finger to his forehead in salute. 'No bother, boss,' he said. 'Although…'

'What?'

'We should maybe think about giving them something. Throwing them a scrap to fight over while we crack on. A quote, maybe.'

'A quote?' Logan ran his tongue across the front of his teeth, considering this. 'How about, "Crawl in a hole and die, you parasitic bastards?"' he suggested. 'What do you think? Reckon that'll suffice?'

Ben half-smiled. 'I'll maybe leave it for now.'

'Aye, maybe do that,' Logan told him, then he teased another sip of coffee from the slot on the coffee cup lid as Ben hurried off to intercept the news van.

The rain had abated slightly, the drizzle becoming something more akin to a damp mist that hung as tiny droplets in the air. If anything, it only served to make everything wetter, and Logan resigned himself to the fact that the chances of getting any new forensic evidence from the area were now practically non-existent.

A footprint. That was it. A footprint, and *maybe* the sound of a motorbike. Not a lot to go on. Hopefully, the teddy bear and photograph would give them something useful. Otherwise, they were in trouble.

Two days. That was how long Lewis Briggs and Matthew Dennison had been kept alive after their parents had received similar packages. Forty-eight hours. That was it.

And the clock was already ticking.

BAAAAAAA.

Logan blinked and looked around. A long black face with bulging, mournful-looking eyes glared back at him from twenty feet away.

'You've got to be kidding,' he muttered.

Clicking his fingers, Logan beckoned to one of the uniformed officers standing nearby.

'You. What the hell is this?'

The PC pushed back his cap a little. 'It's a sheep, sir.'

'No, I know it's a fu—' Logan pinched the bridge of his nose. 'I can see it's a sheep. I know what a sheep is. What's it doing on my crime scene?'

The constable regarded the sheep. 'Just standing there, sir.'

'Jesus Christ. How did you get into the polis, son? Was there a raffle?' Logan snapped. He gestured angrily with a thumb. 'Get rid of it.'

For a moment, the uniformed officer just stood staring, his head tick-tocking between the DCI and the offending animal. Then, with a determined nod, he squatted down beside the sheep and tried to wrap his arms around it. It shrugged him off, *baaa'd* in protest, then scuttled a few feet along the path.

'Go on. Shoo. Piss off,' ordered a female uniformed officer, clapping her hands and stamping her feet. The sheep shot her a dirty look, then obligingly pissed off, picking its way through the scrub and tree stumps, headed for the rest of the flock standing gathered in the distance.

'Thank you,' Logan said. 'Good to see someone's got some sense around here.' He glared at the male constable. 'I mean, *picking it up.* Jesus.'

'Happy to help, sir,' said the female officer.

She was young—early twenties, barely out of the cellophane—but carried herself like someone with ten years more experience. Aye, she was bluffing it, Logan could tell, but then weren't they all on some level?

'What's your name?'

'Sinead.' She shook her head, admonishing herself. 'PC Bell, sir.'

'You down from Inverness?'

'No, sir. Local.'

Logan drained the final dregs of his coffee. 'Know the family?'

Sinead nodded. 'My brother's in school with Connor. Year above, but it's not a big school so they all hang out.'

'You've met his mum and dad?'

'A few times, aye. Don't know them well, but know them to see.'

'Good. I'm heading over to speak to them. You can come with me.'

'I can't, sir.'

Logan's brow furrowed. 'What? How not?'

'I'm finishing in twenty minutes.'

Logan felt himself bristle. His face must've shown it.

'I'd stay on if I could, but it's my brother, sir. He's at the babysitter, and I need to pick him up.'

'Well, can't one of your parents do it?'

Something flashed across Sinead's face—there one minute, gone the next.

'No, sir.'

'Why not?'

'They're not available, sir,' the PC explained. 'But... I could maybe ask the babysitter to hang onto him for a couple of hours.'

'Right. Good. Do that, then. I'd appreciate it.'

Sinead fished her phone from inside a vest pocket and turned away to make the call.

Logan clicked his fingers and pointed to the male officer again. 'You. Captain Obvious. Think you can manage to keep the wildlife off the scene?'

'I'll do my best, sir.'

'Good man,' said Logan. He started to head for the car, then stopped a couple of paces in. 'Oh, and try to resist molesting anything next time, if you can. It doesn't reflect well on any of us.'

Chapter 9

The Reids lived in a mid-terrace house with a front garden that was roughly the size of a postage stamp, but immaculately cared for. A multi-coloured monoblock path led up to a rustic-looking front door that was completely out of character with the house, and different to the other three doors in the block.

The number eighteen was embossed on the frame above the door, but an ornate wooden sign announced the house name as 'The Willows'. It was, from what Logan could see, the only house with a name on the block, and probably in the whole of the estate.

The street leading up to the house was dense with polis and news vans. A couple of uniforms out front were keeping the scrum of journalists from getting too close. One of them shifted a traffic cone as the Focus arrived, making room for the car directly in front of the house.

The excitement levels of the journo crowd picked up. Microphones were produced. Cameras were trained. Throats were cleared.

'You ready for this?' Logan asked.

In the passenger seat, PC Sinead Bell nodded. 'Ready.'

'OK. Keep your mouth shut. Don't swear. Try not to punch anyone.'

Sinead gave a thin smile. 'Will do.'

'Hmm? Oh, no. I wasn't talking to you. That was for me,' Logan said, then he opened the car door and stepped out into the rabble of press. The questions came thick and fast.

'Any update?'

'What are you doing to find Connor?'

'What do you think happened?'

Logan ignored them, letting the uniforms keep them at bay. He opened the garden gate and indicated for Sinead to go ahead of him. He was about to close it behind him when a familiar voice rang out over the general hubbub.

'Is it happening again, DCI Logan?'

Logan stopped momentarily. His eyes met a silver-haired journalist with all the plastic insincerity of a used-car salesman. He held an iPhone in one hand, extended like a microphone. One eyebrow was raised, and there was the beginning of a smirk tugging at one side of the man's mouth.

Ken Henderson, freelance journalist and thoroughly horrible bastard. Granted, those two things usually went hand-in-hand, but Henderson seemed to take it to another level. Annoyingly, he was also a good reporter with an eye for a story and a brass neck that could deflect bullets. He'd covered a lot of the 'Mister Whisper' stuff back in the day, and had asked a lot of difficult questions about the accident that had left Petrie in his current condition.

Logan groaned inwardly at the sight of him but did his best not to let it show on the outside.

Is it happening again? Why the hell was he asking that? What did he know?

He looked across the faces of the gathered press. There were only nine of them for now, but that would be just the beginning.

'The only thing happening again is you lot getting on my tits,' Logan told them. 'I'll answer one question, and one question only.'

The mob erupted, firing questions at him. He ignored them, and pointed to a young, hapless-looking lad who practically screamed *local press*.

'You.'

The young lad's eyes widened in shock. 'What, me?'

'Aye. And that was your question. Threw that opportunity away, didn't you?' Logan said. He briefly met Henderson's eye, then shot the rest of the group a contemptuous glare. 'Now, how about you all try pretending to be human beings for once and give the family some peace, eh?'

With that off his chest, and feeling marginally better about the world, Logan clacked the gate firmly closed, and stalked up to the front door with Sinead hurrying along in his wake.

–

After the handshakes and the introductions, Logan sat on a big, solid-looking brute of a couch that immediately tried to swallow him into its cushions. He perched himself near the front, sitting upright, and smiled gratefully as Catriona Reid handed him a cup and saucer.

Connor's mother was awkwardly tall, with a short, feathered haircut that gave her a vaguely elf-like appearance. Her eyes were like dartboard bullseyes—red in the middle, a ring of black running around them. She had tried to disguise her grief with make-up, but it hadn't held up well.

Given the circumstances, Logan wasn't going to hold it against her.

She was doubtlessly exhausted, but her movements were alive with nervous energy, her face twitching, her fingers knotting together, her gaze darting to the window at every sign of movement.

'Thank you,' Logan told her.

Catriona's eyes blurred with tears, like this simple expression of gratitude was the thing that might finally break her. She sniffed and pulled herself together, though, and turned to PC Bell who stood off to the side of the couch.

'You sure I can't get you anything, Sinead? Tea? Coffee?'

'I'm fine, thanks,' Sinead replied, smiling kindly.

'Juice? There's apple juice.' Catriona's lips went thin. Her throat tightened, the thought of the unused carton of apple juice in the fridge almost cutting through her defences again.

'Honestly, I'm fine. Thanks, Catriona,' Sinead assured her. 'You should take a seat.'

'How can I take a seat?' Catriona snapped. The venom in her voice caught her by surprise and her eyes went wide. 'I'm sorry.'

Sinead shook her head. 'Don't be.'

Catriona bent, brushed some fluff off the arm of a big round armchair, then perched on it next to her husband. If Catriona Reid was a bundle of anxious energy, Duncan was the polar opposite.

He sat slouched in the armchair, one elbow leaning against the armrest, his hand jammed against the side of his head like his skull was too heavy to stay up without support. There was something haunted about his expression. A step removed from the world, or a step behind it, maybe. Logan had seen similar looks before. Too many times before.

His clothes looked slept in. Or, more likely, not-slept in. They were a stark contrast to the figure-hugging jeans and neatly-pressed purple shirt his wife wore.

'That's a good cup of tea,' the DCI said, setting the cup back in the saucer. He looked around for somewhere to sit it, then settled on the polished wooden floor at his feet. 'Now, I hope you don't mind, but I'd like to ask you both a few more questions.'

Catriona was quick with an, 'Of course,' but Duncan gave a vague wave of a hand, as if half-heartedly batting away a fly.

'We've already gone over it. There's nothing more to say. Why aren't you out there finding him? Why haven't you found Connor?'

'Rest assured, Mr Reid, we're working on it,' Logan replied. 'I promise you, we're doing everything we can to get Connor home safely, and as quickly as possible.'

Duncan's hand dropped into his lap. He exhaled. 'Sorry. Aye. I know. I know you are. It's just…' He sighed again.

'It's frustrating having to go over it all again. I understand it's a difficult thing to have to relive,' Logan told him. 'But we all want Connor home, and you can help make that happen.'

Duncan nodded, and drew himself upright in the chair. His wife's hand slipped into his and he squeezed it.

'You're right. You're absolutely right, detective…'

'Jack. Please.'

'Jack.' Duncan took another steadying breath. 'Go for it. What do you want to know?'

Logan caught Sinead's eye, then pointed to the couch beside him. She hurried over and sat down, producing her notebook without having to be prompted.

Promising, Logan thought.

'The package that arrived last night. The teddy bear,' he began, eyes flitting between husband and wife. 'Who found it?'

'It was the policewoman,' said Catriona. 'The... what do you call it?'

'Liaison?'

'Yes. Her. Jess, was it?'

Logan shot Sinead a look. She nodded to confirm. 'Jess French.'

'There were a few things left on the step. Flowers, mostly. Someone left chocolates,' Duncan continued.

'Roses,' Catriona added.

Sinead paused, mid-scribble. 'Which?'

The other three occupants of the room looked at her, and she wilted slightly. 'You said 'roses.' Did you mean the flowers or the chocolates?' She deliberately avoided meeting the DCI's gaze. 'Because it... it can be both.'

'The chocolates,' said Catriona.

'Does that matter?' asked Duncan.

'Well, I mean...' Sinead began, then she finally relented and caught the look from Logan. She quietly cleared her throat. 'Sorry, no. Go on.'

'You sure?' Logan asked.

Sinead blushed and nodded, fixing her gaze firmly on her pad as she jotted down the now-clarified information. Logan offered a smile by way of apology to the Reids.

'So, the liaison officer arrived in the morning, picked up everything on the step and then brought it in?'

'Right,' Duncan confirmed.

'She's lovely,' Catriona added. 'She's been very kind.'

'I'm glad to hear that,' said Logan. 'And, when did you notice the teddy?'

Duncan and Catriona exchanged glances. 'Must've been... what? Just after seven?' Duncan ventured.

'About quarter past,' Catriona clarified. 'The Yoga alarm had just gone off.'

Sinead looked up from her pad, began to open her mouth, then thought better of it. Luckily, Logan asked the question for her.

'Yoga alarm?'

'I do Yoga every morning,' Catriona explained. 'Seven-fifteen.'

'She sets an alarm,' said Duncan.

'I set an alarm,' his wife confirmed. 'Keeps me from forgetting.'

Logan set out the timeline in his head. 'So, Yoga alarm, liaison turns up, find the teddy. That right?'

'No. The liaison turned up around seven,' Catriona corrected. 'We were looking through everything that had been left—well, I was. Duncan wasn't really in the mood, but I think if people are going to go out of their way to show support, it's the least we can do to look at it.'

She shot her husband a sideways look. Clearly, this had been a bone of contention between them.

'The cards looked nice up on the mantelpiece,' Catriona continued. Her eyes went to the bare mantle and she deflated a little. 'Of course, the other policemen took them away.'

'We'll try to get them back to you as soon as we can, Mrs Reid,' Logan told her. 'Now, you were saying about the alarm?'

'Right. Yes. The alarm rang, I turned it off, and it was around then that I spotted the teddy.'

She gave a little shudder and seemed to shrink into herself. Duncan gave another squeeze of her hand, but if she noticed, she didn't let on.

'There was something about it. Something... I don't know. Do you believe in energy?'

Logan tried to keep his face relatively impassive. 'Energy?'

'Spiritual energy. Positive, negative. *Energy*,' Catriona continued. 'I just got a bad feeling from it, that was all. A bad vibe. It was dirty. Like it had been in a puddle,' Catriona continued. Her eyes were glassy, as if she could see the soft toy in the air in front of her.

'Was it one of Connor's?' Logan asked.

Catriona and Duncan both looked surprised by the question.

'I don't know,' Duncan admitted. 'Maybe. He has one similar, I think. I mean, not all manky, but... maybe.'

'If you could try to find out for us, that would be useful,' Logan said, then he turned his attention back to Catriona. 'So, sorry. You got a bad feeling from the teddy bear. And then...?'

'And then we saw the envelope.'

Her voice went higher, her throat tightening. The sentence ended in a breathless sob, and Duncan gave her another hand-squeeze before taking over.

'We thought it was another card,' he said, his own voice not much better. 'And then... And then...'

He looked away. His jaw tensed, the effort of holding everything back making him shake. 'We opened it.'

'Who did?' Logan enquired, as gently as possible.

Duncan gestured wordlessly to his wife. If she'd looked upset when recalling the soft toy, the thought of the image in the envelope was positively haunting her. Her face seemed to grow thinner before Logan's eyes, the features drawing together as if finding comfort and safety in numbers.

'I didn't realise what it was. Not at first,' Catriona said. She was whispering, but not through choice. It was as if her throat had constricted to the point that only the faintest suggestion of words could escape. 'It was just... it was just...'

She pressed the fingers of her right hand against her skull, as if trying to push down something bubbling up inside it. 'It was just a shape. That was all. I wouldn't... I couldn't...'

The tears came then, big silent sobs that contorted her face into something ugly and raw. If she was hiding something, she was bloody good. Whatever else might have happened, the grief was real.

Not that Logan had any reason to suspect her of being involved. Neither of them. Not officially, anyway. And yet, he couldn't help himself. It was right that the courts worked on the 'innocent until proven guilty' principle, but Logan tended to approach investigations from the opposite end.

Still, if Catriona Reid was involved in the abduction of her son, two decades of polis instincts had let him down.

He gave the couple a moment to console each other, then offered an apologetic smile. 'I know it's difficult.

You're doing really well. Maybe we can go back to Friday?'

Catriona nodded hastily, relieved to be able to switch out this recent nightmare for one that was less vivid and fresh.

'Mr Reid, you were with Connor?'

'Aye. We went for a walk after school,' Duncan confirmed. 'With the dog.'

Logan glanced around the room.

'Meg. She's out back,' Duncan explained. 'She goes mental at new people.'

'She doesn't bite. She's not like that,' Catriona quickly added. 'Just barks.'

'She's a biddable big thing when you get to know her,' Sinead confirmed. 'Just… noisy.'

'Meg is certainly that!' Catriona said. She half-laughed, then everything about the situation came rushing back in, shattering her moment of respite.

'Can you talk me through what happened?' Logan asked, keen to get past the dog chat. 'You went for a walk after school…'

Duncan sat up straighter in the chair. 'We drove up to Leanachan. It's a good walk. You don't see anyone. We were just doing that, just walking and then…'

He took a breath, centering himself.

'Meg ran into the trees. We shouted, but she wasn't coming back. And so…'

He ran his tongue across his lips, his eyes locked on Logan. There was a hopelessness there. A desperation. A cry for help.

'So, you went after her,' said Logan. 'It's OK. I'd have done the same.'

Duncan nodded wordlessly.

'And then what?'

'I… I shouted. I kept shouting to him. To make sure he was OK,' Duncan continued. 'I didn't want him to get scared. He… he gets scared. We have to leave the light on for him.'

This time, it was Catriona's turn to do the supporting hand-squeeze.

Duncan's nostrils flared and his mouth turned downward. His eyes filled with fear, self-loathing, and everything in between. His tears, when they fell, were like the waters of purification, cleansing everything away and allowing him to struggle on.

'So I shouted, and he shouted back. And then, one time, he didn't.'

He stared past the DCI to the wall beyond, as if watching everything play out there. 'I knew something was wrong. I don't know how, but I *knew* it. I ran back, and he was… he was gone.'

Duncan raised his eyes to his wife, like a penitent man before God. 'I only left him for a couple of minutes. Just a couple of minutes, that was all. I swear.'

'I know,' Catriona told him. She slid down onto the seat beside him, and he sagged against her. 'I know.'

'And you didn't see or hear anything?' Logan asked. 'There was no sign of anyone else in the area?'

Duncan shook his head. 'No.'

'They said he was probably hiding in the trees,' Catriona said. 'Is that true?'

'We're looking into it. But aye, that's our theory at the moment,' Logan told her. He shifted his attention back to Duncan. 'How was Connor during the walk? Anything seem different?'

'He was quiet.'

'Doesn't sound like him,' said Sinead, glancing up from her pad.

'No,' Duncan agreed. He frowned. 'He was talking and everything. Just… Not the same. Not his usual self. He normally doesn't shut up. And they had swimming at school that day.'

'He never stops talking about swimming,' Catriona added. The words seemed to take a physical toll on her, and she sagged further into the armchair.

'Did you ask him about it?' Logan pressed.

'Aye. He said he was fine. But, he just… I don't know. There was something.'

Logan glanced down at Sinead's notebook to make sure she was writing this down.

'Did he say anything else? Had he fallen out with anyone at school, maybe?'

'At school?' said Catriona, incredulous. 'You think someone from school did this? They're eight!'

'Just pursuing all avenues, Mrs Reid,' Logan told her.

'You already know who it is!' she replied, her voice rising. 'We looked on the internet. We know all about him.'

Logan bristled. 'About who?'

'Mister Whisper. He's done this before, hasn't he?' Catriona continued. Duncan tried to quieten her, but she pulled her hand free from his and batted his protests away. 'It's him, isn't it? It's the same thing. The teddy. The photo. It's the same!'

'We caught him, Mrs Reid. I can assure you, whoever took Connor, it wasn't…' He rolled the words around in his mouth, as if unable to spit them out. '*Mister Whisper*. Owen Petrie, the man responsible for those children's…'

He caught himself just in time. 'The man who took those children, he's in Carstairs. We believe the individual who took Connor is trying to emulate Petrie's abductions.'

'He killed them. Didn't he?' Catriona asked, her tone harsh and accusing, daring him to say no. Or praying he would, perhaps. 'He killed those boys.'

Logan hesitated, then gave a nod. 'He did, aye. But we're not dealing with the same man. There's no saying that's his intention with Connor.'

'*There's no saying?*' Duncan yelped. He jumped to his feet, his eyes blazing. 'That's the best you've got? Our boy's out there, and that's all you can tell us? *There's no saying?*'

'Like I say, I understand it's frustrating, Mr Reid, but—'

'It's not fucking frustrating!' Duncan bellowed, looming over the DCI. 'A Rubik's Cube's frustrating. A jar you can't get the lid off. Not this. Not *this!*'

Sinead stood up and took Duncan gently by the arm. 'We know. We understand, Duncan. We do. And we're going to do everything we can to get him back home, all right?'

At the back of the room, the kitchen door opened, and Jess, the family liaison officer looked in. Logan dismissed her with a shake of his head and she slipped out of sight again.

The fury that had propelled Duncan to his feet was already burning itself out. He locked eyes with Sinead, and the hand on his arm became the only thing holding him up.

'I'm sorry,' he whispered. 'I just… I just…'

'You're fine. We get it,' Sinead told him. 'I understand.'

'Of course you do, sweetheart,' Catriona said. She reached up and took one of Sinead's hands for a moment. 'After what happened with your mum and dad.'

Sinead smiled awkwardly, and very deliberately did not meet Logan's inquisitive gaze. Instead, she helped Duncan back down into the chair beside his wife. Duncan kept his eyes on the floor, embarrassed by his outburst.

'He didn't mean that,' Catriona said, putting a hand on her husband's shoulder.

'He did,' said Logan. 'And he's absolutely right. Cards on the table? I can't begin to imagine what you're going through. None of us can. And I don't have a lot of information I can give you right now, but what I can give you is my word. I—we—will not stop until we find who's responsible for this, and get your son back. Whatever it takes, whatever we have to do, we will bring Connor home. That's a promise.'

The Reids said nothing, but both seemed to grow in stature a little, buoyed by the speech. Duncan wiped his nose on the sleeve of his creased shirt, screwed the heels of his hands into his eye sockets for a few seconds, then gave a nod.

'What else do you want to know?'

Logan caught Sinead's gaze, then flicked his eyes to the couch beside him. She sat again, pencil poised.

'You said he seemed out of sorts, but was there anything else? Anything specific he said that seemed unusual?'

'No, he was just worried about the dog getting lost. It was only because he was panicking that I...'

His forehead creased. He blinked, caught off guard by something.

'Wait. Ed.'

Catriona shifted in the chair so she could look at him. 'What?'

'Ed. He asked about Ed.'

'Ed who?' Logan probed.

'Next Door Ed?' Catriona asked. 'Why was he asking about Next Door Ed?'

'I don't know. He just… He asked if I liked him.'

'If you liked *Ed*?'

Logan cleared his throat, drawing their attention back to him. 'Sorry, who is this we're talking about?'

'Sorry. Ed, uh, Walker, I think,' Duncan said. He looked to his wife for confirmation. 'Walker?'

'Ed Walker, yes,' Catriona said. 'He lives next door.'

'Only bought the place a few months back,' Duncan said.

'Renting,' his wife corrected. She dialled back the certainty a touch. 'I think he's renting, anyway.'

Duncan shook his head. 'He must've bought. He was working on converting the loft just before he moved in, I think. Lot of racket, anyway.'

'Which direction?' Logan asked, steering the conversation back on track.

Catriona drew a look to the wall on her left, but said nothing.

'That way,' Duncan said, gesturing in the same direction. He sat forward, his frown deepening. 'He asked if I liked him, and then he asked if *you* liked him.'

Catriona gave a little snort. 'What, me?'

Duncan nodded. 'Aye. He said, 'Does Mum like Ed?''

'Why would he ask if I liked Ed?'

'I don't know. I asked him, but that's when he got panicky about Meg.'

'I'm sure it was nothing,' Catriona said. The abruptness of it made Logan's Polis-sense tingle, but he let it slide for the moment.

'Almost certainly,' Logan agreed. 'But we'll arrange to have a chat with him.'

He stood up. Sinead hurriedly finished scribbling a note, then got to her feet.

'Thank you for your time. You've been very helpful,' Logan told them. 'If you need anything—anything at all— please just ask...'

He clicked his fingers softly a couple of times.

'Jess,' said Sinead.

'Jess. She'll keep you up-to-date and get you anything you need. And, if the press lot start to get too annoying, you have my full permission to set the dog on them.'

Duncan and Catriona moved to get up, but Logan motioned for them to stay seated. 'It's fine. We'll see ourselves out. Thank you again.'

He turned, caught sight of the pack of vultures loitering out front, and then turned back. 'The back garden. Can I get next door from there?'

'Aye, but the dog'll go mental,' Duncan said.

'I'm sure we'll cope,' Logan told him.

'Are you going to see Ed?' Catriona asked. She shot the briefest of glances at her husband. 'Next Door Ed, I mean?'

'Aye,' said Logan. He looked over at the dividing wall, then down at the couple in the chair. 'We'll at least pop our heads round the door.'

Chapter 10

True to form, the dog went bananas when Logan stepped out through the back door and into the garden. Meg raced for him, barking furiously, fur rising on the back of her neck.

Logan ignored her and plodded down the steps onto the path. The back garden was a little larger than the front, but less neatly turned out.

There were no raised flowerbeds here, no manicured lawn. Just a shed, some stacks of planks, and a whisky cask the size of a caravan. It had roofing felt on top, and Logan had a vague recollection of seeing something similar before.

'Is that a sauna?' he asked, as Sinead stepped out of the house behind him. The dog redoubled its efforts to be an annoying wee bastard.

'Yes, sir.'

'A sauna. In Fort William?' the DCI continued. He gestured at the smirr of fine rain falling from the dark grey clouds overhead. 'Isn't this, like, the wettest place in Europe?'

'Three years running, sir,' Sinead replied, almost proudly. 'We got a certificate.'

'Well, I hope to Christ it was laminated,' Logan replied, pulling his coat closed. He sized the sauna up. 'Is that normal?'

'Well, I've not got one myself, sir. But it's got a roof, so I don't imagine the rain's a big problem,' Sinead said. 'Anyway, I think he makes them, or sells them, or something. He's always advertising them on Facebook.'

Down at their feet the dog upped its barking game from 'bananas' to 'batshit'.

'Hello! Yes, I see you. I see you!' Sinead said, baby-voicing the bloody thing. She squatted down, making the dog skitter back away from her, all its weight on its hind legs. 'What's all the noise about? Hmm? What's all that noise for?'

'Ignore it,' Logan told her.

'Sorry, sir?'

'If you ignore them, they eventually shut up,' he explained. 'It'll just keep going if you make a fuss.'

Sinead held the back of her hand out to the dog. Meg sniffed it, then gave a tentative lick. Her tail wagged as Sinead stroked the top of her head.

'There you go. That's better. See? No need for all the noise.'

She stood up, looking just a tiny bit smug.

Logan raised an index finger. 'Wait for it.'

Meg erupted into barking again, and it was Logan's turn to look pleased with himself. 'See?' he said. 'Told you. Ignore them. They get bored eventually.'

The dog ushered them down the back path and continued to announce their departure as they pushed through the gate and into the alleyway that ran behind the block.

'I'd never endorse cruelty to animals,' Logan said, heading for the next gate along. 'But I'd happily strangle that bugger if it kept that up.'

'Sounds *quite* cruel, sir,' Sinead pointed out.

'I'd make it quick,' Logan told her. 'Big hands.'

He held up his hands to demonstrate that they were indeed big.

Sinead smirked. 'Should I be writing this down?'

'Probably best not,' Logan told her.

They stopped at the back gate of the neighbouring house. Unlike the Reids' gate, this one and the surrounding fence were double-height, making it difficult to see much of the garden or the lower half of the building.

The curtains upstairs were closed in one bedroom, but there were no lights in any of the windows.

'Right. Next Door Ed, then,' Logan announced. 'Thoughts?'

Sinead's eyes widened a little, caught off-guard. 'Uh… he's got a big gate.'

'He *has* got a big gate,' Logan confirmed. 'I was hoping for something a bit more insightful and that wasn't currently staring me in the face, but that's a start.'

He put a hand on the handle. It had a thumb-operated latch that clacked metallically when Logan pushed it down. The gate was a little too wide for the gap, and he had to give it a shove to budge it.

Logan stopped then, the gate ajar. 'What happened to your parents? If you don't mind me asking?'

'Road Traffic Accident, sir,' Sinead replied. The answer snapped out of her in an instant, like it had been pre-programmed. 'Eighteen months ago.'

She coughed gently. 'Well, nineteen,' she corrected, and something about the way she said it told Logan she could've given it to him in hours and minutes.

'Christ. I'm sorry. You should've said,' Logan told her. 'So now it's…'

'Me and my wee brother, sir, aye,' Sinead confirmed.

Logan exhaled through his nose, looked up at the house, then pulled the gate closed. 'Let's get you home. I'll come back later.'

Sinead frowned. 'Are you joking, sir?'

'What?'

'Well…you think he might be in there, don't you? Connor, I mean.' Sinead asked. 'You jumped up off the couch as soon as they told us he'd asked about Ed.'

'Not necessarily…' Logan began, but it was clear from the way she looked at him that she wasn't buying it.

'That's why you wanted to come in the back way, so the press didn't see.'

Logan chuckled drily. 'Maybe I'm the one who should be taking notes.'

He glanced up at the house again. 'Do you know him? Ed, I mean.'

Sinead shook her head. 'No. Never met him.'

'Right.' Logan pushed the gate open. 'Stay close, follow my lead, and don't do anything stupid.'

'Should I radio it in?'

'Remember that 'don't do anything stupid' bit? That would qualify,' Logan told her. 'We don't want to put the wind up him. Not yet. It's just a routine door to door at this stage.'

'Won't us going to the back door make him suspicious?'

'Trust me, if he's kidnapped the boy, we'll soon be the last of his back door's worries.'

It took Sinead a moment to understand what the DCI meant. 'Oh. Prison?'

'They've been known to be somewhat unwelcoming to certain categories of prisoner,' Logan confirmed. 'Or overly welcoming, depending on your point of view.'

He dropped his voice down low. 'Now, mouth shut, ears open. Ready?'

'Ready, sir.'

'Well, you fell at the first hurdle on the whole 'mouth shut' thing, but we'll let it slide this time.'

Raising a hand, he knocked on the door. It was a classic policeman's knock—loud, no-nonsense, and clearly announcing its intention not to go away until someone answered.

When no-one did, Logan knocked again, even louder this time.

He stepped back and looked up at the windows. The smirr of rain had been promoted to a drizzle, and he had to squint in order to see the top half of the house.

There was a set of chrome-coloured blinds on the kitchen window, slanted at an angle that only let Logan see the ceiling when he tried to peer through.

'Mr Walker? Can you come to the door, please?' he called.

'Maybe he's not in,' Sinead ventured, then she immediately realised this was the most obvious thing she could've said, and cursed herself inside her head.

'We'll make a detective of you yet,' Logan told her, absent-mindedly. The living room curtains were open, but the window itself was too high to see through.

Logan found a cracked terracotta plant pot and turned it upside down below the window. It creaked ominously when he stood on it, but somehow managed to take his weight.

'See anything?' Sinead asked.

Logan wiped a layer of grime off the window with the sleeve of his coat. The room was dark inside, and barely resembled a room at all. It was more like a campsite, with the only furniture a folding camping chair, a little plastic table, and a pyramid of Tennent's Lager cans, presumably all empty. He wasn't sure that last one technically qualified as 'furniture' but it wasn't the time to split hairs.

A *Pot Noodle* sat on the table, a fork sticking up through the peeled-back foil lid. From his angle, Logan couldn't tell if it was empty, full, or somewhere in-between.

'Not a lot,' he said, stepping down. 'But it doesn't fill me with confidence.'

He put a hand on Sinead's shoulder. 'You should go.'

'What? Why?'

'Because I'm telling you to, constable,' Logan said, his tone becoming officious. 'You've done well. You show a lot of promise, but you should get home. Call it a night.'

Sinead looked past him at the living room window, then up at the closed curtains above.

'But… I want to help.'

'And that's to your credit.' He jabbed a thumb back over his shoulder. 'But in a minute, I'm going to hear a cry for help from within this house, giving me no choice but to break this door down and investigate. It wouldn't be wise for you to be here when that happens.'

Sinead chewed her bottom lip. Her eyes searched the house again. 'What if we both heard it, sir?' she asked. 'I just don't think you should be going in there by yourself.'

'I'm a big boy. And I've been in a lot worse places, believe me,' Logan told her. He smiled, not unkindly. 'Go home, Sinead. That's an order.'

Sinead hesitated, then nodded. 'Yes, sir,' she said. 'But… can I make a suggestion?'

Logan nodded. He watched as Sinead leaned past him, turned the handle, and pushed the door open. 'It's the Highlands,' she told him. 'We don't always lock our doors.'

'Daft bastard,' Logan muttered, although it wasn't clear if he was referring to himself or to Next Door Ed. 'Thank you, Sinead,' he said, pulling on a thin smile.

Reaching into his pocket, he produced a pair of thin blue rubber gloves, and began the laborious process of wrestling his oversized hands into them.

'Now, piss off before you get us both into trouble.'

Chapter 11

The air in the kitchen was old and stale, flavoured with something damp that clawed up inside the nostrils and down the back of the throat.

Logan eased the door closed behind him and listened for any sign of movement from elsewhere in the house.

Nothing.

There were no appliances in the kitchen, just the open voids and trailing wires where a washing machine and oven should've been. Water pooled from the end of a hose in one of the cavities, forming a puddle on the scuffed lino floor.

Outside, the evening was drawing in, and the last of the sunlight had a fight on its hands to get through the blanket of cloud. The kitchen was washed in a gloomy half-darkness, but Logan could see just enough to know that there wasn't a lot worth looking at.

He quietened his breath and moved to the door leading out of the kitchen, the bottom of his coat brushing against his knees.

The living room looked much like it had from the window. Camping chair. Plastic table. Stack of lager cans. They were empty, as he'd guessed, but there were a few unopened tins in a *Spar* bag under the table.

The *Pot Noodle* was two-thirds eaten. Logan touched the side of the pot. Cold, he thought, although the gloves made it difficult to be sure.

There was another window at the far end of the room that looked out onto the street at the front. Logan could see a couple of press vans out there, but the journos themselves were still assembled outside the Reids' house, waiting in the rain for him to come striding down the path.

They'd be disappointed.

Keeping as far from the window as possible, Logan made for the room's second door. It rubbed against the carpet as he eased it open, and he stopped a couple of times to listen for the sound of anyone moving around upstairs that would suggest someone had heard him.

Silence.

On the other side of the door was a small hall, barely larger than the inside of a hotel lift. The house's front door was on Logan's right, an internal door on his left, and then a staircase led up to the floor above.

There was no furniture in the hall, either, just a worn-out old mat, a stack of letters on the floor that mostly looked like junk, and a little mirror fixed to the wall around Logan's chest height.

The door on the left led to a cupboard. A disposable waterproof jacket hung from a hook, and a couple of pairs of trainers had been left on the floor. Logan squatted and picked a couple of the shoes up. There were no size markings inside one of the pairs, but the other had a tag sewn into the inside of the tongue.

Size ten.

Setting the trainers down again, Logan returned to the hallway, and crept to the bottom of the narrow stairs. A bathroom door stood open at the top, the light through the dimpled window mottling the shadows on the staircase walls.

Logan held his breath. Listened.

A couple of cars passed outside. One of the uniforms ordered some over-eager press bastard to, 'Keep back from the gate.'

But from inside the house, there was nothing.

There were thirteen steps. Every single one of them creaked and groaned beneath the carpet as Logan made his way up, sounding out a fanfare to anyone lurking above.

By the fourth step, Logan decided to abandon his attempts at stealth and just charge up the stairs as quickly as he could. He braced himself as he reached the top, fists clenching, ready for someone to come swinging at him from behind the bannister.

No-one did. The cramped upstairs landing was as empty as the floor below.

There were four doors, including the bathroom. Logan spent a second giving that room a cursory once-over. A similar damp smell to the one in the kitchen loitered around in there, too, thick and claggy in the DCI's throat.

Two of the other doors were open. The other had been pulled fully closed. Judging by position, it was the room with the closed curtains he'd seen from outside.

He checked the other two first. Both bedrooms, he supposed, although they both lacked anything in the way of beds. They both lacked anything in the way of very much, in fact.

One had a threadbare carpet, while the other had bare floorboards that had been badly painted in an ill-judged shade of lilac at some point in the dim and distant past. The décor in both was shabby and long past its best, and

Logan got the sense that neither room had been in use for some time.

More importantly than any of that, neither room was occupied, so no big bastards were likely to come rushing up behind him when he entered the other room.

He stole a glance down the stairs, listened for a moment, then turned his attention to the fourth and final door.

The floorboards upstairs were more solid than those on the staircase, and he was able to approach the door in relative silence. He waited outside it, breath held, ear pointed to the wood, ready for anything but prepared for nothing.

There was no point doing all the announcement stuff. He wasn't officially here. Instead, he pushed down the handle and simultaneously put his shoulder to the wood, throwing the door wide.

The smell hit him almost immediately—the sour tang of sweat mixed with the sweeter notes of cannabis. The heavy curtains and lack of light from elsewhere made it hard to make out the details of anything, but there was a single mattress in the corner of the room, a dark lump curled up on top of it.

Child-sized.

Motionless.

No. God, no.

Not again.

Logan flicked the light switch and a bare bulb sparked into life, pushing back the darkness. Logan saw the mattress properly, and the knot in his stomach slackened a little.

A sleeping bag. Just a sleeping bag. That was all.

He gave it a nudge with his foot.

Empty.

The rest of the room was a graveyard of crisp bags, pizza boxes, *Irn Bru* bottles, and other junk-food detritus. Logan carefully opened the lid of one of the cardboard pizza containers. There was half a slice left. Ham and pineapple.

'Bloody savage,' he muttered, nostrils flaring in distaste.

Closing the lid, he took out his phone and snapped a photo of the logo and phone number printed on the box.

That done, he patted down the sleeping bag. Tucked in at the bottom was a little wooden box containing half a packet of green Rizla, some torn-up strips of what looked like a cereal box, and a few crumbs of hash that'd struggle to choke a mouse.

He replaced the box, then turned, still crouched, and took another look at the room. It was grim, no doubt about that, but there was nothing to suggest that Connor had been here. Which meant that Logan was officially breaking and entering without anything even vaguely resembling an excuse.

Time to go.

He began to stand, then hesitated. On a hunch, he slipped a hand beneath the mattress. Almost immediately, the side of his pinkie finger bumped against something solid.

Raising the edge of the mattress, Logan found himself staring down at an old battered laptop.

'Shite,' Logan spat, torn by the discovery.

Two very different 'next steps' presented themselves to him. He spent a few moments considering the implications of each. Then, reluctantly, he lowered the edge of the mattress again, covering the laptop.

He made for the door, took another look around the room, then switched the light off before stepping out onto the upstairs landing and pulling the door closed.

Logan was at the top of the stairs when a thought that had been niggling at him for the past few minutes pushed its way forward.

His eyes crept up to the ceiling, and to the hatch built into it.

He was working on converting the loft.

A tingling crept up the back of Logan's neck. The thin rubber of his gloves *creaked* as he flexed his fingers in and out.

And then, he stretched up and slid the snib aside. An exhalation of stale air hit him as the hatch swung down, revealing a yawning chasm of blackness.

There was a ladder attached to the hatch. Logan fiddled with the hook until the bottom half slid down to the floor at his feet.

Reaching up, he took hold of one of the rungs and shook it, testing its sturdiness.

And then, with his heart thudding in his chest, he began to climb.

Chapter 12

If Next Door Ed was converting the loft, it wasn't immediately apparent what he was converting it into. Logan swept his phone's torch across it, taking it all in.

A few planks had been nailed across the exposed ceiling beams, forming a haphazard pathway leading to the wall that divided this attic space from the one next door.

Or, what was left of the wall, at least. A hole had been knocked through it, the crumbling bricks stacked up on another clumsily floored area. The planks used for the flooring looked like the same ones in the Reids' back garden. Presumably they had been nicked at some point.

The rafters creaked ominously as Logan made his way across the makeshift floorboards. The hole in the wall wasn't particularly big, but large enough for an adult to clamber through, provided dignity wasn't high on their list of priorities.

The loft on the other side of the wall was empty, aside from some thick rolls of insulation between the ceiling joists, and another couple of the same planks Logan was standing on. They had been laid across the insulation but weren't nailed down.

Logan snapped a couple of pictures of the hole, a few of the loft beyond, then did another sweep of the space around him. The wind whistled through gaps in the sloping roof. A percussion of rain played on the tiles overhead.

The oval of torchlight tracked across the exposed beams, and probed the corners where the floor met the roof. Just like downstairs, there was nothing to actively suggest that Connor had been there.

Still, even before venturing into the attic space, Logan had been keen to talk to Ed Walker as a matter of urgency. Now, after this, he was suspect number one.

Technically, suspect number *only*, but Logan didn't really want to dwell on that right now.

After taking another few pictures, he clambered down the ladder, the rungs groaning in protest as he picked his way to the bottom.

Once down, he manhandled the bottom part of the ladder back up into position, then closed the hatch and fastened the snib.

He was halfway down the stairs when he stopped.

Logan stood in the mottled darkness, chewing his bottom lip.

'Bollocks,' he muttered.

His eyes flitted upwards in the direction of the closed door.

–

The journos hadn't expected him to approach around the side of the house, and Logan was almost back at his car before they spotted him. They moved through the rain like a single organism—one that was generously endowed with limbs and heads, but distinctly lacking in moral integrity.

'Detective Chief Inspector!'

'What is the family saying?'

'Do you know where Connor is?'

Their voices were raised, shouting to be heard over the growing wind. Logan muttered something deeply uncomplimentary and fished his car keys from his pocket. The Focus chirped as he thumbed the button, its wing mirrors unfolding as if giving him a welcoming wave.

'Is the boy alive?'

'When will you be making an official statement?'

'Do you have any leads yet?'

Logan shot the approaching throng a glare. If looks could kill, this one would've taken out the whole front row, and probably left the rest of them fighting for their lives in the ICU.

He had just hauled the driver's door open when one voice in particular rose up above the others. One familiar, fork-scraping-on-a-plate voice that stirred some primal response deep in Logan's gut.

Ken Bloody Henderson.

'Is it true there was a teddy and a photo, Jack?'

Logan tried to rein in the look of shock he could feel spreading across his face, but only managed to temper it a little. He stood there, frozen, the car door held open.

The rest of the journalists had fallen quiet. For a moment, it was just Logan and Henderson, eye-to-eye, the reporter holding his phone out, the microphone aimed at the DCI.

'What?' Logan asked. His mind raced. 'Where did you hear that?'

Henderson shrugged nonchalantly. He said nothing, but there was a little smirk on his face that Logan would've dearly loved to wipe off. Ideally, with the sole of his shoe.

'No comment,' Logan told him. He jumped into the car and slammed the door shut.

He sat swearing below his breath for a moment, then glanced in the wing mirror and caught sight of Henderson and his gaggle of bastards hanging around behind the car. Grimacing, he fired up the engine and slipped a gloved hand inside his coat.

He took out the *Spar* bag containing the laptop, placed it carefully on the passenger seat, and spent a few seconds considering the ramifications of it.

The car's automatic windscreen wipers kicked in, swishing a slick of rain from the glass and drawing Logan's gaze away from the bag with the battered computer inside.

With a final glance back at the houses, Logan crunched the car into first, pulled away from the kerb, and set off into the strengthening storm.

Chapter 13

DI Ben Forde and the rest of the Major Investigations Team eyed Logan warily as he stormed into the Incident Room with a face like thunder.

'It's out,' Logan barked. 'They know. About the bear. They know.'

'Shite,' Ben groaned.

'Aye. Shite. You can say that again.'

Logan paced back and forth, exorcising the tension that had been steadily building during the drive over.

'Who knows?' asked DC Neish. He had been pinning photographs of the abduction scene to a board on the wall that was already heavily decorated with other pictures and notes. A school photograph of Connor Reid smiled out at Logan, jarring disturbingly with a blown-up version of the image that had been delivered to the parents earlier that day.

'The press. Who do you think?' Logan snapped. 'Someone told them. Someone blabbed.'

He pointed to the only female detective in the room and clicked his fingers. 'DS... sorry.'

'McQuarrie, sir,' Caitlyn replied.

'Ken Henderson. He's a journalist. Freelance, but writes for *The Herald*, I think. Bring him in. Put him in cuffs, if necessary. Hogtie the bastard, if you have to.'

Caitlyn glanced at DI Forde, then back to Logan. 'On what pretext, sir?'

Logan stopped pacing. 'On the pretext that I said so,' he snapped.

'Jack,' Ben soothed. 'Wherever it came from, it didn't come from in here.'

For a moment, it looked like Logan might dispute that, but then he sighed and shook his head. 'Aye. No. I know,' he admitted, his tone losing some of its edge. 'But there's a leak, so let's find out where.'

'On it, boss,' said Caitlyn. 'Ken Henderson, did you say?'

Logan nodded. 'Aye. He might refer to himself as 'Kenderson,' though, on account on him being a massive arsehole. Get him in, and let me know when he's here.'

Caitlyn confirmed, unhooked her jacket from a hook by the door, then hurried out, already drawing her phone from her pocket as she left.

With the immediate drama over, Tyler went back to pinning up the crime scene photos. DC Khaled sat at a desk, rifling through a depressingly small bundle of paperwork, and dividing it into different piles.

'Hamza, wasn't it?' Logan asked.

'Aye, sir,' Hamza said, looking up. He had a hopeful look on his face, like he might be about to be reassigned to do something more interesting.

'Know anything about computers?'

'A bit, aye. Why?'

Logan fished the *Spar* bag from inside his coat and deposited it on top of the paperwork piles. 'See what you can get from that laptop, will you?'

Hamza reached for the bag.

'Wear gloves,' Logan instructed. 'It could be evidence.'

'Shouldn't it go to forensics?' Hamza asked.

'Eventually, aye. But take a wee look first, eh? See if anything jumps out.'

'Right, sir.'

While DC Khaled went to fetch himself a pair of gloves, Logan rounded on Tyler. 'Come back to that later. We need to put out a shout. Ed Walker. Lives next door to the Reids, right-hand side looking from the front. Don't know the number. I think he might be our man. I went round, but there was no-one home.'

'Why? What did you find out?' asked Ben.

'The father says Connor was acting strangely when they were out walking. Quieter than usual.'

'Aye, that's in his original statement,' said Hamza, snapping on a pair of thin blue gloves as he returned to his desk.

'Connor also asked about Walker. "Next Door Ed", they call him. He asked if his dad liked him, then he asked his dad if he thought his mum liked him.'

'Liked Ed?' said Ben.

'Aye. Connor asked his dad if his dad thought his mum liked Ed,' Logan explained, trying to clarify but not making a particularly good job of it.

'And does she?' Tyler asked.

'That's not really the point, is it, son?' Ben said, shooting the younger officer a dismissive look.

'Maybe not, no,' Logan agreed. 'But I did get the impression that she knew him better than the husband did. Nothing concrete, but I wouldn't be surprised.'

'An affair, you think?'

Logan tilted his head from side to side in a sort of weighing gesture. 'Doubt it. Maybe, though. But I reckon she's a woman who likes the finer things. Or would like the chance to like them, anyway. Not sure Next Door Ed would fit that description. The house is a shithole.'

'Maybe she just likes a bit of rough, boss,' suggested Tyler. He waggled his eyebrows suggestively and grinned at both superior officers.

'Is it my imagination, or is he still here?' Logan asked Ben.

'Unfortunately,' Ben said. He clapped his hands twice. 'What are you standing around here for? Go put out the shout.'

'Sorry, Boss,' Tyler said, then he turned and hurried out of the room.

Ben waited until he was gone, looked over to where Hamza was hunched over the laptop, then sidled closer to Logan.

'House is a shithole? I thought he wasn't home?'

Logan nodded, not looking at him. Instead, his eyes were fixed on 'the Big Board', as he'd always referred to it, and the all-too-sparse collection of leads currently pinned to it.

'Door wasn't locked.'

'Jesus, Jack,' Ben whispered. He pointed to the computer Hamza was working at. 'And did you get that...?'

Logan nodded.

'Christ. That's a big bloody risk,' Ben warned. 'And not just for you, for all of us.'

'Aye,' Logan admitted. He finally turned in the DI's direction, and there was something dark and hollow behind his eyes. 'But you didn't see them, Ben. Last time, I mean. Those kids. You didn't see them.'

Ben said nothing. What was there to say?

'I know it's not him doing this. It can't be him,' Logan said. 'But someone has done a bang-up job of copying him this far, and if they stick to the script and see this thing through, then we have less than two days to find that boy.'

He cleared his throat, inhaled through his nose, pulled together his fraying edges. 'So, I'll be the one to take the risks. It won't reflect on anyone else. Buck stops with me. You're all just following orders.'

'You know that's not how it works, Jack. They won't buy that.'

Ben sighed and rubbed a finger and thumb against his forehead, kneading away the beginnings of a migraine.

'What are you saying?' Logan asked.

Ben dragged his top teeth over his bottom lip, scraping at the smoothly shaved skin.

He stopped rubbing his head and nodded, a decision reached.

'I'm saying that the buck stops with both of us,' Ben said, keeping his voice low. 'We're both responsible. The rest of them aren't.'

'Ben…'

'That's the deal on offer, Jack.'

Logan briefly considered protesting, but he knew the DI well enough not to waste his breath. Instead, they shook hands and patted shoulders.

'I'll take it, then,' Logan said. 'And thank you.'

'He's a wee boy, Jack,' Ben said. 'Fuck the risks. Let's just get him home.'

'No arguments from me,' Logan said, shrugging off his coat.

'Oh, but before you get too comfy, the Chief Inspector wants to see you,' Ben said.

'The Chief Inspector? Of what? This place?'

Ben gave a nod. Something mischievous sparkled behind his eyes.

'Shite. Who is it?' Logan asked, recognising that expression. He quickly flicked through his mental Rolodex but came up blank.

DI Forde's mouth curved up into the beginnings of a smirk.

'Jinkies.'

A groan burst unbidden from Logan's lips. He finished taking off his coat and let it flop down onto his desk. 'Of course,' he said with a grimace. 'I should've bloody guessed.'

Chapter 14

Chief Inspector Hugh Pickering was sitting behind a large, well-organised desk when Logan entered the office. He was writing studiously in a large notebook, the shiny top of his head pointed to the door, a fountain pen scratching across the paper.

Without looking up, he gestured to the chair across from him. Logan closed the door, stood behind the chair, and waited.

The pen continued to scratch across the page.

'You're making the place look untidy, Jack.'

Logan recognised the power play, but had no interest in competing. He pulled out the chair, sat in it, then leaned forward with his hands clasped, so his forearms were resting on the edge of the desk.

'You wanted to see—'

Pickering raised a hand, still not looking up.

Once Logan fell silent, the Chief Inspector lowered his hand and returned to writing.

'I won't keep you.'

Logan resisted the urge to point out that he was already keeping him, aware that it would only drag things out further. He sat back and waited.

Pickering had earned the nickname 'Jinkies' on his very first day of training at Tulliallan. It had been coined

93

due to the then constable's striking resemblance to Velma, one of the characters from the cartoon series, *Scooby-Doo*.

At first glance, there had been a passing resemblance, mostly down to Pickering's reddish-brown hair and thick-rimmed glasses. Weirdly, though, the longer you looked at him, the more he resembled the canine-accompanied ghost-hunter.

He had a round face—'Bawchops,' had been another popular designation for a while—and a scattering of freckles across each cheek. Someone had got him drunk one night and talked him into putting on an orange roll-neck jumper, thus cementing his status as, 'What, that guy who looks like Velma out of *Scooby-Doo*?' for the rest of his career. And, if Logan had anything to do with it, far beyond.

Poor Velma had let herself go in recent years, though. Jinkies' distinctive hair had been vacating the premises for a while now, and only a few stragglers were hanging around the edges like the last revellers at a school disco.

His already round face was now substantially rounder and was carrying some extra baggage under its chin. He still wore the glasses, though, and if Logan didn't know better, he'd have sworn they were the same pair.

Jinkies had never been cut out for frontline policing. Not really. In some ways, it wasn't his fault. It couldn't have been easy to walk through Sauchiehall Street after closing on a Saturday with some mouthy wee bam shouting, 'Fuck me, is that no' her out of Scooby-Doo?' at you at the top of his lungs.

He'd taken a desk job as quickly as humanly possible, and hadn't stepped out from behind one since. At least, not to do anything useful.

From the looks of him, he'd been golfing today. He wore a V-neck Pringle jumper with no sleeves and an eyeball-melting diamond pattern knitted into the front. Beneath it, he wore a short-sleeved polo-neck with the top button done up, presumably in some token nod to formality.

Logan couldn't see Jinkies' legs, but he was picturing some truly horrifying checked trousers. Or worse—shorts.

He pushed the image away and was giving serious consideration to grabbing the Chief Inspector's pen and ramming it up his arse when the scratching stopped. Logan watched impatiently as Jinkies scanned over what he'd written, lips moving silently.

Then, with a nod, the Chief Inspector slid the page aside, interlocked his fingers on the desk in front of him, and finally raised his head.

'Jack! Good to see you,' he said.

'Hugh,' replied Logan, non-committal. 'Ben said you wanted to see me.'

Jinkies frowned, as if this was news to him. Then his eyes widened behind his glasses and he bumped his hands against the desktop.

'Ah, yes. I did. That's right.'

Logan waited.

But not for long.

'Well? What for?' he asked. 'Not sure if you've noticed, Hugh, but we've got a live abduction going on.'

Jinkies smiled magnanimously. 'That was why I wanted to see you, Jack. I just wanted to let you know that whatever you need, it's yours. "Mi casa, su casa. My house is your house".'

95

'I know what it means,' Logan grunted. He checked himself and managed something that was within spitting distance of being a smile. 'Thanks, Hugh. I appreciate that.'

Jinkies leaned forward a fraction. 'But, so we're clear, it is *mi casa*, Jack.' He tapped a pudgy finger against the desk. 'My house. My rules. You have your team, I have mine. We will offer any and all assistance we can, but they answer to me. Is that clear? To me. Not you. I'm not interested in a *who's got the biggest willy* contest.'

This was understandable. Logan had seen Jinkies in the shower. It was a contest the Chief Inspector couldn't hope to win.

'Got it? Mi casa, mi...' The Chief Inspector realised, too late, that he had exhausted his Spanish. '...rulios. Capiche?'

'I'm not here to get in anyone's way, Hugh,' Logan said. The words were designed to be reassuring, but the tone of his voice didn't back them up. 'But this is a major investigation, and I'm heading the Major Investigations Team. In about...'

He checked his watch.

'...six hours the whole world is going to be watching this case, scrutinising every bloody thing we do. And that's going to be on me, Hugh. Not you. So I'm going to do whatever I have to do to get that boy home. If I tell your lads to jump, I want to hear, 'How high?' and not, 'I'll have to run it by the boss. While that boy is missing, I'm the boss, all right?'

He tapped a finger against the desk, just as Jinkies had done.

'*Mi* casa.'

Across the table, the Chief Inspector leaned back, his face searching for an expression but not quite finding one. 'We both know that's not how it works, Jack. There's an order of—'

'Today, that's how it works,' Jack said, standing up. 'And tomorrow.'

Two days.

'After that… We'll see where we are.'

Logan looked the Chief Inspector up and down, scarcely bothering to hide his distaste. 'But don't you worry about it. You enjoy your golf.'

He made it to the door without Jinkies saying a word, but stopped when he got there and turned.

'What's the story with PC Bell?'

'Which one's she?'

'Sinead. Young lassie. Parents died in an RTA.'

'Oh, her. Yes. She's promising,' Jinkies said. He puffed out his ample cheeks. 'Nasty business with the accident, though. It was down by the lochside. They were headed back up the road from Glasgow, or somewhere, if I recall. Sinead was first on the scene.'

'Jesus.'

'Don't think it was pretty, by all accounts.'

'I can't imagine it would be, no,' Logan said. 'I want her assigned to my team for this.'

Jinkies looked the DCI up and down, then raised a salacious eyebrow. 'Bit young for you, isn't she, Jack?'

'Don't judge us all by your own standards, Jinkies,' Logan told him. He enjoyed the little flinch the Chief Inspector gave upon hearing his old nickname. 'She's a well-known face. Local knowledge. Seems bright. She'll be an asset.'

'Plain clothes?'

Logan shook his head. 'We'll keep her in uniform. For now, anyway. Could be handy.'

Jinkies clicked his tongue against the back of his teeth, then nodded. 'Fine. You can have her on your team.'

Logan smiled grimly. 'Thanks,' he said, pulling open the door. 'But I wasn't really asking.'

–

If the sight of Jinkies' face had wound him up, the next one Logan saw almost tipped him over the edge.

'All right, Jack? You going to give me an exclusive?'

'Henderson,' said Logan, practically spitting the word out.

The journalist was being led along the corridor by DS McQuarrie. She hadn't cuffed him or, to Logan's immense disappointment, set about him with a baton.

Logan intercepted them outside a closed door. He caught Henderson by the arm, shot Caitlyn a look, and jerked his head in the direction of the door.

'This an interview room?'

'Uh, no. Cleaning cupboard, I think,' Caitlyn replied.

'It'll do.'

Shoving the door open, Logan bundled Henderson inside. The smug wee bastard went clattering into a shelf of polishes and sprays as a single light automatically blinked on above them.

'Watch it, Jack,' Henderson smarmed, his weasel smile showing off the gap in his two front teeth. 'Don't want to get yourself in trouble again.'

'Uh, boss?' asked Caitlyn, peering into the cupboard from out in the corridor. 'I'm not sure we should be...'

'It's fine. We go way back,' Logan told her, just as the door squeaked closed between them.

Henderson straightened and brushed himself down. 'No need to be so rough, Jack. You know I'm always happy to help a fine establishment such as yours.'

'Who told you?' Logan demanded.

'Who told me what?'

'You know what. Stop wasting my time.'

'People tell me a lot of things, Jack. You'll have to remind me what—'

Logan's hand caught him by the front of the jacket. Henderson's smile only broadened as he was pinned against the shelves.

'Police brutality is still a hot topic, Jack. I could get a centre spread out of this.'

'Centre spread? Is that still a thing? I thought you'd all been replaced by blogs and Twitter.'

'Not quite yet,' Henderson said.

Logan sneered. 'Are you no' tired of trailing the country looking for dirt to dig up?' he asked. 'Aren't you a bit old for all this shite?'

Henderson held the detective's gaze, his smile fixed in place. 'Aren't you?'

For a second, maybe two, Logan and Henderson just stared at each other, combatants sizing each other up before a duel.

Then, with a grunt, Logan released his grip.

'Aye. Maybe,' he admitted. 'The teddy. Who told you about the teddy?'

Henderson smoothed himself down for the second time in as many minutes. 'A good reporter never reveals his sources, Jack. You know that.'

Logan's jaw tensed. He eyeballed Henderson, but turned his head a fraction towards the door.

'DS McQuarrie?'

'Yes, boss?' Caitlyn's voice was muffled through the door.

'Go get yourself a cup of tea, will you?'

There was a pregnant pause. A moment of hesitation.

'Shouldn't I maybe hang on in case...'

'Caitlyn. Go get yourself a cup of tea.'

Another pause, shorter than the last one.

'Yes, boss.'

Logan listened until he heard the DS's footsteps fading along the corridor. Then he unbuttoned the cuff of one shirt sleeve and began to roll it up.

'Come on now, Jack. There's no need to go acting the Big Man,' Henderson told him.

Logan said nothing. He finished rolling up the first sleeve, then set to work on the second.

'I'm sure we can figure something out,' Henderson said, his eyes darting briefly down to follow the sleeve's progress. 'I'm sure I could be persuaded to help if you were to, say, offer me something I could use. You tell me something, I'll tell you something.'

Logan finished rolling up the second sleeve, then opened and closed his fingers a few times, flexing the tendons. He cracked his knuckles. He cricked his neck.

'Nothing major, just a nugget or two. A crumb, that's all,' Henderson said. 'A fair swap.'

'We're talking about a boy's life,' Logan reminded him.

'And a man's career. Namely, mine. Maybe that's not as important to you, but it's all relative, isn't it?' Henderson said. He eyed the DCI's hulking great hands, then smiled. 'You said yourself, those arseholes online are cannibalising us. Come on, Jack. Scratch my back. What have you got?'

Logan balled his fingers into fists, and the smug look slid from Henderson's face, swept aside by various flavours of panic. Logan allowed himself a moment to savour it, before throwing the journo a bone.

'Ed Walker.'

Henderson's eyelids fluttered as if Logan had thrown a punch at him but stopped short of landing it.

'What?'

'Ed Walker,' Logan said again. 'The neighbour. We're interested in speaking to him.'

'You think he did it?' Henderson asked.

'We're interested in speaking to him,' Logan said again. 'That's all. We're going to announce it in the morning if we haven't found him, so I'm giving you the jump on it. Ed Walker. Write it down.'

Henderson tapped the chest pocket of his jacket and smiled. 'Don't worry. I'm recording every word.'

'Aye. No, you're not,' said Logan. He produced a phone from one of his own pockets and passed it back to the journalist. 'You need to be more careful with that thing, Ken. They're no' cheap.'

Henderson gave his jacket a more thorough pat down.

'How the fu—' he muttered, then he snatched the phone back.

'Now,' Logan began. 'I've scratched your back. Who told you about the teddy?'

Henderson sniffed and shrugged. 'One of the local press boys. Works for one of the weeklies. Tom something. The guy who threw the question away outside the Reids. Him.'

'And where did he hear about it?'

'Well, I don't know, do I?' Henderson said. His eyes blazed as he scrutinised Logan's face. 'True then, is it?'

Logan sighed. 'Aye. Aye, it's true. Looks like we've got a copycat.'

'And you think it's this Walker fella?'

'He's a person of interest,' Logan said. 'That's all at this stage.'

'How much interest? Scale of one to ten.'

Logan pulled the door open. 'Get out, Henderson. We're done,' he instructed. 'And leave the parents alone, eh? They've already suffered enough.'

'Suffering sells papers, Jack. Not nice, but it's how it is,' Henderson told him. He followed the DCI out of the cupboard and into the corridor. 'Thanks for the inform-ation. Very interesting. I'll see myself out.'

'Aye, nice try,' Logan told him. He beckoned over to where DS McQuarrie was hovering by the canteen door. 'Escort Mr Henderson off the premises, would you? And keep an eye on him to make sure he doesn't try to sneak back in.'

Henderson grinned, showing off his crooked teeth again. 'You know me too well, Jack.'

'Well, we've all got our crosses to bear,' Logan replied.

Along the corridor, Caitlyn scanned her pass and opened the door that led out to the reception area. Henderson shuffled towards it, head down, already tapping out a number on his phone.

'Oh, Jack?' he said, stopping a pace or two before he reached the door.

'What now?'

'The boy. I hope you find him.'

A flash of surprise registered on Logan's face.

'Aye,' he said, once it had passed. 'You and me both.'

Chapter 15

DI Forde was talking to a couple of shirt-and-ties when Logan returned to the Incident Room. One of them, who had been perched on the edge of the DCI's desk, jumped up as if an electrical charge had just shot up his arse.

'DCI Jack Logan, this is DS Boyle and DC Innes,' Ben said, hand-signalling his way through the introductions. 'They're CID. Offered to clue our lot up with the local gen.'

'Good. That's good. Thanks,' said Logan, shaking both offered hands in turn. 'Don't suppose you know anywhere to get something decent to eat nearby?'

DS Boyle sucked air in through his teeth. 'Sunday.'

'There's J.J.'s along the road,' suggested DC Innes, gesturing off in the direction of the town centre. 'They do a good breakfast.'

Logan's eyes went to his watch.

'Aye, an All-Day Breakfast, I mean. Sausage, egg, nice bit of black pudding. *Mushrooms*, if you like that sort of thing.'

From the way he said it, and the expression on his face, it was evident that DC Innes very much did not like that sort of thing one little bit.

'Sounds good,' said Logan.

'J.J.'s is shut.'

All eyes went to DS Boyle.

'Shut?' said Innes. 'J.J.'s?'

'Aye.'

'What, like *shut* shut? Or just shut?'

'Well, no' *shut* shut, but no' just shut. *Shut*,' said Boyle, with varying degrees of emphasis. 'They're on holiday.'

'Oh, so *shut*. Right.' Innes nodded, then turned to Logan. 'J.J.'s is shut.'

'Aye, I picked up on that,' Logan said. 'Anywhere else?'

Both CID detectives gave this some thought.

'Pizza place in the village,' suggested Innes.

'Aye! What time is it?' asked Boyle. He checked his watch. 'Aye. That'll be open.'

Pizza Place. Logan remembered the photo on his phone.

'Want me to ring you something in?' Ben asked.

'Actually, no. Leave it,' said Logan. 'I might go round in a bit. What time does it shut?'

'Same time Sean Connery gets to Wimbledon, sir,' said Innes.

Logan and the others all looked at the DC blankly. Their expression remained unchanged when he continued in an utterly dire Sean Connery impression.

'*Tennish*.'

From the look on their faces, it was obvious that nobody was impressed. Innes wilted, his cheeks burning. Logan decided to gloss right over it and pretend it had never happened. He turned his attention to DS Boyle instead.

'Ed Walker. Next door to the Reids. Anyone talk to him?'

'Not sure. I'll check. Probably, if he was in,' Boyle said. 'I'll find out.'

'Thanks. And Tom... something. He's been blabbing about the teddy bear. I want to know how he knew about it. He's a reporter for one of the local papers.'

'There's just the one,' said Boyle.

'Reporter?'

'Paper. Don't know him, though. We'll see what we can find out.'

Boyle put a hand on DC Innes's shoulder and guided him towards the door. 'If there's anything else, just shout. We all want to see the wee lad home safe.'

Logan nodded. 'Thanks.'

'And try the pizza place. It's good. Well, not *good*, but... good.'

'Will do,' said Logan.

He watched the DS manhandle the junior officer out into the corridor, and caught a hissed, 'Fucking *tennish*,' before the door clunked closed behind them.

'They're a good bunch,' Ben said. 'You'd think they've probably got it a bit easy up here, but they know their stuff. Made some big drugs collars. Like, major.'

'Good to know,' Logan said.

He looked across to Hamza's desk, where the DC was still hunched over the laptop, his blue-gloved fingers tapping away at the keys.

'Getting anywhere?'

'Well, I'm in, so aye. Getting somewhere. Nowhere exciting, mind. There's not a lot on it.'

'Shite.' Logan groaned. 'Still, good job on getting in. That was quick.'

Hamza shrugged. 'His password was '12345.' It wasn't exactly rocket science, sir.'

'Keep looking. See if anything turns up.'

The door to the Incident Room flew open, and Tyler came rushing in clutching a bundle of printouts.

'What have you got?' Logan asked.

'Ed Walker, sir. He's got previous,' Tyler announced, waving the bundle. 'Just out of a stretch at the Big Hoose.'

'Barlinnie? What for?'

'Possession of a Class A, and assaulting a police officer,' Tyler replied. He thrust the folder of paperwork into the DCI's waiting hands. 'Shocking beard, an' all, although I suppose that's not technically a crime.'

Logan flipped open the folder, then whistled quietly through his teeth when he saw the mugshot within. Walker glared sheer contempt back up at him.

'Jesus,' Logan muttered. 'That is a shocker, isn't it?'

He skimmed through the first couple of pages, then handed the folder to Ben. 'We should put it up on the board.'

DI Forde opened the folder. 'God. You're right. That is a shite beard.'

'Any word on his whereabouts?' Logan asked.

Tyler shook his head. 'Not yet, boss.'

'Keep an eye on the house and start knocking doors,' Logan instructed. 'Find out if anyone's seen him coming and going since Friday.'

'It's getting late,' Tyler pointed out, glancing at the clock.

'Good, then we might actually catch some of them at home,' Logan replied. 'Check if there's any family or known associates in the area. And get his photo and description out in circulation. We need to find him and find him fast. CID said they'll help. Hold them to that.'

'Yes, boss.'

Logan glowered at him.

'Oh, you want me to… now? Right.'

Tyler scuttled off. Logan pulled the swivel chair out from beneath the desk he had claimed as his own and flopped into it.

He sagged for a moment, tiredness slackening his muscles and dragging him down into the cracked leather of the seat.

A headache had been making itself at home in his skull for the past couple of hours, and felt like it was settling in for the long haul. Hunger wasn't yet gnawing at him, exactly, but it was certainly making its presence felt.

It had been hours since Tyler had brought him that biscuit. Even then, it had only been a Rich Tea, and man could not get by on mere Rich Teas alone.

Well, he probably could, but it'd be a fucking miserable existence.

'You all right?' Ben asked him.

Logan sat up and nodded. 'Aye. Aye. Just a long day.'

'Looks like your hunch might be right,' Ben said. 'Ed Walker, I mean.'

'Hm.'

Ben rolled another chair over and took a seat. 'What's "Hm"?' he asked. 'You don't think it's him?'

'I think we need to talk to him,' Logan said. He waved a hand. 'It probably is. I mean, it's looking like it.'

'But…?'

'But how would he know about the envelope? The writing on the front? That's the bit I don't get.'

Ben flipped idly through the paperwork. 'He'd have to have come into contact with someone who knew. Someone from the original case?'

'Aye. Who, though?'

'Petrie?' Ben hazarded.

'Petrie's a cabbage. Or, so he wants us to believe. He's got a cushy wee number in Carstairs. Compared to where he should be, I mean. He wouldn't risk giving the game away by blabbing to some scrote he didn't know,' Logan reasoned.

'Unless he did know him,' said Ben.

Logan's eyes narrowed, but he looked unconvinced. 'What is Walker? Fifties?'

Ben flicked back a few pages. 'Forty-three,' he said. He studied the photo again. 'Bloody Hell. The years have not been kind.'

'We could look for a link between him and Petrie, but I doubt we'll find one. Still, worth a try. Get DS McQuarrie on it,' Logan said. 'And check for any connection with the original families, too. But discreetly.'

Logan's headache stabbed at him. The families. Shite. The arrival of the teddy was going to catapult the story to the front page of every newspaper in the country. It had been twenty years since Mister Whisper had taken Dylan Muir. His parents—not to mention the parents of Lewis Briggs and Matthew Dennison—were about to have it raked up all over again.

He'd have to phone the Gozer, ask him to send officers round to help prepare them for the media shitestorm. Probably too late tonight, but first thing in the morning. The last thing they needed was the polis hammering on their doors in the wee small hours. Not again.

'We need to get forensics into Walker's house,' Logan said.

'Going to take time to get a warrant.'

'Not necessarily. I'm pretty sure he's squatting there. Find out who owns it, then we can go in.'

Ben nodded and reached for the phone.

'Hamza? Get anything yet?'

'A lot of porn, sir. Aye, I mean a *lot* of porn,' Hamza said. He tilted his head a little, frowned like an art critic trying to work out the meaning of a masterpiece, then his eyes widened and he quickly clicked the trackpad. 'Didn't need to see that,' he muttered.

'Anything dodgy?'

'Pretty standard stuff, sir. It's more the quantity rather than the content that's worth noting.'

'Anything else?'

'Actually, aye. This is interesting. He did a couple of searches on DNA markers and how DNA evidence gets processed on…'

Hamza tapped at the trackpad.

'Wednesday. Well, no, early hours of Thursday.'

Logan and Ben exchanged glances.

'Still have your doubts?' Ben asked.

Logan stood up. 'We need to find this bastard, Ben,' he said. He flicked his eyes from the DI to Hamza. 'We all know what we're doing?'

Ben nodded and punched a series of numbers on the phone. DC Khaled looked up from the laptop.

'Just got a few more folders to go through, sir,' he said. 'Then, if it's all right with you, there's a couple of things I want to check out on the map.'

'We need all hands on deck.'

'It won't take long, sir. Just a hunch, but… it might be something.'

'Fine. Do it. Then, get yourself a coffee,' Logan told him. 'I can't see any of us getting any sleep tonight.'

Chapter 16

Darkness.

It surrounded him. Smothered him. Claimed him for its own.

He'd always hated the darkness, hated the feelings it conjured up inside him, feelings that burned bright and clear, but which he didn't yet have the vocabulary to put a name to. 'Fear,' yes, but it was something more than that, something deeper, more pure.

The ties were cutting into his wrists. The gag tasted bad in his mouth. Oily. Sour. Foul. A shiny film of snot coated the outside of it, glistening like the trail of a slug.

He snorted in some air. Gulped it down. Tried to breathe. The gag made it difficult. Impossible, sometimes, and his chest held more panic than breath.

He wanted to sob, to scream, to make himself heard. To make the whole world know where he was.

But that would bring the man back. He didn't like it when the man came back. Hated it, in fact. Hated the way he looked at him, hated the way he smiled, hated the way his voice came as a breathless whisper in the half-dark.

He couldn't scream anyway, even if he tried. There was another gag somewhere deep down in his throat—a slab of solid fear preventing everything but the occasional whimper from escaping.

During his more rational moments—those times when he calmed down enough to think straight—he thought he was in a cupboard. The walls felt close and oppressive, his cheeps and

*whimpers rebounding inside the narrow space. It stank of stale
and damp. Foosty, his mum would've said.*

He thought of his mum, and sobbed silently in the darkness.

*The stench of his own urine had permeated everything in
the confined space, but the warmth of it had long since become a
cloying coldness around his thighs. His cheeks burned with shame
when he thought about it.*

*The man had seemed annoyed when it had happened. The
boy with him had laughed and laughed and laughed until the
man had closed the door.*

He didn't like the man.

But he liked the boy even less.

Chapter 17

DS McQuarrie stepped back from the Big Board and admired her handiwork. Walker's mugshot had been stuck up, shocking beard and all, and she'd added a few key details about what they knew so far. She'd connected some of it together with lengths of red wool. There weren't many strands, but those there were all led back to Walker.

DCI Logan had handed her another folder full of paperwork to add to the board but had then decided against it and taken it back. It sat on his desk now, open slightly, teasing her with its contents.

It had been over an hour since the shout had gone out about Walker. The forensic team were on their way down the road from Inverness, and extra uniforms had been drafted in from the surrounding areas to help with the search. Fort William was in the process of being turned upside down, but so far there was no sign of the bastard.

'Done, boss,' Caitlyn announced. 'Anything I've missed?'

Ben Forde twisted in his chair and looked back at the board over his shoulder. 'Nothing jumping out. Good work. Jack?'

Logan looked up from a typed-up copy of the notes Sinead had made back at the Reids'. She'd dropped them in at the station on the way home, surmising that Logan probably hadn't had her write everything down for a laugh.

She was going to go far, that one.

He scanned the board. 'Shoes.'

Caitlyn frowned. 'Sir?'

'Shoes. Trainers. He had size tens in the cupboard under the stairs,' Logan told her. 'And he's knocked a hole through the loft wall into the Reids' loft next door.'

'When did he do that?' Ben wondered. 'Wouldn't they have heard?'

'They did. The husband, what's his name? Duncan. He thought Walker was doing a loft conversion.'

Logan stood up. 'Is the liaison still round there? Ask her to find out when they heard it. And has anyone told them about Walker yet?'

'Not that I know of. We were waiting until you gave the word.'

'Good. I want to tell them myself,' Logan said. He pulled on his coat. 'But first, is anyone else hungry?'

'I could eat, sir, aye,' said Caitlyn.

'Hamza?'

Across at his desk, DS Khaled looked up from the laptop. What he'd thought were just a few more folders to check had led to dozens more, and he was still clicking through, hunting for anything that might help them figure out Walker's motive, whereabouts, current state of mind, or anything else that might prove useful.

'Sir?'

'Hungry?'

'Eh, aye. Pretty famished, actually. Want me to get something?'

'I'll get it. It's fine. Ben? Pizza?'

DI Forde shook his head. 'I've got a packed lunch in the fridge.'

Logan hesitated, his coat halfway on. 'Packed lunch?'

Ben patted his ample stomach. 'Wife's orders.'

'Wife's no' here.'

Ben looked torn, but it only lasted for a moment. 'Go on then. Something meaty. And maybe some of them cheese bite things.'

Satisfied, Logan pulled his coat on the rest of the way. 'Right.'

'And double chips.'

'Jesus. I'm no' the Sultan of Brunei.'

Ben reached for his wallet.

'Shut up, I'm kidding,' Logan told him.

He crossed to the Big Board, took out his phone, and snapped a close-up of Walker's mugshot.

'Anyone else got any particular preference, or will I just get a mix of meat and veggie?'

'Not fussy,' said Caitlyn.

'Hamza? Do you need, like… halal or…?'

DC Khaled's face split into a grin. 'Nah, you're all right, sir.'

Logan nodded a little awkwardly. 'Right. Grand. Won't be long. Phone me if anything comes up.'

He marched out of the Incident Room.

A moment later, the door opened again and his head popped around the doorframe.

'By the way, anyone have any idea where the shop is?'

–

'Oh, and double chips. In fact, double chips twice.'

The lad behind the counter glanced up from the till. 'Quadruple chips?'

'Aye. If you like,' Logan replied. He fished his wallet from his coat pocket. 'How much is all that?'

The till bleeped a few times. Logan shifted impatiently from foot to foot, watching the lad pick a path through the buttons. 'That's…'

Logan sucked air in through his teeth. 'That's…?'

'Thirty-eight forty—Wait. No.'

More bleeps.

'Forgot the chips.'

Logan stood, wallet poised.

'Forty-four forty-five.'

Logan muttered something about 'double chips,' then produced his debit card.

'Sorry, we don't take cards.'

'What?'

'We don't take cards.'

Logan looked down at his card, then up at the kid behind the counter. His face was contorted in confusion, like none of this made any sense.

'You don't take cards?'

'No.'

'How can you not take cards? What are we in, the Roaring Twenties?'

The lad shrugged.

'You seriously don't take cards? In this day and age?'

'There's a cash machine up the street,' the kid offered. 'But you'll have to be quick, we shut in forty-five minutes.'

'I thought you shut at ten?' Logan said.

'We do.'

Logan glanced at his watch. 'Jesus. Right, fine. How far up the street?'

'About… a mile and a half.'

'Fuck off!' Logan retorted, the words tumbling out of him before he could stop them. '*A mile and a half*? It's pissing down.'

The kid glanced at the big windows like he hadn't previously noticed the onslaught of water hammering against the outside.

'You could order online,' he suggested. 'We take cards online.'

Logan's mind, which had already been struggling to deal with the fact that this place didn't accept card payments, practically exploded.

'I can pay by card *online*, but not in person?'

'Cash only in person,' the employee confirmed. From the expression on his face, it was clear that he'd had this same conversation on several occasions before, and very probably had to go through it on a daily basis.

'Jesus.' Logan slotted the card back into his wallet. 'Fine. Where's this cashline, then?'

The lad rattled off a concise but detailed explanation without very much thought, reaffirming Logan's suspicions that he was an old hand at this particular conversation. Logan made a mental note of the directions, then opened the door. A gust of wind and a blast of icy rain swirled in, scattering a bundle of menus piled up on the counter.

'Stick it all on now, I won't be long,' he said.

'We don't usually start making the food until people come back,' the employee explained. 'Because a lot of the time they don't bother.'

'I'll be back,' Logan told him, a touch more *Terminator*-like than he'd intended.

The kid wavered, unsure. Logan let the door close, crossed to the counter, and flashed his warrant card.

'I'll come back. All right? Pinkie swear.'

'Right. OK. Good,' the lad said, snapping to a sort of panicky attention. 'I'll get it all put on for you now.'

'Thank you,' said Logan, trying not to sound sarcastic, but failing. As he turned, his eyes fell on the logo on the pizza box. He took out his phone and opened the photo app. 'Quick question. Does this guy look familiar?'

He showed the kid the snap he'd taken of Walker's mugshot, and watched as the boy looked at it, his eyes lifeless and disinterested.

'No. Don't know him.'

'He's not a customer?'

'Not that I've seen. Why?'

Logan returned the phone to his pocket. 'Nothing. Doesn't matter. I'll go get that cash.'

He was halfway to the door again when the phone rang. He paused, listening to the kid rattle off a robotic salutation and take an order.

Once the lad had hung up, Logan approached the counter. 'Do people phone in orders a lot?'

'Huh? What?' The kid's eyes went to the phone, like the answer might be written there. 'Yes?' he said, more like a question than an answer.

'For delivery?'

'Um, yeah. Why?'

'What about Cowie Avenue?'

'What about it?'

'Number sixteen. Ever get orders phoned in from there?'

The kid looked blank.

'Ham and Pineapple.'

'You mean a Hawaiian?'

Logan's eye twitched. 'I don't want to debate the semantics. Does he ever phone an order in?'

'What?'

Logan rapped his knuckles on the stainless steel counter.

'Wake up. The guy at Sixteen Cowie Avenue. Ham and Pineapple. Does he ever phone in?'

'I think so. Yeah. Yeah, a few times. Why? Is that the guy in the picture?'

'When was the last time he ordered anything?'

'I don't know. I don't work every night.'

Logan's nostrils flared. 'Well, when's the last time you remember?'

He watched the kid thinking, could practically see the steam coming out of his ears as he ploughed through his memories.

'Thursday, maybe?' he decided. 'I think it was Thursday.'

Logan sighed, unable to hide his disappointment. 'Thursday. Right.' He turned to the door. 'Get the food on. I won't be long.'

'OK,' the kid said. Then: 'Actually, wait.'

Logan stopped.

Turned.

'I *think* he might've phoned in last night, too,' the lad said. 'But he didn't get it delivered to the usual place.'

Something lit-up inside Logan's head. Something fluttered in his chest.

'Do you remember where?'

'It'll be written down,' said the kid, jabbing a thumb over his shoulder in the direction of nowhere in particular.

Logan's hand slipped into his pocket, reaching for his phone again. 'Good. Then hold the food, son,' he instructed. 'And get me that address.'

Chapter 18

The Caledonian Canal was a world-renowned tourist attraction, apparently. Logan couldn't really figure out why. It was, as far as he could tell, just a canal like any other. Water. Lock gates. Boats. The usual. Nothing startling about any of it.

Sure, if you were into that sort of thing it was probably nice enough, but it didn't do a lot for him. Maybe because it was getting dark.

Or, more likely, because he had more pressing issues to think about.

He sat behind the wheel of the Focus, peering ahead through the gloom at a long wooden houseboat moored a few hundred yards along the canal path, just off a little wooden jetty. It sat low in the water, rocking gently as the wind shoved it around.

The curtains were drawn over the boat's windows. Behind them was mostly darkness, but occasionally an oblong of light would sweep across the curtains from the inside, as if someone was moving a torch around.

'How long until armed response gets here?' Logan asked. He clicked the windscreen wipers on for a moment, clearing the rain away.

'Forty-five minutes, maybe,' said Ben from the passenger seat.

Logan drummed his fingers on the steering wheel.

'We can't wait that long.'

'Aye, we can,' Ben argued.

'No saying what's going on in there,' Logan said, his gaze boring into the side of the boat as if some previously latent X-Ray vision might suddenly kick in.

'Well, no, but...'

Ben sighed.

'You couldn't have got me the bloody chips first?' he muttered, then he sighed a second time for effect. 'Fine. What's the plan?'

'It's no' really a "plan" as such. "Plan" would be stretching it,' Logan said. 'Is everyone in position? Path blocked further up?'

'Tyler's got a couple of cars and a van up around the corner,' Ben replied, motioning ahead to where the towpath curved around to the right. The area on the right of the path was fenced off and thick with trees that nicely hid the vehicles stopped round the bend. 'Caitlyn has a crew covering the exits behind.'

'Good,' said Logan. The door clunked as he pulled the handle and shouldered it open. 'Right, then. You stay here. Eyes peeled.'

As Logan exited the car, Ben clambered clumsily across into the driver's seat. 'For Christ's sake, be careful,' he warned.

Logan gave him a curt nod, then gently pushed the door just far enough for the mechanism to click into place. He didn't want to risk fully closing it, in case the sound of it alerted Walker.

Pulling his collar up against the rain, then thrusting his hands deep into his pockets, Logan set off walking up the path. He kept to the right, away from the boat, eyes fixed on the path ahead like he had a very specific destination planned, and it wasn't anywhere around here.

His boots made a series of soft crunching sounds on the limestone surface of the path, but he reckoned the sound of the wind and rain against the boat's windows should mask that, with a bit of luck.

The torchlight licked the inside of the curtains. Logan picked up the pace.

He was twenty feet away when the door at the back of the houseboat opened and a wild-haired man in a leather jacket launched himself onto the path.

'Shite!' Logan spat. 'Walker, stay where you are!'

Walker clearly wasn't great at following instructions. He set off at a clip, racing away from the DCI, headed in the direction of the bend. He glanced back, and the sight of Logan kicked his legs into higher gear.

'Get him, I'll check the boat.' Ben's voice came in snatches from behind Logan, sliced and diced by the storm.

Logan didn't need telling twice. He knew the coat would only slow him down, so he shrugged it off. Then, head down, arms pumping, he set off after the bastard.

His old P.E. teacher had always told him that, 'You might be a big lad, but you can fair move.' Logan demonstrated that again now, his size twelves slamming against the limestone path, propelling him on through the rain like pistons.

Walker was almost at the bend, and was about to run straight into Tyler's team, but Logan very much wanted to be there to see him getting collared.

With a final glance back at the pursuing detective, Walker lumbered around the curve and out of sight. Being unable to see him spurred Logan on. Digging deep, he found some extra reserves of speed, and was soon clattering around the corner himself, chest heaving beneath his now almost-transparent shirt.

The curve went on for a couple of dozen yards. Logan was halfway around it when the worry kicked in. There was no shouting. No raised voices. No barked commands.

He stumbled onto the straight, then hissed when a set of car headlights illuminated, blinding him.

'Stay where you are!' barked a voice from beyond the lights.

Tyler.

'It's me, you daft bastard,' Logan spat. 'Where is he?'

'We haven't seen him, boss. We thought you were—'

'Bastard! He's gone into the trees.'

Logan vaulted over the wire fence that ran alongside the path, misjudged the landing, and went staggering down the grassy incline on the other side, branches whipping at him.

'Well, don't just fucking stand there!' he bellowed back over his shoulder as he plunged on into the woods, gravity and momentum pulling him down the steepening hill.

A van door slid open. Two car doors slammed. Logan heard the fence shake and feet come thudding onto the wet grass as he pushed through the trees.

'On the right!' called someone from behind. Logan's eyes shot in that direction and caught a glimpse of a burly figure haring away from him.

The route in front of Logan was uneven and choked with scrub and branches, but it was a dream compared to what Walker had to go through. The beardy-bastard alternated between cursing and sobbing as he struggled through a tangle of jaggy bushes, the thorns ripping at his legs through his faded jeans.

There was a path or road ahead through the trees, maybe fifty feet away. Walker was desperately making his way towards it, but Logan was going to make bloody sure he never got there.

Thundering down the hill, the detective skirted the jaggies, used the trunk of a tree as an anchor point, and swung himself sideways into Walker, hammering him with a shoulder-barge that sent him crashing into the undergrowth.

'Right, then—' Logan wheezed, making a grab for Walker's arm. Walker twisted, swung. Logan caught a fleeting glimpse of something metallic, and then pain exploded across the side of his skull and his legs turned to jelly.

He sensed Walker's movement more than saw it, and grabbed for him. His fingers found the leather jacket, but Walker shrugged him off.

The forest spun. The rain, which had been falling from above now came at Logan from all directions at once, a cyclone of icy droplets that twirled him around and sent waves of nausea flooding through him.

'You all right, boss?'

'Get after him!' Logan hissed. He shook his head and Tyler's face blurred into focus.

Tyler set off again. Logan started to run, but his legs objected, and his head voiced its own concerns with a series of stabbing pains that almost dropped him to his knees.

An uneven line of uniforms in high-vis vests came scrambling past him. Blinking against the rain, Logan was just able to make out Walker stumbling the final few feet towards the edge of the tree-line.

He was going to make it. The bastard was going to make it.

A blue light illuminated directly ahead of Walker as he launched himself onto the road. Logan heard a shout, a grunt, a clatter.

'Get off me! Get the fuck off me!' Walker howled.

'Edward Walker? I am arresting you on the suspicion of the abduction of Connor Reid.'

That was DS McQuarrie's voice. Logan let out a little groan of satisfaction and slumped against the trunk of the nearest tree, his semi-transparent shirt pinking down the front with his blood.

'You are not obliged to say anything, but anything you do say will be noted and may be used in evidence.'

Logan raised his eyes to the sky, letting the rain wash over him.

'Got the bastard,' he said, and then he pushed himself away from the tree, dabbed at his wound with his sleeve, and set off down the hill.

By the time Logan reached the bottom, Walker was already cuffed and in the process of being bundled into the back of one of the cars with the lights flashing. He had been putting up a bit of a struggle, but the sight of the blood-soaked Logan striding closer made him practically throw himself into the back seat.

'I didn't do nothing, all right?' he protested. 'I didn't do it.'

DS McQuarrie, who had been standing back while a couple of uniforms manhandled Walker into the car, pulled her phone from her pocket and glanced at the screen.

'Boss,' she said, showing Logan the message she had received.

Boat empty. No sign of boy.

Logan's face darkened. He tore his eyes from the screen and marched to the car.

'Where is he? Where's Connor?'

'I told you, I don't know!' Walker protested. He was vibrating, tears streaming down his cheeks. 'I knew this would happen. I fackin' knew it. I didn't have nothing to do with it, all right? I ain't seen him.'

Logan's fists clenched. His teeth ground together.

He slammed the door before he could do anything stupid.

'Get him to the station. Log him in, then get him in an interview room,' he instructed anyone and everyone within ear shot. 'Do not let him talk to anyone. Do not let him eat or drink. Don't even let him go for a slash. Get him booked in, get him sat down, and get him warned that he had better start talking.'

Logan raised his voice to ensure Walker heard the next part. 'Or I may not be responsible for my actions.'

'You need your head looked at,' Tyler said.

Logan turned on him, eyebrows furrowed. 'Sorry?'

'I mean, no. I'm not saying you're mental, or anything, sir. I mean…' Tyler pointed to the side of Logan's head, just above the temple. 'That might need stitching.'

Logan dabbed at the wound with the back of a hand. It came away bloody. Very bloody, in fact.

'Bollocks. Fine. DS McQuarrie, can you…?'

'Hop in, boss,' Caitlyn said, indicating her car. 'We'll swing by the hospital.'

'Right. Thanks,' Logan said. He eyeballed Tyler while stabbing a finger in Walker's direction. 'Not a bite to eat, not a drop to drink, not a moment to piss. All right?'

'Got it.'

'But try to get him talking before you get him in. If he knows where Connor is, we need to find out pronto.'

'Will do, boss.'

Bending, Logan brought his face close to the back window of the police car. Walker slid a little further along the seat away from him as Logan glowered at him through the tinted glass.

'I'll see you soon, Eddie.'

Chapter 19

Half an hour later, Logan sat in the front seat of Caitlyn's car, gingerly brushing his fingers across three neat sutures on the line of his head where skin met scalp. The car's wipers were thunking away, working overtime to push back against the rain.

'I'll tell you, for a wee hospital, they're good,' Logan said. 'What was that? In and out in twenty minutes? You wouldn't get that down the road.'

'Aye, pretty good,' DS McQuarrie agreed. 'I mean, you did go in flashing your ID and declaring it a police emergency, but still...'

'Never hurts to light a fire under them,' Logan said. He gazed out through the windscreen at the police station looming ahead of them. 'Does it ever stop raining around here?'

'Occasionally, aye. Nice when it does.'

'Shite when it doesn't, though, I'd imagine.'

'Oh God, aye,' Caitlyn confirmed.

She pulled into a parking space at the side of the station, then flipped the little lever that activated the automatic handbrake. The fact you had to flip a lever seemed to negate the 'automatic' bit, she'd always thought, but it was still better than wrestling with the pull-up handle she'd had in her previous cars.

'Right then,' said Logan, unclipping his belt. 'Let's go see what Mr Walker has to say for himself.'

He caught the door handle, but didn't pull it yet. 'I want you sitting in on the interview.'

'Me? What about DI Forde?'

'He's tired. He needs a break,' Logan told her. 'Besides, Ben'll let me get away with murder. I want you keeping things by the book. All right?'

Caitlyn nodded. 'Sure. Aye. No bother.'

'Right. Good,' Logan said. He pulled the handle and opened the door. 'Let's go find that boy.'

'You might want to get changed first, sir,' Caitlyn suggested.

Logan looked down at his shirt. It was in a hell of a state, quite frankly—soaked through, smeared with dirt, and stained down one side with blood. Between that and the stitches, he reckoned he must've made for a truly horrifying sight.

'Nah,' he said, stepping out into the downpour. 'Adds to the effect.'

-

Logan and Caitlyn sat across the table from Ed Walker in one of the station's two interview rooms, audio and video recorders listening in and watching on.

Someone suitably junior from one of the local legal firms had been dragged out of his warm house and was scanning through a bundle of documents DI Forde had presented him with when he'd arrived. Lawrence, someone had said his name was, although Logan didn't know if this was his first name or his last name. Nor did he care.

'Sorry. Sorry, won't be...'

Lawrence licked a finger and flipped on a page. His lips moved silently as he quickly read.

Logan's chair creaked as he leaned back and sighed, very deliberately.

'Sorry!'

Walker's head was down, his eyes fixed on the table in front of him. Like Logan, he was still wet, although nowhere near to the extent the detective was, his leather jacket having protected him from the worst that the weather had thrown at them.

'Right. Aaaaand done. Sorry,' said Lawrence, dragging his eyes up from the page and setting the document back on the table. 'Now, what did you—?'

'Where is he?' Logan asked, brushing the young solicitor's question aside before he could finish it. 'What did you do with the boy?'

'I told you, I ain't seen him,' Walker said, raising his gaze to meet the DCI's.

'Then why hide? Eh? Why run? Why clout me with a bloody torch?' Logan asked, indicating the sutures on his head. 'If you had nothing to do with Connor's abduction, why do all that?'

'Because I've been inside, ain't I?' Walker spat. 'I know what you lot are like. Ex-con living next door. Kid goes missing? I know what you'll be thinking.'

Logan leaned forward, interlocking his fingers on the desk before him. 'Trust me, Eddie, you have *no idea* what I'm thinking. If you did—if you had even the *faintest notion* of what's going on in my head right now—you'd be much more forthcoming with information, I can assure you.'

Lawrence shot a look across the table at DS McQuarrie, but she ignored it.

'Where is he?' Logan asked again.

'I told you, I don't know. I only heard about him going missing on Friday night. I haven't seen him since… I don't know, Wednesday, maybe.'

'Where did you see him on Wednesday?'

'Coming home from school.'

'Did you follow him?'

Walker tutted. 'Out the window.'

'Right. Out the window. Got you,' said Logan. 'So, not through the holes you made in his bedroom ceiling, then?'

Walker snorted. 'What holes? What are you on about?'

'We'll come back to that,' Logan told him. 'We're circling around the big issue here a bit, don't you think?'

He slowed his voice down, speaking each word very deliberately in turn. 'Where. Is. Connor?'

Walker ran his tongue across the front of his bottom teeth. He ran his fingers through his beard, which was even worse in real life than it had been in the photograph.

'Neverland.'

'What?'

'Through the Looking Glass. Outer space.' Walker leaned in closer, his voice rising. 'I keep telling you, I don't fackin' know where he is! I'd never hurt any kid, never mind him. If I did know where he was, I'd say, but I don't. All right? I don't.'

Logan's eyes became narrow slits. He squeezed his hands together. As long as they were together, they weren't around Walker's throat.

He was annoyed at himself for bringing DS McQuarrie in. And yet, at the same time, relieved she was there.

'What do you mean 'never mind him'?' Logan asked. 'What's so special about him?'

'What? Nothing,' said Walker. He settled back in his chair, his eyes darting away from Logan.

'Aye there is. You singled him out. You wouldn't hurt any kid, *never mind him*. Why wouldn't you hurt him in particular?' Logan pressed.

'Because he's my neighbours' kid, ain't he?'

Logan laughed. 'Neighbours? It's no' Ramsay Street. You're squatting, Eddie. Illegally. Which, in case your crack legal team here hasn't already informed you, is a clear violation of your parole.'

Lawrence half-smiled and frowned at the same time, like he'd just heard a joke he didn't quite get, but which he suspected he was the punchline of.

'Isn't that right, DS McQuarrie?'

'Blatant breach, sir,' Caitlyn confirmed.

'Shocking violation,' Logan reiterated. 'Although, would you say it's currently Mr Walker's biggest problem?'

'Far from it. I'd say it's the least of his worries, sir.'

'Hear that? The least of your worries.' Logan jabbed a thumb in Caitlyn's direction. 'And she knows her stuff. Believe me.'

He started to count on his fingers. 'Let's look at those worries, shall we? Breaking and entering. Squatting. Criminal damage. Possession of a Class B drug. Resisting arrest. Clouting a police officer with a dirty great torch, and… oh, aye. Lest we forget. Kidnapping.'

He shot Caitlyn a sideways look. 'Anything I missed?'

'Did you count B&E twice, sir?' DS McQuarrie asked. 'The boat.'

'The *boat*. God, aye. I forgot the boat.' He beamed a broad grin across the table at Walker. 'Told you she's good. That's potentially a long stretch. A *long* stretch. I mean, I've been doing this a while, I could probably get you six months for just the state of this shirt alone, never mind what you'd get sent down for the rest of it.'

Sucking in his bottom lip, he shook his head. 'No. It is *not* looking good, Eddie. It's not looking good at all.'

Logan stopped there for a while, letting the silence worm its way into Walker's head and do his talking for him.

It was important to give it all a bit of time to sink in. Bed down. If you knew what you were looking for during an interview, you could actually see the moment the full gravity of the situation hit them, and watch as the idea of a lengthy sentence and all its horrible repercussions took root in their heads.

Walker was no different. His breathing became short, his eyes shimmered, and somewhere in that badger's arse of a beard, his bottom lip gave a wobble.

Bingo.

'Of course, we could make a lot of that stuff go away,' Logan said, dropping his voice to a conspiratorial whisper. 'Breaking in. The drugs.' He indicated the wound on his forehead. 'I'm even prepared to overlook this, Eddie, and I do not say that lightly. Do I, Detective Sergeant McQuarrie?'

'No, boss. You do not say that lightly.'

'I do *not* say that lightly,' Logan reiterated. 'We can do it, too. Me and her. We can make all that other stuff go away. We're nice like that. But you have to tell us where Connor is, Eddie.'

'I don't know.'

'Come on, Eddie! This is your future we're talking about.'

'I don't *know*!'

'I'm running out of patience fast here, so I'm going to ask you one more time,' Logan said. He leaned forward, his face twisting into an involuntary snarl. 'Where's Connor? What have you done with him?'

'Nothing! I don't fackin' know where he is! I keep telling you!' Walker blurted, tears rolling down his cheeks. 'If I knew, I'd tell you, but I don't! I swear, I don't!'

'I think you're lying to me, Eddie.'

Walker's face was a scrunched up mess of tears and snot now. His shoulders shook as he sobbed silently, eyes closed.

'Maybe we could take a break,' Lawrence volunteered.

'He'll get a break when he tells us where the boy is,' Logan said.

'He says he doesn't know,' the solicitor said, his tone bordering on apologetic.

'I know what he said. I don't believe him,' Logan countered. 'What about the teddy? The envelope? How did you know about that?'

Walker sniffed and wiped his eyes on his sleeve. 'What teddy? What are you on about?'

'Don't give me your shite!' Logan snapped. His fist thumped the table. Lawrence jumped in his chair. 'The teddy you left on the doorstep. With the photo. How did you know about the writing?'

'What teddy? What photo?' Walker asked. He looked to his brief for support. 'I don't know what he's talking about.'

There was a knock at the door. Logan tutted. 'What?'

The door opened a crack, revealing a narrow strip of DC Khaled. 'Boss. You got a minute?'

'Kind of busy right now.'

'It's important. You're going to want to see.'

Logan eyeballed Walker. 'I'll be right back. You use this time wisely, Eddie. Think about your options. It shouldn't take you long.'

He stood up so he towered above the other man. 'You've no' got all that many left.'

Chapter 20

'This had better be bloody important.'

'It's major, sir,' Hamza told him, leading the DCI back into the Incident Room. Tyler Neish stood a good eight or nine feet from DS Khaled's desk, where the laptop was sitting open. Hamza gestured to it wordlessly, then hung back with Tyler while Logan approached.

'What am I meant to be looking…?' Logan began, then his voice trailed off as he got closer and saw what was currently displayed on the screen. 'Hang on. Is that…?'

'Aye. Looks like it, sir,' Hamza said. 'Didn't notice at first, but I spotted it when going back through.'

A jumble of thoughts spun around inside Logan's head, none of them quite falling into place. The photo was a game-changer, no question about it. He just had no idea what the game was going to change into, that was the problem.

'Can you run me off a couple of copies of this?' he asked, pointing to the screen.

Hamza nodded. 'It'll take about fifteen minutes. I'll have to get a USB to take—'

'Do whatever you need to do.'

Logan turned his attention to Tyler. He noticed that the younger officer had got himself tidied up after the chase through the trees. He looked immaculate, with only a few hairs out of place, and even those had been styled that way deliberately.

'Is the liaison still with the Reids?' Logan asked him.

'Not sure, sir.'

'Check and find out. Then, send someone to get Catriona Reid. In fact, you go. Tell her we need to ask her a few questions. Nothing major, tell her, just some background stuff. Keep the husband at home in case anyone tries to get in contact.'

'Got it.'

Logan looked around the Incident Room. 'DI Forde around?'

'He's getting his head down for an hour, sir,' Hamza explained. 'Thought it was a good time. Plans doing the nightshift, if we need to.'

'Right. Fine.'

'What do you want me to do with Catriona Reid when I bring her in?' Tyler asked.

'There's another interview room, right? Stick her in that, then come get me.'

'It's occupied, sir,' Hamza said.

Logan frowned. 'What? Who by?'

'Your journalist,' Tyler volunteered.

'Henderson?'

Tyler shook his head. 'Nah. The other one. The local guy. Fisher, is it?'

'Thomas Fisher,' said Hamza.

'All right, you fucking swot,' Tyler teased. 'We didn't have to go far to find him, he was out front with the rest of them.'

'Right, aye. I'd forgotten about him. Anyone spoken to him yet?'

'Not really, boss, no,' said Tyler. 'He's sitting in there looking fit for tears, though.'

Logan sighed. 'Fine. Tyler, go get Catriona Reid. Hamza, I don't hear that printer going.'

Hamza practically snapped to attention. Tyler took out his car keys and spun them on a finger, like a Wild West Sheriff with a six-shooter.

Logan turned to the door. 'Right, Mr Fisher. Let's get you out of the road.'

-

Tom Fisher gave a throaty little sob at the sight of Logan when the DCI threw the Interview Room door wide open. He stood there in the doorway, one hand on the handle, a shoulder resting against the frame.

The young journalist's eyes widened in horror as he took in the blood on Logan's shirt, and the cakes of dried crimson on the side of his neck.

'I d-didn't do anything!'

Logan smiled, good-naturedly. 'Relax, Mr Fisher. You're not under arrest. I just need you to help clarify something for us.'

He entered the room but didn't close the door all the way. Tyler had said that Fisher had been close to tears, but by the looks of him now he'd fully succumbed to those at some point, and was now all red-ringed eyes and dried snot.

'Don't worry, Mr Fisher. We're going to have you out of here in just a couple of minutes,' Logan soothed. 'I just have a question about Ken Henderson.'

Fisher frowned. He was younger than most journalists Logan had dealt with, although a lot of the local reporters tended to be that bit less experienced. Not all, of course—Logan had come across some right terriers in the local press over the years—but for some it was the first rung on a career ladder that would ultimately take them all the way to the bottom.

'Who's Ken Henderson?'

'Another journalist. Freelance. Grey hair. Smarmy bastard.'

'Oh. Yes. Him. From Glasgow?' Fisher asked. He nodded even before Logan had volunteered an answer. 'Yes. I was talking to him this morning. He seemed nice enough.'

'Oh, aye. He does seem nice. He seems *lovely*, in fact, when he wants to,' Logan agreed. 'He isn't, though. You'll want to watch yourself there.'

Fisher said nothing. He'd had acne in his younger years, and the scars of it dotted his cheeks. Logan vaguely recalled seeing him in the scrum outside the Reids' house earlier in the day. He couldn't place exactly where he'd been, but he seemed familiar enough.

'Henderson said you told him about a teddy bear that was delivered to the home of Connor Reid. Is that true?'

Fisher was quick to nod. 'Yes.'

Logan closed the door. Fisher's eyes darted from the DCI to the door and back again. He shifted anxiously in his seat.

'And how did you come to know about this teddy bear?'

'The Spar. You know, down the road from the house? Not the one up the hill.'

Logan had no idea where either of the shops were, but didn't say as much.

'Go on.'

'Someone in there was talking about it,' Fisher continued. 'Well, I mean, everyone was, really. Two women were chatting about it. And an old fella. They said something about it having a ransom note?'

Fisher sucked in a steadying breath, then swallowed. 'Is that... is that true?' he asked.

'I think we'll stick to me interviewing you, son, if you don't mind?' Logan told him.

Fisher blushed and immediately looked away. 'I wasn't...' he began to protest, but then clearly thought better of it. 'Sorry.'

'We're all just doing our jobs. I get it,' Logan told him. 'So, it was general chatter, was it? About the bear, I mean. You didn't see anything yourself?'

'No. I mean, yes. I mean... People talking. That was all. I just... I passed it on. Ken, was it? He said we should keep each other in the loop with stuff, so I told him about it.'

'Aye. That sounds like him,' Logan said. 'I'm guessing he hasn't been quick to keep you "in the loop" at his side?'

Fisher blushed again and shook his head.

'No, thought not.'

'There was...'

The young journo's voice fell away.

'What?'

'Nothing. I mean. No. I mean... it was just that he didn't seem surprised or anything,' Fisher said. 'About the teddy and the ransom note, or whatever it was. He didn't seem surprised.'

'You think he already knew?'

'I'm not saying that, no. I'm not...' Fisher shook his head. 'He probably was surprised, just didn't show it.'

'Aye,' said Logan. 'Probably.'

He opened the door.

'Right, thanks for your time.'

Fisher's face almost collapsed in on itself with relief. 'That's it? I can go?'

'You can go,' Logan told him.

The legs of the young journalist's chair scraped on the floor as he rushed to his feet. He was at the door when Logan stopped him.

'One thing, just quickly,' the DCI said. 'Could you tell me where you were on Friday around one-thirty in the afternoon?'

The boy looked flustered. For a moment, Logan thought he might burst into tears again right there in the doorway.

'It's just for our records, that's all. Nothing to worry about.'

Fisher's brow furrowed. His eyes flitted left to right, desperately searching. 'I don't... Friday? I'm not...'

Something slotted into place and he let out something that was part-sob, part-cheer. 'Friday. Lunchtime? Yes, I was doing an interview!' he said, sounding like he'd never been more happy about anything in his life. 'Mary Grigor. Her cats keep going missing.'

It was Logan's turn to frown. 'What?'

'Her cats. They keep going missing. She's had four disappear in the last three months.'

Fisher squirmed a hand down into the pocket of his too-tight jeans. 'Hang on, I've got a picture.'

Producing his phone, he tapped the screen a couple of times, then swiped with his thumb. 'No, no, no, not that... there.'

He turned the phone so Logan could see the photograph displayed on screen. A woman in her eighties, or thereabouts, sat in a worn old armchair, keeping a firm grip on an unhappy-looking cat.

'She had five,' Fisher explained. 'Well, no, she had three, then she lost two, so she got another—'

'It's fine. I don't need her life story,' Logan said, gesturing for him to put the phone away. 'And there's been no sign of them? The cats.'

Fisher shook his head and slipped his phone back into his pocket.

'Has she reported it?'

'I think so, yes. She said she had, but she's a bit... dottled.'

'Aye, I can imagine. Someone at the paper can verify you were at her house around lunchtime?'

'No, probably not,' Fisher admitted. 'They know I covered the story, but... wait. No. They can! I sent the photos across right after. Probably about... ten to two? I'm sure if you check with Mary, she'll be able to tell you I was there, too.'

Logan flashed him the thinnest of smiles. 'That won't be necessary, Mr Fisher. Like I say, just for our records. Thank you again for your time, and sorry for the inconvenience.'

He held the door open and motioned for the journalist to go through. 'I'll have someone see you out.'

DS Khaled was lurking out in the corridor when Logan and Fisher emerged from the room. He immediately offered the DCI an unmarked cardboard folder. 'Those printouts you wanted, sir.'

'Grand. Swap,' said Logan, taking the folder. 'Can you see Mr Fisher out? Get someone to give him a run home.'

'It's OK. I've got my bike,' Fisher said. 'I only live around the corner.'

Logan looked past him to the window. The rain was no longer sideways, but was still coming down. 'You sure? You'll get soaked.'

For the first time since arriving, Fisher smiled. 'It's the Highlands. We're used to it.'

'Ha. Aye. Fair enough,' Logan said. 'Thanks again for your time.'

He gestured for Hamza to lead the journalist out to reception, then turned and flipped open the folder. Two faces gazed up at him, both smiling.

'Right then,' he muttered, when the door through to reception clunked closed behind him. 'Let's see what this is all about.'

Chapter 21

How long had it been quiet, out there beyond the door? An hour? A day? He couldn't tell. All he knew was it was dark, and he was cold, and he was scared, and that he wanted, more than anything, to go home.

His wrists hurt where they were tied. His legs were numb. His throat was raw from keeping his sobs inside. He risked letting one out now. It was muffled by the gag across his mouth, but the sound was enough to startle him, to send electric shocks of panic coursing through his veins.

What if they heard? What if they got angry? What if they hurt him?

Tears came at the thought of them hurting him. He didn't want them to hurt him.

Not again.

He'd seen what they had done to the cat. What was left of it. It had looked like roadkill when the boy had brought it to him on the tray, all bright red flesh and exposed white bone. The smell had been horrible. It had forced its way up his nostrils, turning his stomach and making him feel sick.

He had almost been sick when the cat had moved. Its head had twitched. A wet, mournful sort of sound had emerged from its mouth, and the boy had erupted into delighted laughter before skipping off with the tray held high like some sort of trophy.

The man had appeared a moment later. The man had stared in around the edge of the door as he inched it shut, sealing him back inside the cupboard.

That had been a while ago. He hoped, for the cat's sake, that it was dead by now.

Alone in the darkness, he prayed that he wouldn't be next.

Chapter 22

'Have any changes of heart while I was away, Eddie?' Logan asked, settling back into his seat. 'You ready to tell us where Connor is yet?'

'I already told you. I don't—'

'You don't know, aye. You did mention that,' Logan said.

'For the benefit of the recording, DCI Logan has now re-entered the room,' Caitlyn announced.

'Sorry, aye. Always forget that bit,' Logan said.

He placed the folder on the desk in front of him, one hand on top of it to keep it closed.

'How do you know the Reids, Eddie?'

Walker's eyes went to the folder, then back to the DCI. 'How do you think? I live next door to them.'

'And that's it, is it? That's the extent of it.'

'What do you mean?' Walker asked.

'It's not a hard question, Eddie. I think it's pretty clear. Before you illegally moved in next door to them, had you ever met either Mr or Mrs Reid?'

The eyes flicked to the folder again. This time, they lingered for a moment before Walker dragged them back up.

'No.'

'No? You've never met them?'

The solicitor, Lawrence, cleared his throat. 'Detective Chief Inspector, I think—'

'Shh,' Logan told him. He tapped a finger on top of the folder, beating out a slow, steady rhythm. 'I'm going to ask you again, Eddie. And I want you to *really think* about the answer this time, all right? Really try for me. OK?'

He leaned forward in his chair. 'Did you know either Mr or Mrs Reid prior to the day you moved into the house next door to theirs?'

Walker opened his mouth to respond. Logan raised a hand to stop him.

'At–at–at. Think before you answer, Eddie. Take your time to consider your response before you say anything.'

Logan tapped his finger against the folder again. Slow. Steady.

Tik. Tik. Tik.

'No,' said Walker, although he sounded even less convincing now than he had been. 'I didn't know either of them.'

'Uh-huh,' Logan mused.

Then, without a word, he opened the folder and slid one of the photographs across the table so it was directly in front of Walker. He handed the other copy to Caitlyn, who looked significantly more surprised by it than Walker did.

'That's you in that picture, Eddie. Right?'

Walker's gaze was fixed on the image. He nodded once, but said nothing.

'And can you tell us, for the benefit of the tape, who that is you're pictured with?'

Walker's eyes met Logan's across the table, wide and defiant. 'Fuck you.'

147

'Language, Eddie!' Logan scolded. He shrugged. 'Fair enough, I'll say it.'

Reaching across the table, Logan tapped the smiling face of the woman next to Walker in the photograph. His arm was around her shoulder, pulling her in close. 'That's Catriona Reid.'

Walker's brief, Lawrence, leaned over and peered down at the photo. His eyes flitted to Walker, then back again. He hadn't come into the interview room particularly confident, but now he looked positively crestfallen.

'So, what happened there then, Eddie? Slip your mind, did it?' Logan pressed. 'Because you look pretty close in that photo.'

He turned the picture around so it was facing him on the desk. 'You look better without the beard, if you don't mind me saying. How long ago was this taken? Ten years?'

Walker ground his teeth together, as if chewing over his answer. 'Eight.'

'Eight? Right, so…'

Logan groaned.

'Jesus.'

'Boss?' asked Caitlyn.

'Eight years. That was *eight years* ago,' Logan said. He glowered at Walker, speaking more quickly as things slotted into place. 'DNA. You were looking up DNA.'

'So?' Walker grunted, shifting in his chair.

'You think he's yours, don't you? Connor. You think you're his dad.'

'What? No! No, nothing like that.'

'That's it, isn't it? You think he's your son,' Logan said. 'Is that why you took him, Eddie? Is that why you grabbed him?'

'I didn't! It wasn't me! You've got it all wrong.'

'Have I? Then explain it to me, Eddie. Because right now, the story I've got up here…' He tapped the side of his head. 'It all makes sense. It's no' pleasant, but it makes sense. You think he's your son, so you took him, and tried to throw us off with the teddy bear and the envelope.'

'What fackin' teddy bear? I don't know what you're on about!' Walker yelled.

And then, like a switch had been flicked, something changed. His breathing and movements, which had both been growing wilder, became slower, more controlled. He clasped his hands on the table top in front of him, a sort of resigned tranquility falling over him.

'I want a lawyer.'

'You've got one,' Logan told him.

'A proper one. Not this useless prick.'

Lawrence looked briefly put-out but didn't voice any objections. If anything, he looked relieved.

'Stop wasting time, Eddie. Where's the boy? Where's Connor?'

Walker leaned forward. 'I don't know. I mean it. I've got no idea,' he said, his voice measured. 'Which means that someone's still got him. He's out there now some-where, and you ain't doing nothing about it. You ain't even trying.'

He sat back. 'Now, I ain't saying anything else until I get a proper lawyer.'

He glanced briefly in Lawrence's direction. 'No offence.'

'None taken,' said Lawrence. He already had his briefcase on the table, and was shoving his notepad and pen inside.

Logan stood, his face a storm cloud of contempt. 'DS McQuarrie. Put Mr Walker in a cell.'

He shot her a sideways look. 'We do have cells in this place, right?'

'We do,' Caitlyn confirmed.

'Good. Right. Pick the worst one and chuck him in it,' Logan instructed. 'We'll continue this after I've spoken to Mrs Reid.' He picked up the photo from the table and tucked it back into the folder. 'Maybe she'll have something more to tell us.'

Chapter 23

Catriona Reid looked drawn and tired, all her previous nervous energy having long-since burned itself out. There was a greyness about her, a flatness to her hair, a lack of flesh-tones to her skin. Logan had seen it before. He'd watched grief and fear sepia-tone too many other parents just like her.

Catriona looked up as Logan and Caitlyn entered the interview room. Her face was in turmoil, wrestling with itself, part resigned acceptance, part refusal to believe what her head was telling her.

'You found him, didn't you?' she blurted, tripping, stumbling, and almost choking on the words. 'You found him.'

Logan closed the door. 'Who?'

Catriona visibly flinched. 'What do you mean, "who"? Connor? You found him. He's dead, isn't he? You found him and he's dead.'

'No. It's nothing like that,' Logan assured her. 'To the best of our knowledge, Mrs Reid, Connor is still alive and unharmed. We have nothing to suggest otherwise, and getting him home safely is still the focus of our investigation.'

'He's… he's alive?'

'We believe so, yes.'

Catriona broke. That was the only way to describe it. Whatever last vestiges of resolve had been holding her together collapsed, and she buried her face in her hands, sobbing with what most people would assume was relief.

And it *was* relief.

Partly.

Logan had never had to go through what Catriona was going through, but he'd seen it often enough, and had been involved in some frank and forthright discussions with other parents at similar moments.

Relief was a big chunk of it. The majority of it, probably.

And yet, as much of a relief as it was to be told their son or daughter was still alive, it only fuelled the little nagging voice that told them that their child might well be suffering somewhere right now, and reminded them there was nothing they could do to stop it.

At this very moment, Catriona was probably picturing unspeakable tortures being inflicted upon her son. She'd be watching him cry, hearing him calling out for her, hopelessly, desperately.

Sure, he's alive, the voice would be telling her. *But at what cost, Catriona? At what cost?*

'Caitlyn, go get Mrs Reid a cup of tea, would you? I'll have one, too, if you don't mind?'

DS McQuarrie glanced sympathetically at Catriona Reid, then nodded. 'Of course. Will do.'

Logan's stomach growled like a hungry animal. This did not go unnoticed.

'And I'll bring the biscuits, sir.'

Once Caitlyn had left, Logan sat across the table from Catriona Reid. He'd had the forethought to bring a box of tissues in with him, and she gratefully plucked a few from the opening on top to wipe her eyes and blow her nose. He set the box and the folder containing the photographs down on the table, the tissues much closer to her than to him.

'Thank you,' Catriona said, her voice taking on a flat, expressionless tone.

Logan had seen this before, too—the battening down of the hatches, hammering any and all emotion into submission before it could bubble over and become unmanageable.

'You're welcome. How are you holding up?' Logan asked. It was a stupid question, and one he already knew the answer to. It was written all over her face.

Catriona sniffed. 'About what you'd think.'

'And how's your husband doing?'

'He still thinks it's his fault,' Catriona said. She looked away. 'I'm trying not to.'

'It isn't. You can't watch your kids twenty-four-seven, much as we'd all like to,' Logan told her. 'The only person to blame for this is the person who took Connor. Your husband shouldn't hold himself responsible. And neither should you.'

Catriona nodded, but it was disinterested, like she was humouring him. 'I'll try,' she said, then her head twitched a little, like something had just flicked her. 'Oh. I almost forgot to say. The teddy. The one that was delivered?'

'What about it?'

'We checked. It isn't Connor's.'

Logan's chair creaked beneath him as he shifted his weight. 'It isn't?'

'He has one a bit like it, but we found that in his...' Her chest tightened as it all hit home again. 'It was in his bed.'

Catriona cleared her throat a few times, trying to free it up. 'But the one that was delivered, it's not his.'

'Right. OK,' Logan muttered, his mind racing as it tried to figure out what, if anything, this new piece of information meant. He filed it away to come back to later. 'Thanks for that. Really useful.'

The door opened behind him, and Caitlyn entered carrying a tray of mugs, a scattering of sugar sachets, and a little carton with a dribble of milk in the bottom.

'Here we go,' she said, setting the tray down. Logan nudged the folder aside to make room, and Caitlyn began distributing the mugs. They were all colourful and mismatched. Logan's had the *Maltesers* logo emblazoned across the side and had originally probably come with an Easter Egg inside.

Catriona Reid wrapped both hands around her mug as if warming them. She stared into the dark depths and breathed in the steam.

'Thank you.'

'No bother at all,' Caitlyn said, relocating the milk, sugar, and a plate of biscuits from the tray to the table.

She placed the tray on the floor, propped up against the table leg, then moved to take a seat beside Logan. He motioned with his eyes for her to sit next to Catriona, instead. It was an interview of sorts, yes, but the last thing the poor woman needed was to feel like they were ganging up on her.

Logan's stomach grumbled. There were three biscuits on the plate—a digestive, a hobnob, and a *Tunnocks Caramel Wafer*. He knew which one he had his sights on, but a nagging sense of decency made him wait.

'Biscuit?' DS McQuarrie asked Catriona, indicating the plate.

Catriona peered at the plate, blinking slowly, as if seeing some sort of weird alien specimen for the first time.

'Oh. No. Thank you.'

Logan had the caramel wafer in his hands before Catriona had finished talking. 'Sorry,' he said, taking a chomp out of the end. 'Starving.'

'DCI Logan has been working around the clock to bring Connor home,' said Caitlyn, filling in while Logan munched his way through the chocolate biscuit. 'We all have.'

'But you haven't found him,' Catriona said, just a touch accusingly.

'Not yet, no. But we think we're close. We have some really strong leads.'

Logan swallowed, spent a few seconds, running his tongue across his teeth, then took a glug of tea. There was no sugar in it, but the lingering sweetness of the *Tunnocks* did the job.

Clearing his throat, Logan picked up the folder. 'Mrs Reid, you're probably wondering why I asked you to come in and see us. First up, let me assure you, you're not in any kind of trouble at the moment.'

'Trouble?' Catriona echoed. She frowned. 'What do you mean *trouble*?'

The tail-end of the sentence hit home.

'What do you mean *at the moment*?'

'What can you tell us about Edward Walker?' Logan asked.

Across the table, Catriona sat up straight, practically squaring her shoulders. 'What? What do you…?'

The effort became too much. She sagged, and as she did all the fight went out of her.

'It wasn't him,' she said. 'I should've told you. But it wasn't him.'

Logan opened the folder and placed the photograph between them. It had been taken in what looked like some kind of American diner, judging by the food on the table, and what could be made out of the background.

Catriona and Ed Walker were sitting on the same side of the table, close together, him with his arm around her. They were both smiling, although Walker looked a touch more relaxed about it than Catriona did.

The photograph seemed to come almost as a relief to her now. Her face attempted something that wasn't quite a smile but was headed in that general direction.

'I never actually saw that picture before,' she said. 'It was in Inverness. We'd arranged to meet up.'

'This was taken around eight years ago. Does that sound about right?'

A jerk of Catriona's head confirmed it. 'A few months before Connor was born. I'd been seeing him occasionally. We were just sort of… getting to know each other, I suppose.'

Catriona took another tissue and blew her nose. 'I never told him. I was going to, but then Ed just disappeared. Prison, I eventually found out, but…' She shook her head. 'No, I never told him.'

'This is going to be a difficult question, Mrs Reid, but it's important you answer truthfully,' Logan said. He watched for something in her eyes that told him she understood, and continued once he'd seen it. 'Is Ed Walker Connor's father?'

Catriona's eyes widened. Her voice, once she found it, was incredulous with disgust. 'What? No! Of course not! Is that what you think? That I'd…? No! No!'

'Could he believe he's Connor's father?'

'No! Of course he couldn't,' Catriona insisted.

'So—and, again, apologies for the bluntness of this question, Mrs Reid—you're saying you never slept with him?'

'Slept with him? What are you talking about? Of course I didn't sleep with him!'

Catriona's voice was becoming higher, her emotions betraying her and making a mockery of her attempts to rein them in. 'He's not Connor's father. *Of course* he isn't Connor's father,' she said.

'He's *mine*.'

Chapter 24

Logan stood in the foyer of the station, watching DC Neish's car pull out of the car park. He caught a glimpse of Catriona Reid in the front passenger seat as the car turned onto the road, but then a streetlight reflected off the glass, hiding her, and the car rolled off into the night.

'Didn't see that coming,' said DS McQuarrie.

'No. Nor me,' Logan admitted. 'Should've, though.'

Catriona Reid's story had seemed legitimate enough, once she'd explained it.

Growing up, she'd never known much about her father, other than the constant reminders from her mother that he was a no-good waster who'd had his wicked way, then cleared out at the first sign of a belly bump.

She'd been trained to hate him by rote, and had always insisted to her then fiancé, Duncan, that she had no interest in ever finding out where he was, what he was doing, or why he had turned his back on her all those years ago.

And then, he'd found her through Facebook, and all that had gone out the window.

She hadn't told anyone about their meetings. It would've killed her mother, and after her claiming complete disinterest in the man for years, Duncan wouldn't have understood.

But she'd met him. She felt she should hear him out. And, more importantly, that he should hear her out. She had a lot of questions, and the opportunity to get some answers had been something she couldn't bring herself to pass up.

To her surprise, he'd answered them all honestly. He'd messed up. He wasn't ready. He let her down. He'd thought about her every night for years, wondered where she was, what she was doing. All that stuff.

To her amazement, she'd found herself warming to him. They'd arranged to meet again. And again. And again. Each time they did, she found herself enjoying his company more. He was funny. Smart. Kind. So far removed from everything her mother had told her.

And then, out of nowhere, he'd stopped contacting her. All efforts to get in touch with him had failed. He'd vanished. He'd left her, all over again. And, she hadn't even got a chance to tell him he was going to be a grandfather.

Eight years later, he turned up. He contacted her online, explained he'd been in prison. She'd resisted at first, but it had been her who had eventually suggested the house next door. Although, to be fair, she'd expected him to rent it, not just move himself in.

'But he didn't take Connor,' Catriona had insisted when Logan had suggested it. 'I went round there on Friday night. I asked him. I even searched the place. He didn't know anything. I could tell. He didn't know anything about it.'

Logan turned from the window, yawning. His eyes went to the clock on the wall. After one. Jesus, when did that happen?

'Still think Walker took him, sir?' Caitlyn asked.

Logan grunted. 'I wish I did. Be easy, then.'

'Where are we if it wasn't him?'

'Back to square one,' Logan admitted.

Caitlyn clicked her tongue against the back of her teeth. 'Aye. I was afraid you might say that.'

'We'll have to talk to Walker again, but it can wait until the morning. My instinct is that he's not a kidnapper, just a bloody idiot,' Logan told her. 'Mind you, have the forensic boys been over the house and the boat yet?'

'They have, sir. Still waiting on the report.'

She looked at the clock, then double-checked on her watch. 'Probably be the morning now.'

'Aye. Probably. You should get some sleep in the mean-time. Not a lot we can do right now,' Logan said. 'Did you get a hotel sorted?'

'I did, sir. Premier Inn. You?'

Logan shook his head. 'No. I'm fine.'

'There's an empty office upstairs. The CID guys some-times use it if they're pulling an all-nighter. You should try to sleep.'

'Hmm? Oh. No.'

'You said yourself, sir. Not a lot we can do right now,' Caitlyn reminded him.

'Thanks for your concern, Detective Sergeant. But I'm all right. Honest.'

'Bollocks you are.'

The voice crackled from a speaker above the reception desk. Officially, the station was shut down for the night, and there was nobody manning the counter.

Even with the echo and slight hiss of static, Logan recognised the voice as that of Detective Inspector Ben Forde. He searched the corners of the room for a camera, then gazed up into its single eye.

'I'm up and about, Jack,' Ben said. 'I'll keep a watch on things. You go get some rest. And, for God's sake, get yourself cleaned up, man.'

Logan looked down at himself, and the dirt and blood that stained his clothes. Jesus, what must Catriona Reid have been thinking?

It wouldn't hurt to get an hour or two, Logan supposed. It had been a long day, and it was going to happen all over again tomorrow, but with the potential to be much, *much* worse. There was certainly an argument to be made for getting some kip.

'Right, well, just make sure—'

'Aye. Don't worry. I'll wake you if anything happens,' Ben told him. 'Now go. You're no use to anyone if you're dead on your feet.'

Logan nodded reluctantly, then turned to DS McQuarrie. 'Back here at eight, all right?'

'Yes, sir,' Caitlyn said. 'See you then.'

'Aye, see you then,' Logan told her. 'Oh, and Caitlyn,' he added, as she headed for the door.

'Yes, sir?'

'Bring some more of them Caramel Wafers when you're coming back in.'

Caitlyn smiled grimly. 'Yes, sir,' she said. 'I'll see what I can do.'

Chapter 25

There was a baton in his hand. Cool. Rigid. Logan couldn't see it, exactly, but he could sense it. He knew it was there. Poised. Ready.

Useless.

The door to the flat was locked, like always. No time for formalities. Never any time to waste. It flew open with a kick—flew away, maybe—and a rush of warm, putrid air rushed past him like the breath of a dragon.

Or the contents of Pandora's Box.

He was inside the flat now. The smell wrapped around him, its flickering fingers of green the only visible thing in the otherwise empty void. He could feel it, hear it, *taste it* all around him. The mulchy stink of rot, and decay, and of things long dead.

His grip tightened on the baton.

From the darkness, he heard a voice. Two voices. Three.

Boys. Children.

Victims.

They clawed at him, tearing at his skin with their scratchy sobs, exposing the flesh beneath.

'Why didn't you save us?'

'Why didn't you come?'

'Why? Why? *Why?*'

The scene shifted. Elsewhere in the flat now. Lights on. Stench stronger than ever.

A cupboard. A door. A hand, reaching for a handle. His hand, he thought, although he wasn't in control of it. He was a passenger. An observer. A bystander, nothing more.

The handle turned. The door opened. Three dead boys cried somewhere behind him.

And from the cupboard came the nightmares. From the cupboard came the sorrow.

From the cupboard came the bones.

Chapter 26

There was a face hanging over him, looking down. Logan had it by the throat before he was fully awake, forcing it back from him, keeping it at bay.

His brain caught up a moment later, and quickly persuaded his hand to release its grip.

'Shite, sorry. Sorry,' he said, wincing and raising his hands in a gesture of surrender. 'You all right?'

'My fault,' said Sinead, rubbing her throat just above the collar of her uniform. 'I shouldn't have startled you. You weren't waking up.'

'No. Wasn't your fault, it was absolutely...'

He blinked in the glow of the sunlight streaming through the blinds. 'Wait, what time is it?'

'Just after eight, sir.'

'*Eight?*' Logan gasped. 'In the morning? Jesus. Why did no one wake me?'

'Maybe worried about being throttled, sir,' Sinead ventured.

Logan gave a little snort. 'Aye. Aye, that might be it. Sorry again. But, Jesus Christ. Eight.'

'Chief Inspector Pickering said you wanted to see me. I reported in, and DI Forde told me to come wake you,' Sinead explained.

'Right. Good. What else did Jinkies tell you?'

'Not a lot, sir,' Sinead replied. 'Just that you wanted to see me.'

It pleased Logan immensely to know that the rank-and-file were fully up to speed on Pickering's nickname. There hadn't been so much as a flicker of confusion on Sinead's face, either, suggesting the name was old news to her.

Excellent.

'Did I do something wrong?' Sinead asked.

'No. Nothing like that. The opposite, actually,' said Logan. He started to stretch, but then caught a whiff of his armpit and hastily aborted. 'You did good. I want you working with the MIT on this. You've got local knowledge, and you seem to know your stuff.'

Sinead looked flabbergasted, but it only lasted a moment. She'd processed the shock quickly, and was now moving on. Always a good sign.

'Thank you, sir. I don't know what to say. I won't let you down.'

'I'm sure you won't, Constable,' Logan said. He yawned into his hand, then gave himself a shake. 'Now, let's go talk to DI Forde and find out the latest.'

Sinead looked him up and down in one swift flick of the eyes. 'You think you should maybe…?' she began, then she pointed over her shoulder. 'I think there's some spare shirts next door.'

Logan regarded his own shirt. It had been in a pretty shocking state the night before, and a few hours spent tossing and turning in an office chair hadn't done it any favours.

'Aye, good call,' Logan said. 'And, if you happen to stumble upon a can of deodorant anywhere, I wouldn't say no.'

'Sleeping Beauty awakes,' said Ben, grinning at Logan as he and PC Bell entered the Incident Room. 'I was starting to think you'd died up there.'

'Aye, you wish,' Logan replied, fastening his tie and adjusting it as best he could by touch alone.

Ben tutted, then stepped in and fixed it properly, before straightening the DCI's collar. 'I'll be wiping your arse for you next.'

'Again, you wish,' Logan said.

Ben's nostrils flared, his face becoming a mask of revulsion as he looked Logan up and down.

'No, I don't actually know why I said that,' Logan admitted. 'Sorry. Probably best we don't ever speak of it again.'

'Aye,' said Ben. 'You wish. That'll be going in the staff newsletter.'

He motioned vaguely in the direction of the reception.

'Tyler's bringing bacon rolls in for us. He should be back in a few—'

The door opened and DC Neish almost walked straight into the back of Sinead.

'Oh, sorry. Didn't see you there,' he said.

'You're all right,' Sinead said.

'Tyler,' said the DC, repositioning his stash of white paper bags until he had a hand free. He offered it to Sinead. 'I mean, Detective Constable Tyler Neish.'

'Sinead. Bell. Sinead Bell.'

'Nice to meet you.'

Sinead smiled back at him, then stepped aside when Logan thrust a hand out in the DC's direction, palm open. 'Hurry up. I'm famished here.'

'What are you on for, boss? Bacon, square sausage—?'

'I don't care,' Logan said.

Tyler selected a bag at random and deposited it in the DCI's hand like an offering to the gods.

'Thank you.'

'Any time, boss.'

While Logan stalked off to his desk, Tyler flashed Sinead an apologetic smile. 'Sorry, I didn't know anyone else would be here. You can have mine, if you like.'

'I'm fine, ta. I ate this morning.'

'Oh, thank Christ,' said Tyler, visibly relieved.

He continued past her, opening one of the bags and peering inside. 'Hamza. Cheese salad roll, you freak.'

Hamza, who had been staring intently at the monitor of his PC, meerkatted up from behind it at the mention of his name.

'Shut it, ya dick,' he said, placing his hands together and opening them for a pass. He caught the bag, winked theatrically to celebrate his catching prowess, then diverted his attention back to the screen.

'Detective Sergeant McQuarrie, bacon, link, or square sausage?'

Caitlyn seemed to wrestle with her conscience for a few seconds, then held a hand out. 'I'll take the link, then, if no-one else wants it.'

'I'm not fussed,' said Tyler, passing over another bag.

'Whatever's going for me,' said Ben.

'Right you are, sir,' said Tyler, holding out a bag.

'Just not the square sausage,' Ben added.

Tyler hesitated for a moment, then swapped bags. 'Sorted. Bacon it is.'

Sinead shifted awkwardly, watching the others settle down to eat. 'Should I make tea, or something?' she asked.

Logan forced down a lump of his dry roll. The bacon was so crispy it could cut glass, and he was pretty sure it lacerated his throat on the way down.

'You're not here to make tea, Constable. You're a valued and respected part of this team, no' a skivvy,' the DCI told her. He gestured with the half-eaten roll. 'Tyler can make the tea.'

'What? I got the rolls!'

Sinead backed towards the door. 'It's not a problem. You're all eating. I don't mind. Might as well make myself useful.'

'I can think of a few ways she could make herself useful,' Tyler muttered, once Sinead had left.

A lump of diamond-hard bacon pinged off the side of his head.

'Ow!'

'DC Neish, if I ever hear you speaking like that again about one of my officers, or anyone else for that matter, then we're going to have a big problem,' Logan warned. 'Is that clear?'

'No, I didn't mean…' Tyler began to protest, but there wasn't really anywhere for him to go with it. 'She seems nice, is all I was saying.'

'That wasn't what you were saying. But you're right. She is. Hence why you're not going to be allowed anywhere near her,' Logan told him.

He addressed the rest of the group.

'If anyone hears DC Neish making similar comments again, or witnesses him attempting to ingratiate himself with Constable Bell, you all have my permission to kick the living shite out of him. Everyone clear?'

The responses were all far too enthusiastic for Tyler's liking. 'It's not what I meant,' he mumbled, then he filled his mouth with a big bite of roll to stop himself getting into any more trouble.

The rolls were polished off. The tea arrived. Introductions were made. And then began the process of getting everyone—Sinead, in particular—up to speed.

As all this was taking place, DS McQuarrie worked her magic with the Big Board, scribbling notes on Post-Its and sticking them in place, connecting Walker and Catriona Reid with another length of red wool, and generally re-organising things based on what they now knew.

'You're good at that,' said DC Khaled, watching her over the top of his computer.

'We sent her on a course,' said Ben. 'Two days of sticking things to a wall. Taxpayers' money well spent.'

'It wasn't *just* sticking things to a wall, sir,' Caitlyn protested. 'I mean, aye, it was *mostly* that, but they gave us lunch, too.'

Once the Big Board had been fully updated, Logan and the others took a few moments to study it. There was more information on it this morning than there had been the night before—no question about that. It was just that Logan had his doubts as to whether any of the information was useful, or if the board was essentially just a collage of meaningless bullshit that told them very little.

'Preliminary forensics on Walker's house and the boat came in around half-seven,' Ben said.

'Anything?' Logan asked.

'Not a sausage. Nothing to suggest Connor was anywhere near the place.'

'What about the loft?' Logan asked. 'Walker was pretty insistent that he hadn't been up there.'

'Nothing back on that yet,' Ben said. 'I'll get them chased up.'

'They'll give us it when they have it,' Logan said, taking a sip of his tea. He considered Walker's mugshot over the rim of his cup. 'I hate to say it, but I don't think it was him.'

'The loft?'

'Any of it,' said Logan. 'Duncan Reid said the work in the loft was done before Walker moved in. Could've been someone else.'

'Walker's our best lead at the minute,' Ben pointed out.

'Best? He's our only bloody lead,' Logan replied. 'But I still don't think it was him. It doesn't make sense. I don't think he knew about the teddy bear, and I can't figure out how he'd know about what was written on the envelope in the original case.'

'He had been inside,' DS McQuarrie reminded everyone. 'Some of the lags talking, maybe?'

'Unless he was locked up with Owen Petrie in Carstairs, nobody should've known about that envelope,' Logan said. His eyes glazed over a little, a memory taking over. 'And the way it was laid out. The spacing, or whatever. It was spot on. I mean, like, *spot on*. He couldn't have heard about it, he'd have to have seen it. And how could he have seen it?'

The others had to admit that they had no idea.

'We'll keep him in for now, we've got a few hours left before we have to decide if we're going to charge him,' Logan reasoned.

'We'll be charging him for the head injury, I assume?' Ben said. 'If nothing else.'

Logan appeared momentarily surprised, then brushed his fingertips across the neat stitches. 'No. Aye. Maybe. We'll see if we need an excuse to hold onto him.'

A silence fell over the Incident Room as they all went back to studying the Big Board. Sinead stood at the rear of the group, her arms wrapped across her middle. She wasn't quite sure what she was meant to be looking at, exactly, but she was looking damn hard at it, regardless.

It was Tyler who eventually asked the question most of them were thinking.

'So, if Walker doesn't have the kid, who does?'

'Not important,' said Logan. He finished his tea and set the mug down on his desk with a thunk.

'Sir?'

'The *who* can wait. It's the *where* we need to worry about,' the DCI continued. 'If the kidnapper is determined to replicate the Petrie case—and he's been doing a bang-up job of it so far—then Connor has less than twenty-four hours left.'

Logan looked across their faces. 'I'll say that again. Connor Reid has less than twenty-four hours left to live, unless we get our fingers out and find him.'

He gave that some time to sink in. But not much. They couldn't spare much.

'So, does anyone have anything? Anything at all?'

'Email in from the forensics guys,' said Hamza, as his computer gave a *ping*. 'They're loading everything they've got so far onto HOLMES. We should start seeing it in ten minutes.'

'That's something,' Logan said.

'I might have something else, too, sir,' Hamza continued. 'But it's a stretch.'

'I'd rather be stretching than sitting here scratching my arse. What is it?' Logan said. He gave Hamza a quick once-over, noting the slightly rumpled appearance, and the fact he was wearing the same clothes as yesterday. 'Have you been at it all night?'

'Aye, sir. Fell down a bit of a rabbit hole with a lead.'

Hamza took a Sharpie from the pen pot on his desk and approached the Big Board. 'You know I said I had a long shot I wanted to look into?' the DC began. 'It might be something.'

He studied the map for a moment, then drew a circle around a spot about three miles north of where Connor Reid went missing.

At first glance, there was nothing in the circle but trees and a section of track. It was only as Logan looked closer that he saw a tiny black rectangle there, slap-bang in the middle.

'What's that? A house?'

'Aye. Well, kind of, sir. It was a croft. *Ravenwood*, it's called. Derelict now, from what I can tell on Google Maps. Been no one living there for decades. There's a few places like this dotted all over the area, so I thought I'd have a check through the Land Registry and see if any of them were interesting.'

'And this one was?' asked Ben.

'It was, sir. Aye. It changed hands about twenty-two years ago. Current owner's some Indian company who probably just bought it for the land, but never did anything with it,' Hamza said.

'You and me have a very different definition of "interesting", mate,' said Tyler. He grinned at Sinead, started to wink, then caught the daggers Logan was shooting in his direction and turned his attention back to Hamza.

'That's not the interesting bit,' Hamza concluded. 'It's the previous owners. Limited company. Shell company, basically, but one of the directors of that company was *another* limited company.'

Something tickled down the length of Logan's neck. Somehow, he knew. Even before Hamza said the words, he knew.

'Petrie Construction.'

DC Khaled tapped his pen against the little black rectangle. 'Owen Petrie used to own that house.'

Chapter 27

He hadn't known. How could he not have known?

Years back, Logan had combed through every file, every document, every damn scrap of paper connected to Owen Petrie, building the case that would keep him inside for the rest of his life.

He'd had access to bank accounts, tax returns, bloody *Primary School reports*. He'd turned the man's whole life inside out and upside down, and compiled a report on everything he'd found.

For a while, he could recite Petrie's assets from memory, including those of his construction company. There was a point when he could've told the court how many teaspoons the bastard owned, and fairly accurately described their condition.

But he had a house. Another house, tucked away in the Highlands.

And Logan had known nothing about it.

'When was he there?' Logan demanded.

Hamza puffed out his cheeks. 'Hard to say, sir. Not sure he was ever actually there. Looks like it was bought by the company with a view to developing, but it never happened. But the company owned it between...'

He consulted a Post-It note he'd left stuck to his computer monitor.

'1992 and 2001,' Hamza concluded.

Logan reeled. 'Jesus Christ.'

He stepped in closer to the map and stared intently at the black rectangle, like he could somehow see through the roof and into the building below. 'Dylan Muir,' he murmured.

'What's that, Jack?' asked Ben.

Logan tore his eyes from the map and turned. 'Dylan Muir went missing in 1999. The bodies of Petrie's other victims were found in or around properties he owned. We never found Dylan. We found his clothes, and Petrie admitted to killing him, but he's never told us where to find the body.'

'Isn't he brain damaged now though, sir?' Tyler asked.

'Allegedly, aye,' said Logan.

'You think Connor could be being held there now?' asked DS McQuarrie.

'Connor? No. That wouldn't make any sense,' Logan said. He looked across their faces. 'Petrie didn't do this. You do understand that, yes? Petrie's not involved.'

'Is it possible that Petrie wasn't responsible for—' Sinead began, then an urgent shake of DI Forde's head cut her off before she could finish.

The warning came too late, however. Logan's face darkened. 'No, Constable, it's not possible that he wasn't responsible for killing those boys. I know, because I was there. I saw what he'd done. All right? Owen Petrie is guilty. And Owen Petrie is safely under lock and key a hundred-and-fifty miles away.'

'Right, sir. Sorry, sir,' Sinead said, her cheeks burning. DS McQuarrie caught her eye, and offered a reassuring smile. Or possibly one of condolences.

'Do I think we'll find Connor Reid at that house?' asked Logan, addressing the room as a whole. 'No. No, I don't. Of course not. Do I think we'll find Dylan Muir?'

He glanced back over his shoulder at the map. 'Aye. Maybe.'

'I'd like to go check it out, sir,' Hamza volunteered.

'You need to get to your bed,' Logan told him. 'You've done enough. That was good polis work, Hamza, but this has waited twenty years. It can wait another few days.'

Hamza gave a grateful nod. 'Thanks. But, I'd really like to see it through, sir. I could take a quick drive up that way on the way to the hotel. It'll only take twenty minutes.'

'Fine. Swing by and take a look. But don't go trampling around the place. We'll have to arrange a full search. Is there a ground radar team locally?'

Logan shook his head.

'What am I saying? Of course not. We'll have to get one brought in. Forensic archaeologists, too.'

'You want to take Tyler with you?' DI Forde asked Hamza.

'No. We need him here,' said Logan. 'We can't spare the resources.'

'Could be dangerous, Jack,' Ben said.

Logan shook his head. 'You're at it, too. Owen Petrie does not have Connor. He can't. Hamza, if you want to take a look, feel free, just be careful. Phone in when you're done, then go get some rest.'

'Will do, sir. Thank you.'

'You might want to go out the side door, mate,' Tyler told him.

'Eh? How come?' Hamza asked.

'You mean, you don't know?'

'Know what?' Logan asked.

Tyler looked from Hamza to the DCI and back again. 'You haven't been outside?'

The penny dropped for DCI Logan. 'Aw, bollocks. Press?'

'Aye, sir,' confirmed Tyler. 'You can say that again.'

—

Logan and Ben Forde stood at an upstairs window, gazing down at the scrum below. Four uniforms were in the process of trying to corral twenty-two parasitic bastards into a makeshift holding pen they'd put together using a couple of plastic barriers they'd borrowed from the building site across the road.

The journos were firing out questions. Logan couldn't hear them, but he could guess the sort of thing— wildly insensitive, massively speculative, and occasionally stomach-turning. The officers down there almost certainly hadn't had to deal with this sort of thing before, but from what Logan could tell, they were handling it admirably, with just the right balance of politeness and utter contempt.

Ben eyed the crowd of reporters. He didn't despise them to the extent that Logan did, but then he didn't have as many reasons to.

They all pushed forward behind the barriers, arms stretching, mouths moving. A zombie horde.

'You'll have to give them something,' he said.

'A bloody good hiding would be my preferred option,' Logan grunted.

He scanned the crowd, expecting to see Ken Henderson somewhere near the front. But no. For once, Henderson wasn't in amongst it.

Small mercies, Logan thought.

Although, if Henderson wasn't making an arsehole of himself here that just meant he would be making an arsehole of himself somewhere else.

'We should get onto the liaison. Check the Reids are all right. If this lot are here, it'll be worse over there.'

Ben nodded his agreement. 'I'll get someone on that.'

He took a breath, then shot the DCI a sideways look. 'You seen the headlines yet?'

'No. But I can guess. 'Mister Whisper Returns!' is it?'

'Pretty much, aye. Just the Scottish papers for now, but a couple of the UK-wides have put it on their websites. The Gozer's coming up the road to handle the press conference later today. Caitlyn's preparing a report for him now.'

'The Gozer? How come he's coming up? I thought someone from up north would handle it?'

'Assistant Chief Constable's request, apparently,' Ben replied. 'She's very keen he should do it. Can't imagine he's thrilled at the prospect.'

'You can say that again. Suits me, though. Means I don't have to talk to this lot,' Logan said. He cast a look to the mostly clear blue sky and sighed. 'The one day you want it to be raining.'

'Aye. Where's a bloody great downpour when you really need one?' Ben agreed.

There was a knock at the door. It opened without waiting to be told, and DC Neish appeared in the doorway. 'Boss?' he said, although it wasn't clear which of them he was directly addressing. 'Update on HOLMES.'

Tyler gave a backwards tilt of his head, indicating for the other two men to follow. 'I think we've got something.'

Chapter 28

Logan stood by Tyler's desk, face to face with a mugshot on the computer screen.

He was an ugly bugger, whoever he was. Scrawny, dirty, and with all the hallmarks of a long standing heroin habit. One side of his face drooped like he'd had a stroke, and his mouth was a graveyard of worn brown stumps.

'Who am I looking at?' Logan asked.

'He's…' Tyler began, but then he stepped aside and motioned to PC Bell like a compere welcoming a new act to the stage.

'Forbes Bamber, sir,' Sinead said. 'Local scrote. Harmless enough, but got a string of shoplifting charges, and various drugs-related stuff. He's a pain in the arse, but I wouldn't peg him for something like this.'

'Then why have we?' Logan asked. 'What's come up?'

'Fingerprint,' said Tyler. 'From the envelope that was delivered with the teddy to the Reids.'

Logan perked up. 'Now you're talking. Delivery man, maybe. He might be able to ID whoever gave it to him.'

'I wouldn't hold my breath, sir,' Sinead said. 'He's usually pretty wasted.'

'Well, here's hoping,' Logan said. He turned back to DC Neish. 'Anything else come through?'

Tyler Alt-Tabbed to another window on his desktop. 'Nothing yet, sir. Shouldn't be long.'

'OK. Fine. Go back to the junkie.'

Tyler clicked the mouse. Bamber's face flashed up like a prop in a Ghost Train.

'You've dealt with him before?' Logan asked Sinead.

'God, aye. We all have. No saying he'll remember me, though.'

'Well, let's go see if we can jog his memory,' Logan said, grabbing his coat. 'Tyler, keep an eye on HOLMES. If anything new comes in, text me.'

'Gotcha, boss.'

Pulling on his coat, Logan took a look around the Incident Room. DS McQuarrie was typing up the report for the Gozer, her fingers darting impressively across the keys in stark contrast to Logan's usual single-digit prodding.

'Hamza left?'

'Aye. He's going to swing by that croft, then go get some kip. We've to phone him if we need him,' said Ben.

'He'll check in though, aye?'

'Aye. Once he's had a look he's going to give us a ring and let us know he's clear.'

'Good. Right. Then, I'll leave everything in your capable hands,' Logan said. He turned to Sinead. 'My car's out front, and I don't fancy walking past that shower of bastards. Am I right in thinking all the polis vehicles are out back?'

'Yes, sir,' Sinead confirmed.

'Good. We'll take one of those. You can drive.'

Logan stood in front of DI Forde and held his hands out at his sides. 'Tidy enough?'

Ben flicked a crumb from the DCI's lapel. 'I suppose you'll do.'

'Right, then,' Logan said. His coat swished behind him as he turned and stalked towards the door. 'Let's go pay Mr Bamber a visit.'

–

'Bloody hell,' Hamza muttered as a front tyre hit another pothole, bouncing his car violently around on the narrow track.

He was crawling along, but the holes were too frequent to avoid, and deep enough that there wasn't much he could do when he hit one except grit his teeth, grip the wheel, and try not to bite off his tongue.

His phone was mounted in its holder on the dashboard, Google Maps open and tracking him. Or trying to track him, at least. It was currently accusing him of being several hundred yards away from the closest road, and seemed to be under the impression that he was driving through a stream.

Occasionally, the little triangle representing his car would randomly teleport to another location nearby, spin in clueless circles for a few seconds, then snap back to its original position.

The phone signal was patchy, and the upcoming section of map hadn't downloaded. As a result, Hamza was about to drive into a perfectly square beige-coloured void, with no idea what awaited him.

So much for bloody technology.

He was reaching into the glove box for the map when a sheep launched a Kamikaze run. It bounded out onto the track directly ahead of him, bleating furiously and stamping its feet like some self-appointed Guardian of Sweet-Fuck-All.

Hamza hammered the brake, churning up the shale beneath the car's wheels. He cursed as the back end spun into a skid, all his police driving training going completely out the window as he wrestled frantically with the wheel.

The car thumped into another pothole. The sudden stop threw Hamza forward in the seat and sent his phone clattering into the passenger footwell.

Hamza took a moment to check nothing was broken, then looked out over the dash. The sheep glowered in at him with its big boggly eyes. It gave an accusing *baa*, then trotted across the track, up the banking, and into the trees that lined the left-hand side.

'Thanks for that,' Hamza called after it.

Then, with a tut, he unfolded the map, glanced around him, and tried to figure out where he was supposed to be going.

–

Forbes Bamber swayed in the doorway of his house, scowling out at the morning sunshine and the two police officers standing on his step. His eyes were taking it in turn to blink, like they'd fallen out of sync at some point, and had never been able to get their timing right since.

If you were being generous, you might describe Bamber's house as a 'detached two-bedroom'. That was, on a strictly technical level, correct. In reality, it was a hideous concrete cube not much bigger than a shoebox, with barely an ant's pube-width gap between it and the two identikit hovels on either side.

A good estate agent could also argue that it had a garden, although they'd gloss over the fact it was eight feet long, made of broken bricks and rubble, and covered in dogshit.

Bamber stood in what might generously be described as a porch. There had presumably been an internal door hanging in the frame behind him once—the holes in the wood suggested the presence of hinges at some point—but it had been removed.

The sound of a child screaming came through the opening. It wasn't a scream of pain or fear, but rather one of those high-pitched screeches some kids liked to do for the sole purpose of being annoying. Judging by the hollered, 'Fucking shut up!' the screams earned from a female voice further back in the house, it was proving to be a successful strategy.

'Ye can't come in,' Bamber said. His voice was a slur that dribbled through his rotten teeth and down onto the front of a filthy t-shirt that was big enough to drown him. A faded print on the front of the t-shirt showed a grinning blue cartoon character with a white hat and glasses.

Irony, thought Logan, *thy name is Brainy Smurf.*

Other than the t-shirt, Bamber was dressed in mismatched socks and faded grey boxer shorts that Logan didn't even want to think about.

'We don't want to come in,' The DCI said. This was true. The last thing Logan wanted was to set foot inside this house.

'Ye need a what-do-you-call-it to come in. The paper 'hing.'

'A warrant,' said Sinead. 'Well, we do, and we don't.'

'Again, though, we don't want to come in,' Logan reiterated.

'Warrant, aye,' mumbled Bamber, his brain slowly catching up. 'Have ye got wan o' them?'

'No. We don't have a warrant,' PC Bell admitted.

'Cos, if ye don't, ye're no' getting in.'

Bamber pointed to the ground.

''At's my garden.'

Logan twitched, irritated. 'What?'

''S my garden,' Bamber said. ''S my property, an' that. Ye're no' allowed on my property.'

'Well, we are...' Sinead said.

'Naw, yer no'. I'll call the polis.'

Sinead shot Logan a glance. 'We are the polis, Forby. That's why I'm dressed like this.'

Bamber leaned back and peered down his nose at her, as if just noticing her outfit for the first time. 'Seriously? You're the polis?'

'Aye.'

He wiped his nose on his bare arm, leaving a silvery trail along it and briefly revealing the crook of his elbow that was a pincushion of red dots and bruising.

'If you're the polis, ye need wan o' them 'hings before ye can get in. What's it called?' Bamber slurred. 'Ye shouldnae even be in my garden.'

Logan had had enough. Bamber yelped as one of the DCI's hands clamped down on top of his head and tore him out of the house. Logan marched along the path, dragging Bamber by the hair.

'Hoi! Fuck off! Ye can't do this!'

Logan opened the gate, pulled the struggling scrote through it, and slammed him hard against the outside of his fence.

'There, now we're not on your property,' the DCI hissed. Ignoring the potential health risks, he was right up in Bamber's face, a hand still clamped on his head. 'Now, Forby. I've got some questions for you. Are you going to help me out by answering them?'

Logan tightened his grip on Bamber's hair, drawing a sob through those rotten tooth-stumps.

'Or am I going to get to do this the hard way?'

Chapter 29

Hamza sat in his car, his eyes flitting from the map sprawled open across the steering wheel to the ramshackle house that slouched in the trees ahead of him.

It was bigger than he'd been expecting, more of a manor house than a croft. The forest had been working to claim the ground back for a while now, and a tree was growing out through one of the building's downstairs windows.

Like the rest of them, this window had been boarded over, but the tree had made short work of that, and the square of plyboard now lay rotten on the ground in front of the house.

'Is this it?' Hamza wondered aloud. He fished around in the footwell until he found his phone, and checked Google Maps. He had one bar of phone signal, but no data connection. According to Google, he was right in the middle of a desert, with nothing of note for miles in any direction.

It wasn't too far off the mark, he supposed.

With nothing to tell him from this distance if he was in the right place, Hamza refolded the map, tossed it onto the passenger seat, then got out of the car.

Birds chirped and tweeted and hoo-hoo'ed from the treetops, singing to him as he turned towards the house. He locked the car, more out of habit than any worry that someone might try to nick it out here. Unless the squirrels were crafty bastards, he was pretty sure he didn't have to worry about that.

The forest had closed in around the back of the house, making it almost completely inaccessible. The front was mostly mud, stones, and weeds, with the track Hamza had followed, leading off past the building to the left. If the map was right, it came to a stop half a mile or so further on, becoming just a footpath that eventually led in a wide loop around to the main road half a day's walk away.

Picking his way through the mud, and avoiding the gloopy brown puddles as best he could, Hamza approached the house.

A nagging voice still told him that this couldn't be the place, although the only thing he had to base that on was the mental picture he had of traditional croft houses. He had no idea where that mental picture had originally come from, though. For all he knew, all croft houses were two storey mini-mansions.

It was only when he saw the sign above the front door that he concluded he was in the right place. A smooth piece of wood had been fixed above the lintel, a single word carved studiously but inexpertly into its well-sanded surface. Moss and time had stained the edges of the letters, but Hamza was able to make the word out.

Ravenwood.

This was the place, all right.

The door, unlike the windows, wasn't boarded up. Hamza tried the handle. Locked. The wood had seen better days, though. One good shoulder would open it.

But, what would be the point? There was no-one here. Or, if they were, they'd been dead a long, long time.

With a final glance up at the house, Hamza headed back towards the car. He was barely halfway when he saw the imprint in the mud. It led from a little further down the track from where he'd left his car, curving towards the front of the house.

Tyre tracks.

Motorbike.

Recent.

Hamza tapped the screen of his phone. The solitary bar had become an empty right-angle triangle in the top right corner.

'Magic,' he muttered.

He stood rooted to the spot, halfway between the house and his car, tapping his phone against the side of his leg.

'Bugger it. I've come this far,' he decided.

And then, slipping his phone in his pocket and adopting his best policeman's walk, DC Khaled approached the building's front door.

Chapter 30

'It was just a guy! Just a guy!'

Logan gave Bamber a shake. Beside the men, Sinead glanced along the street at the twitching curtains and parted blinds.

'What *guy*?' Logan demanded. 'What did he look like?'

'I don't know! Just a guy! He just looked like a guy!'

Logan produced his phone, opened the photo app, and swiped until he found the mugshot of Ed Walker. 'Was this him?' he asked, holding the phone up in front of Bamber's face.

'I don't know, I cannae see it. It's too close,' Bamber said, his eyes blinking in turn as he tried unsuccessfully to focus.

Muttering, Logan released his grip on the scrote's hair and brought the phone back a foot.

'Naw. Naw, that's no' the guy. He looked different.'

'Different in what way?' Logan asked.

'Just different. Like... different,' Bamber slurred.

Logan sighed. 'Jesus Christ. Older? Younger? Fatter? Thinner? Different how?'

'His face was like...'

Bamber gestured vaguely to his own face.

'...different. Aye, like, it wisnae the same. Know?'

'I know what 'different,' means, aye.'

'He didnae have a beard for wan thing,' Bamber said. 'Aye, like no' like a *beard*.'

'Right. OK. Now we're getting somewhere.'

Bamber's pock-marked brow furrowed. 'Or maybe he did. I cannae mind.'

Logan clenched his jaw, swallowed back his rage.

Behind him, Sinead's radio squawked into life on her shoulder. 'Control to PC Bell. You there, Sinead?'

Sinead looked to Logan for his approval, then retreated when he gave her the nod. 'It's Sinead, Moira. What's up?' she asked.

Bamber watched her, his face fogged with confusion. 'That's a shite phone,' he remarked. 'I've got a better phone than that.'

Logan caught Bamber's chin and turned his head so the junkie's glassy eyes were focused vaguely in the DCI's direction.

'You're wasting my time here, Forby. Right now, we've got evidence that connects you to the abduction of a child. I could haul you into the station now and keep you there for *days*,' Logan told him. 'When did you have your last fix, Forby? How do you fancy a week of cold turkey in a wee grey box?'

His eyes went to Bamber's house.

'A different wee grey box, I mean.'

The expression on Bamber's face made his thoughts on the matter very clear.

'No, thought not,' Logan said. 'So, you need to give me something useful. Something more than "just some guy".'

A few yards along the street, PC Bell swore urgently.

'Shit, shit, shit,' she said, scrabbling for her phone.

'What's the matter?' Logan asked.

'It's my brother, sir,' Sinead said, hurriedly thumbing through her contacts. 'School's been on the phone to the station. He hasn't turned up.'

Logan checked his watch. 'Ten past nine. Could he no' just be late?'

Sinead shook her head. 'He goes to Breakfast Club at eight. I walked him to the end of the road before I came in. He wasn't there, either, so I don't—'

A car trundled past. Sinead put her finger in one ear, pressing the phone more firmly against the other. 'Hello? Hello, Anna? It's Sinead. Harris's sis—Aye. No. No, he definitely left. He should've been at Breakfast Club.'

She listened for a moment, her face telling the story of what the person on the other end was saying. 'Well, where is he?' she asked, her voice rising. 'Where is he?'

Logan jabbed a finger in Bamber's face. 'Don't leave town. I'm not finished with you,' he said, then he placed a hand on Sinead's back and guided her towards the car.

'Get in,' he told her. He held his hands out for the keys. 'I'll drive.'

Chapter 31

'Roundabout! *Roundabout*!'

Logan held steady, siren screaming as he flew across the junction in a near-perfect straight line.

'It's painted on. It doesn't count,' he said, shooting a glance back in the car's rear view mirror.

A bus chugged along ahead of them. Jerking the wheel, Logan swung out onto the other side of the road, then immediately swung back in again to avoid a head-on collision with a delivery van coming the other way.

'Jesus, is everyone deaf around here?' he asked. 'Sirens, people, sirens.'

He made a non-specific but almost certainly rude gesture to the driver of the van, then eased out enough to see past the bus. It had indicated to the left and was slowing down to let him by, but the road ahead was clear now, so he gunned the engine and roared on past it, blue lights licking across the *Shiel Buses* logo painted along the vehicle's side.

'Where now?'

'Left past the traffic lights. Across the bridge, then left again.'

Traffic lights. Traffic lights.

There.

The lights were on red. He ignored that fact and sped through, hanging a left at another roundabout—a proper one, this time—just beyond them.

Sinead gasped and grabbed for the solid plastic handle of the door as the car swung around the corner, rear tyres smoking.

'Been ages since I've done this,' Logan said.

'I couldn't tell,' Sinead hissed, bracing herself against the seat. 'Left up here past *Farmfoods*.'

More lights, but the filter arrow was green this time. The tyres howled in protest as Logan skidded the car around the bend. Sinead caught a glimpse of a terrified-looking older driver in the opposite lane, but then they were past it, leaving the junction behind them in a cloud of burning rubber.

'And there's nowhere else he'd go?' Logan asked, crunching up into third and kangarooing past a couple of cars whose drivers had had the foresight to pull into a bus stop.

'No. Nowhere. He must've gone back home. He has to be there,' Sinead said. 'If he's not...'

Logan shot her the briefest of sideways glances, before returning his eyes to the road. 'He'll be there. Don't worry. He'll be fine.'

He added the '*Please, God*' silently in his head so Sinead couldn't hear it, then he jammed his foot down on the accelerator and powered the car along the narrow, winding road towards whatever awaited them ahead.

–

DC Neish looked up from his computer screen. 'Email in from up the road, boss. There was a hold-up with the DNA stuff. We'll have it in the next twenty minutes.'

'Good. About time,' said Ben. He was perched on the edge of his desk, studying the Big Board. 'Any word back from Hamza yet?'

'Nah. Want me to give him a ring?'

'Please.'

Standing, Ben followed the strands of wool around the board, pausing to take in the contents of the Post-It notes dotted all over it. He'd read them so often now that he knew most of them off by heart but he read them again, anyway, in case this time they triggered some new idea, or potential line of enquiry.

'Dead, boss,' said Tyler.

Ben turned. 'What?'

'His phone. It's dead. Probably no signal.'

'Oh. Right. Aye.'

DI Forde turned back to the board. He sucked in his bottom lip, his gaze falling on the little black rectangle circled on the map. He scratched his chin, his fingernails rasping across a day or two's worth of stubble.

'You fancy checking on him?'

Tyler looked down at the phone. 'Already tried, boss. Told you, no signal.'

'No, I get that. I was asking if you fancied taking a drive up there and checking on him,' Ben said. He looked back over his shoulder. 'And, to be clear, I wasn't *actually* asking.'

–

Sinead rattled the handle of her front door, finding it locked.

'He's not in. He's not here,' she said, panic rising like a bubble in her throat. She pushed back a jolly-looking garden gnome that stood at the edge of a small lawn that hadn't seen a mower in a while. Something metallic shone from the dirt below.

'The key's still there. He can't get in without the key.'

Cupping his hands around his eyes, Logan peered in the downstairs window into the living room. A pair of blue pyjamas was spread across a couch, one leg turned inside-out. A mug and a plate sat on a little coffee table, half a slice of toast left on top.

'Can't see him in there,' Logan remarked. 'Is there a back door?'

'Aye, but it's locked. The key's in it on the inside. There's no way in,' Sinead said. 'Shit. Where can he be?'

'We'll call it in, get folk out looking for him,' Logan told her. 'We'll find him.'

Sinead chewed her thumbnail, her eyes shimmering with worry. 'Right. Aye,' she mumbled. She reached for the walkie talkie on her shoulder and was about to thumb the button when Logan caught her by the arm, stopping her.

'Wait. Hang on,' he said, lowering his voice. 'Listen.'

Sinead listened, as instructed, but the thumping of her own heart and the traffic passing out beyond the end of the garden path made it difficult for her to hear anything.

'What? What is it?'

'Round the back,' Logan said.

Sinead moved to hurry past him, but he blocked the way. 'Wait. Let me go first.'

'Why?' Sinead demanded. She searched his face. 'What is it?'

'I don't know. But stay behind me.'

Constable Bell shook her head. 'No. Sorry, sir, but no.'

She ran up the path and out of the front garden, then sprinted off towards the house at the end of the block.

'Bugger it,' Logan grunted, hurrying to keep up. Sinead was twenty years younger, though, and Logan had never been built for running.

He caught up with her at the back gate. She stood there at the end of the house's back path, watching a boy in school uniform digging with a rusty spade. The spade thwacked when it hit the grass—the sound Logan had heard from out front.

Halfway between the gate and the boy, the shed door stood open. A badly weathered padlock hung from its broken latch.

The boy had his back to the gate and hadn't noticed Sinead and Logan's presence yet. He grunted with effort as he plunged the blade of the spade into the grass, and prised a little mound of dirt free.

'Harris? Harris, what are you doing?' Sinead asked.

Her little brother jumped with fright. He turned the spade clutched before him like a weapon.

It was then that they saw the blood. It plastered the front of his jacket and smeared up his chin. It pooled between his fingers and ran down the handle of the shovel in long, weaving strands.

Harris swallowed when he saw his sister and Logan standing there.

'Sinead,' he said, his voice an anxious squeak. 'Am I in trouble?'

Chapter 32

What Hamza had assumed was the front door had, in fact, opened into a good-sized kitchen and dining area at the back of the house.

The size was the only good thing about it.

It had been tiled once, but damp had cancered the walls behind them, and most of the tile-work now lay smashed on the floor.

Cabinets had fallen from their mountings, smashing through the rotten wood of the lower storage units below. An old-style porcelain sink had cracked in two, spewing a greenish-black gunge through the gap.

The lino flooring was curling up in places, the edges pitted and gnawed away by rats. Alternate layers of mulch and moss and dust clung to most surfaces, and as Hamza creaked into the room, a carpet of woodlice hurried to clear a path.

'Shit,' he ejected, burying his face in the crook of his elbow. He coughed, his eyes watering, his gag reflex demanding to know what the hell he thought he was playing at.

His eyes travelled to the corners of the room, saw things there that they wished they hadn't, then shot a longing look back at the fresh air of outside.

The place wasn't just giving him the boak, it was gift-wrapping it for him and presenting it on a silver platter.

Every instinct told him to get out of there before he caught something. Every thought was of turning around and walking away.

Logan was right, he'd had a long night. He needed to be in bed, not poking around in a decaying old death trap filled with beasties. He forced himself to look at the squirming mound of woodlice, then shuddered at the sight of them, and at the thought of the millions of others no doubt roaming around in the house like they owned the place.

Something clacked onto the floor beside him, making him jump. Another of the fat, wriggling bugs lay on its back, legs bicycling frantically in the air. Hamza looked up, then jumped back into the doorway when he saw the ceiling was heavy with more insects. Not just woodlice but spiders, beetles, centipedes, and a variety of other bugs he didn't know the names of but despised on sight.

Part of the ceiling had collapsed, the plasterboard buckled, to reveal part of a wooden beam and the underside of some floorboards above. Hamza retreated until he was standing under the doorframe. He'd heard somewhere that it was the safest place in an earthquake, as the house was less likely to fall on your head.

He wasn't expecting the ground to start trembling, but the house spontaneously collapsing on him felt like a very real possibility.

Taking out his phone, Hamza snapped off a few photos. The light from the door didn't stretch far into the room, so he took a few more with the flash on. The brightened images revealed more detail about the place but fell well short of conveying the horror of it.

There were a couple of doors leading off from the kitchen area. Both doors were open, and by leaning forward a little, Hamza could see what looked like a small utility room through one of them.

The angle of the second door blocked his view in that direction, but he guessed it must lead into the rest of the house. A living room or hallway, maybe. The window with the tree sprouting through it was in that direction somewhere, and while he was quite interested in getting a look at that, he was even more interested in getting back into the fresh air of outside, and away from this shitehole of a place.

Besides, if Dylan Muir's body was here somewhere, he didn't want to contaminate the place.

He cast a final glance around at the filth and debris.

Contaminate it any more than it already was, anyway.

Hamza was turning to leave when he heard the sound. Short. Sudden.

Thump.

He stopped, tensed, breath held, head cocked. His eyes moved left to right, seeing nothing as he listened.

A few seconds passed.

A minute.

Hamza's heart rate slowed. He allowed himself to breathe again.

Nothing. Probably just his imagination going into over—

Thump.

There was no mistaking it, that time. No denying it. A sound. But not *just* a sound.

A movement.

Upstairs.

Slowly—ever so slowly—Detective Constable Khaled leaned back, his eyes creeping to the ceiling above him.

Chapter 33

'Harris? What have you done? What did you do?' Sinead whispered, edging along the path towards her brother.

Harris shook his head. 'It wasn't me.'

'What wasn't you, son?' Logan asked, eyeing the boy's blood-soaked clothes and the spade in his hands.

'I just found it.'

'Found *what*?' Sinead demanded.

The sharpness of her voice made the boy jump, and brought tears bubbling to the surface. He tried to speak, but the words wouldn't come, so he stepped aside and pointed, instead.

A cat lay on the grass beside the hole Harris had been digging. Most of a cat, anyway.

An oblong of fur and flesh had been torn from its side, exposing part of its ribcage and a purple jelly of intestines. Its back legs hadn't been broken so much as mangled, bones jutting through meat at a range of stomach-churning angles.

'Jesus,' Sinead hissed.

'It was... it was on the pavement,' Harris said.

'And what? You picked it up?' Sinead yelped. 'What were you thinking?'

Harris sniffed. His blood-spattered face burned with shame.

'You can't just pick up dead cats, Harris! That's *mental*!' Sinead continued. 'You should be in school. Do you have any idea how worried I was? Do you?'

Harris shook his head, keeping his gaze fixed on the ground between them.

'It's not just me, is it?' Sinead asked, turning to Logan. 'It's mental?'

'Well, I mean…' was all Logan could really add.

'It had been in an accident,' he croaked. His shoulders shook. 'Like… like Mum and Dad were. I couldn't just leave it. I couldn't just… I couldn't just…'

Sinead was at him in three big steps, her arms around him, pulling him in. He dropped the spade and buried his face against her high-vis vest, his body wracked by big breathless sobs.

Logan watched Sinead's bottom lip start to wobble, then had the good grace to look away. Bending, he retrieved the spade.

'Why don't you two go inside?' he suggested. 'I'll take care of this.'

'You've got to bury it,' Harris told him, turning his face but not releasing his grip on his sister. His words were wobbly, carried on unsteady breaths. 'When things die, we bury them. That's just what we do.'

Logan nodded. 'You're right, son. We do. And I will. I promise.'

Sinead shot him an apologetic look, but he dismissed it with a shake of his head. 'Away inside. Get him calmed down and cleaned up. It's fine.'

'Thank you,' she mouthed, then she turned with her brother and steered him out of the garden and around the block.

Logan waited until they were out of sight before squatting down, leaning on the spade for balance as he examined the cat.

It could've been an accident, he supposed, but the hole in the animal's side was neater than he'd have expected to see, the size and placement making it a near-perfect window into the poor thing's insides.

Similarly, the leg breakages were messy, but calculated. It was *possible* that a car could've done damage like that, but unlikely. The bones had splintered in opposite directions, so each leg was a mirror image of the other. Unless the animal had been lying with its legs spread in an open invitation to an oncoming tyre, Logan couldn't imagine how they had broken the way they had.

The front of the cat was in perfect condition, other than the redness matting its black and white fur. Its eyes were closed, its mouth open. It was missing a few teeth, Logan noted, although nothing out of the ordinary.

He wanted to believe it was an accident. He wanted to believe that nobody would do something like this on purpose. But, the unfortunate truth of it was, he'd seen similar to this before.

Too similar.

Once, in particular.

Fishing a pen from his pocket, he carefully prodded around at the edges of the wound, trying to figure out if the flesh had been torn off or cut away. The smell from the cat's insides snagged at the back of his throat and filled his mouth with saliva. He swallowed it down, still leaning on the spade as he continued his inspection.

He was looking closely at the injury when the cat twitched, its eyes opening, its face contorting in pain.

It mewed desperately, piteously, its front paws kicking at nothing, its tail sticking straight out behind it.

Logan jerked back and jumped to his feet, the cat's pained cries carrying across the garden and up towards the house. Its head twisted. Its eyes met Logan's. Frightened. Desperate.

'Poor wee bugger,' Logan muttered.

And, with that, he raised the spade.

Chapter 34

Hamza stood halfway up the stairs, darkness hanging heavy and oppressive overhead.

The lack of signal had rendered his phone mostly useless, but at least the shite *Vodafone* service didn't affect the torch function. He clutched the phone in his rubber-gloved hands, directing the torchlight upwards. It pushed back against the gloom, sending shadows scurrying across the peeling wallpaper and the blooms of black mould.

Each step groaned beneath his weight, a chorus of suffering singing him up the stairs.

There had been no more sounds since he'd left the kitchen beyond those he made himself. Creaking floorboards. Rustling clothes. The odd panicky gasp whenever something scurried out of a hole in the plasterboard or scuttled across the floor.

From the rest of the house, though, came only silence.

The upstairs landing was L-shaped, with six doors that Hamza could see, and probably at least one that he couldn't because of the corner. None of the doors looked particularly inviting. One had a little brass plate fixed to it that announced it as the 'Little Boys Room'.

Bathroom. Almost certainly. And yet, that particular choice of words meant Hamza had no choice but to check.

The door opened with a nudge. Hamza shone the torchlight inside, then stepped back, burying his face in his arm again. An overflowing toilet stood in the corner, a jagged hole in front of it where the floor had collapsed down into the room below. He flashed the torch across the rest of the room, finding nothing but a wash basin, an empty bath with a mildew-stained curtain hanging limply from a rail above it, and a generous amount of decay.

Hamza closed the door again, and turned his attention to the rest of the landing. The five other doors were unmarked. One stood ajar, giving him a glimpse of a carpet so damp it was literally sprouting mushrooms.

He decided to leave that one for now, and considered the others, instead. He thought about calling out, but a tightness in his throat prevented him. He told himself it was his body's way of resisting the urge to vomit. That was all.

Not fear.

His feet scuffed on the bare floorboards of the landing as he turned to the next door. An army of ants swarmed across the edges of the frame and up the wall between that door and the next.

Hamza had just decided to give this door a miss for now, too, when he saw the blood.

He didn't realise it was blood. Not right away. It was a dried puddle, a stain, a congealed pool of blackish red that had seeped out under the door and glossed the floor-boards.

The truth of what he was looking at hit him with a sudden jolt that forced him back a step and brought a hissed expletive to his lips.

He should go, get out, drive until he found a signal and call for back-up. That was what he *should* do. No question.

He reached for the handle. Turned. Pushed.

The door remained closed. It took him another couple of attempts before he discovered it opened outwards.

The smell hit him first. It was unlike anything he'd ever smelled before—richer, blacker, more pungent.

The bones came next. They rattled and clunked out of the cupboard and onto the floorboards as an avalanche of yellows and browns. Long. Thin.

Child-sized.

'Fuck, fuck, fuck!' Hamza croaked, the phone shaking in his hand, the trembling torchlight making the bones' shadows dance.

Dylan Muir. Had to be.

THUD.

Everything but Hamza's eyes froze. They darted instinctively in the direction the sound had come from.

Around the corner. The other leg of the L.

He held his breath. Stood his ground. A voice in his head screamed at him to run. Another voice—Logan's, he thought—warned him not to fucking dare.

Do your job, that one told him. *Just do your bloody job.*

He checked his phone screen again, just in case. Still no signal.

The floorboards shifted noisily as he crept towards the corner and peeked around it into a shorter branch of the upstairs hallway. A single door stood at the far end. Mounted to the wall above it, the antlers of a deer's skull stabbed up at the decaying ceiling.

He heard the thump of movement from beyond the door again. There was more though, this time. A squeak. A sob. The whimper of a wounded animal.

Or a frightened child.

The uncertainty that had been crippling Hamza evaporated and he knew, with crystal-clarity, what he had to do.

He reached the door in three big creaks, and threw it open.

Hamza didn't notice the room. Not at first. All he saw was the chair, and the ropes, and the wide, staring eyes of a boy whose face he had previously only seen in photographs.

'Connor,' Hamza exhaled. 'Connor? It's OK, I'm with the police. I'm with the police, OK? I'm here to rescue you.'

Bound to the chair, Connor Reid wheezed desperately into his gag. He kicked his bare feet, thudding his heels against the rotten carpet, squirming and thrashing in panic.

'Shh, it's OK, it's OK,' Hamza promised. 'I'm going to get you out. I'm going to get you home.'

He took a step closer. The floorboards squeaked.

Twice.

A voice came from right behind him.

No, not a voice.

A whisper.

'Naughty, naughty,' it said.

And then, before Hamza could turn, something cold and sharp was buried low down in his back, and his world fragmented into shards of pain.

Chapter 35

Logan stood by the kitchen window drinking tea from a chipped mug and admiring the view. The house looked directly onto Ben Nevis, and the mid-morning sun was dappling the mountain's snow-covered peak.

He'd never been much into climbing himself, but looking up at the mountain now—The Ben, as the locals referred to it—he could almost see the appeal.

Almost.

A train rattled past just up the road from the house. There was a steam train that ran along this route, he knew. Part of the track up towards Glenfinnan had featured in the *Harry Potter* movies, and fans flooded the area during the summer, trying to get a glimpse of the train, or paying through the nose to ride on it.

It was a bog-standard old diesel that came thundering past now, though, vibrating the breakfast dishes in the sink. Probably headed to Glasgow, Logan thought, and part of him wished he was sitting on it.

Although, he noted with interest, maybe not as big a part of him as he'd have thought.

He turned away from the window. Sitting at the kitchen table, Harris immediately turned his head, trying not to let on that he'd been scoping the DCI out. Logan could hear Sinead through in the living room, explaining the situation to the school. By the sounds of things, she was glossing over the 'he'd picked up a dead cat,' thing. He couldn't really blame her.

'How you doing, son?' Logan asked the boy.

Harris looked young for his age. Physically, at least. Not behind the eyes, though. Behind the eyes, where it counted, he was old. Older than his sister. Older, perhaps, than Logan himself.

Harris shrugged.

'Aye. Get used to that. When you get to my age, that's pretty much the default,' Logan said. 'In fact…'

He shrugged.

'…is a good day once you're past forty. Enjoy your…'

He shrugged again.

'…while it lasts.'

Harris smiled. Logan rewarded himself with another sip of tea.

'Do you think I'm mental?' Harris asked.

Logan did him the courtesy of not answering right away.

'I think we're all mental, son,' he told the boy. 'Some of us more than others. If it's any consolation, you're way down near the bottom of the list.'

Harris's brow furrowed.

'No. I don't think you're mental,' Logan clarified. 'I think you tried to do a good thing, even though you knew it'd get you into trouble. There's hee-haw mental about that.'

Harris relaxed a little, the lines of confusion lifting from his forehead.

'I mean, did you *look* mental plastered in blood and waving a spade around? God, aye,' Logan told him. 'You did. But looks can be deceiving. Take me, for example.'

Harris looked him up and down, not understanding.

209

'Ballet dancer,' said Logan over the top of his mug.

Harris exploded into laughter.

'What?' Logan demanded. 'What's so funny?'

'No, you're not!' the boy giggled. 'You're not a ballet dancer.'

'Aye, I am! What are you saying, like?' Logan retorted, mock-offended.

Sinead came in from the hallway, thumbing the hang-up button on the phone. She looked from the DCI to Harris and back again. 'What's going on?'

'Your brother is casting aspersions on my dancing skills,' Logan told her. 'Can you believe the bloody cheek?'

'Ballet dancer!' Harris exclaimed.

Sinead smiled weakly. 'Right. I'm really sorry about this, sir.'

Logan waved the apology away. 'I helped myself to a cup of tea.'

'No, it's not fair, sir. We're up against the clock with…'

She shot Harris a look and stopped herself before she finished the sentence.

'…everything. This is slowing us down.'

'It's fine. I can multi-task. I texted DI Forde. He's getting your man… what's his name? Bamber, brought in. CID are going to give him a going-over, see if they can figure out who 'just some guy' is. Asked him to have Social Services pop their heads in, too, to check on the wean.'

Sinead nodded. 'OK. I'm really sorry, though.' She began jabbing digits on the phone. 'I'll see if I can get Maureen down the road to watch him. I've told the school he's not coming in.'

She looked between them both. 'You OK here for a minute?'

'Aye. As long as he doesn't start having a go at my singing voice next, I'm sure we'll get on just fine.'

'OK, that's…' Sinead turned and marched out into the hall. 'Hello? Alan? Is Maureen…? Aye. Aye, that's right. Thanks.'

Logan tipped the rest of his tea down the sink, swirled out the mug, then sat it on the draining board. Harris was watching him when he turned and leaned against the kitchen worktop.

'So. This cat, then,' Logan said.

'Did you bury it?' Harris asked. The question came out of him in a flash, like he'd been holding it back until now.

'I did,' Logan said.

A lie, but a necessary one. The boy never needed to know the animal's remains were currently stashed in a Bag for Life in the boot of the polis car.

Harris nodded, satisfied. 'Good. That's what you're meant to do.'

'It is,' Logan agreed.

He took a seat across the table from the boy. 'You remember where you found it?'

Harris shifted uncomfortably, like he was resisting the memory.

Then, just when Logan was about to tell him not to worry about it, he nodded.

'Can you tell me where it was?'

Harris nodded again. 'You know where the Co-op is?'

'No.'

The fact that someone didn't know where the Co-op was appeared to momentarily blow the boy's mind. He sat in silence for a while, his eyes fixed on Logan, an expectant expression on his face like he was waiting for a punchline.

'I'm not from around here,' Logan explained. He brought out his phone and tapped the Maps icon. 'Can you show me on this?'

He handed the phone over. 'You can move the map around by…'

Logan opted to shut his face when Harris took the phone, pinch-zoomed in, and swiped a finger across the screen.

'Aye, like that,' the DCI said, when the boy handed him the phone back. He'd marked the spot with a little red flag.

How the bloody hell had he done that? Was that a thing you could do? Logan hadn't had a clue.

'Right. And it was there, was it?'

Harris nodded. 'It was beside the road. Just lying there. A car must've hit it.'

'Aye. Aye, it must've,' said Logan.

Another lie, probably. Forensics would have to confirm.

'Did you see anyone around?' Logan asked.

Harris frowned. 'What do you mean?'

'Just, like, anyone watching. Or acting strange.'

'There was an old woman,' Harris said. 'She shouted at me.'

'Did she? What did she say?'

Harris shot a look in the direction of the hallway. 'I'm not allowed to swear.'

'I won't tell anyone,' Logan promised.

The boy chewed his lip for a moment, then spat it out. 'Put that f'ing thing down. You don't know where it's f'ing been,' he said. He glanced furtively in the direction of the hall. 'Except she didn't say f'ing.'

'Right.'

'She said 'fucking.''

'Gotcha. And what did you say?'

'Nothing. I just ran past her. I was nearly home by then.'

Logan nodded. 'Ah, OK. No-one around where you found the cat, though?'

'No. Not that I saw,' said Harris. He wrung his hands and looked up at the DCI. 'Are you going to find who killed it?'

'I'm going to do my best,' Logan told him, then they both turned as Sinead entered from the hallway, a child's jacket held open before her like a Matador's cape. It was not the same jacket he'd been wearing earlier. Considering that one now resembled a butcher's apron, Logan reckoned this was probably for the best.

'Right, you. Jacket on. Maureen's going to watch you for the day.'

Harris hopped up from his chair and inserted an arm into a sleeve.

'And for God's sake,' Sinead told him. 'Don't mention the cat.'

Chapter 36

Tyler bent and peered in through the driver's side window of DC Khaled's car, then up at the ramshackle house a few dozen yards ahead.

The journey up here had taken longer than he'd expected, largely on account of him getting completely lost twice. Quite how he'd managed to get lost on what was, essentially, a single road with no junctions, he wasn't sure. One thing he did know, though—he'd never mention it to anyone, and especially not to Hamza. The bastard would never let him live it down.

'Ham?' Tyler bellowed in the direction of the house. A flock of birds rose from the trees at the sound of his voice, cawing and squawking their displeasure. 'Helloooo?'

He checked his phone. One bar. Just. He tried calling Hamza, but was met by a lengthy silence, then— eventually—the dulcet tones of the voicemail greeting.

'Bollocks.'

The door to the house stood open. Even from that distance, it wasn't exactly inviting.

Tyler looked across the boarded windows and moss-coated stone of the building's frontage. 'Hamza, you in there, mate?'

He waited for an answer that didn't come.

'I swear to God, if I come in there and you jump out at me, I'll kill you,' Tyler warned.

Silence.

Tyler reiterated the 'Bollocks,' and then set off in the direction of the door.

Something stopped him a few paces in. A doubt. A niggle. A creeping sensation down his spine that told him something wasn't right.

Returning to his car, he popped the boot, grabbed the torch and extendable baton that were in there, then closed it again with a clunk.

He flicked the torch's switch, checking the battery. All good.

Flicking his wrist, Tyler extended the baton to its full length.

'Right, then, Detective Constable Khaled,' he muttered. 'Good luck to you if you come jumping out at me now.'

–

'Thanks, Maureen, I really appreciate this. I owe you one.'

Logan stood back at the car, watching Sinead express her gratitude to the white-haired woman in the doorway for about the third time since Harris had disappeared inside. Maureen, for her part, looked thrilled to have the boy, and had beamed from ear to ear when he'd hugged her briefly on his way into the house.

Still, time was getting on. Logan cleared his throat just loudly enough to catch PC Bell's attention. She shot a look back over her shoulder, smiled apologetically, then beat a hasty retreat up the path.

'If there's anything, just call the station. You've got the number.'

'He'll be fine. He's always fine. Off you go. We'll give him his dinner.'

'Thank you!'

'Christ, are you rehearsing for your Oscars speech?' Logan asked, holding the gate open. 'You're grateful. She gets it.'

Sinead gave the old woman a wave, and mouthed another silent, 'Thanks!'

'It's short notice. I don't like dumping him on her at short notice.'

'Dumping him on her? Did you see her face? I think you just made her day.'

He held out the car keys. 'Not sure your nerves'll handle me driving.'

'Aye, they've had enough for one day, I think,' Sinead agreed. She took the keys. 'Sorry again, sir.'

'Not at all. It was… enlightening,' Logan said, pulling open the passenger door.

'You're good with him. Harris, I mean. Have you got kids?'

Logan hesitated, the door open. 'Aye. A daughter. Older, though. Not a kick in the arse off your age.'

'Oh? What does she do?'

'Eh… I don't know. Not too sure, actually.'

Sinead swore at herself inside her head.

'Oh. Right,' she said, then she pulled open her door and got into the driver's seat. She spent a few moments adjusting the position of it, then pulled on her belt.

'By the way, thanks,' she said, as Logan clambered in beside her. 'You know, for burying the cat. You didn't need to do that.'

'The cat. Aye,' Logan said. He clipped in his own belt, then shot her a sideways look. 'About that…'

Moira Corson turned from the reception desk as Logan and Sinead came in through one of the front office's side doors. There was a soft thud as the DCI deposited a *Marks & Spencer* Bag for Life on the desk beside her.

'For me?' she asked, peering down at it. 'What is it?'

'It's a cat,' Logan told her.

Moira's face remained largely impassive. 'I don't want a cat.'

'Well, you certainly won't want this one,' Logan said.

Moira leaned forward to look into the bag. Logan motioned for her not to. 'I wouldn't. I need a postmortem done on it ASAP.'

'A postmortem?' said Moira. 'On a cat?'

'Aye. On a cat. On this particular cat.'

Sighing, Moira reached for her notepad. 'What do you need to know? Cause of death?'

Logan shook his head. There was a bag of Mint Imperials open on Moira's desk. He helped himself to one, drawing a furious glare from the receptionist.

'I already know how it died. It was whanged on the head with a spade.'

Moira flicked her gaze down into the opening at the top of the bag. 'How do you know that?'

'Because I'm the one who whanged it,' Logan told her. 'I need to know if the other injuries were accidental or deliberately inflicted. Can you get that processed for me?'

Moira's face said 'no,' but her words said otherwise. 'Fine. Yes. I'll see what I can do.'

'Thanks,' said Logan. He took another mint, then held it back over his shoulder for Sinead. 'Sweetie?'

'I'm all right, thanks,' said Sinead. It was one thing for Logan to get on Moira's bad side. He could clear off back to Glasgow when the case was over and done with. Sinead, on the other hand, was stuck with the old bat.

'Suit yourself,' said Logan, popping the mint in his mouth. He gave the receptionist a nod. 'Give us a shout when they come back with something.'

Moira's response was ejected through gritted teeth. 'Will do, Detective Chief Inspector.'

Logan led Sinead through the back into the corridor that led to the Incident Room. As they walked, he prodded experimentally at the stitches on his forehead. Pain stabbed through him, making him hiss.

'You shouldn't fiddle with it, sir.'

'I'm not fiddling with it. I'm assessing the damage.'

'You're fiddling with it. You'll start it bleeding,' Sinead told him.

'Fine. There. I'm not touching it,' Logan told her, pushing open the door to the Incident Room. 'Happy now?'

He strode in, ready to start barking orders, then stopped when he saw DI Forde hurriedly pulling on his coat.

'Ben? Everything all right?' Logan asked, but he knew the answer to that already. If the urgency of Ben's movements hadn't told him, then the look of shock on DS McQuarrie's face certainly had. 'What's happened?'

'Tyler's just been on the phone. He's in a panic. Hasn't had a signal until now.'

'And?'

'It's Hamza,' Ben said. 'Tyler's got him in the car. Didn't trust the ambulance to be able to find the place.'

'Ambulance? What are you talking about?' Logan asked. 'What ambulance?'

DI Forde glowered at Logan. And, although the DCI had a substantial height and weight advantage, in that moment he was sure that Ben could've leathered seven bells out of him.

'Hamza's been attacked, Jack,' Ben said. He shook his head, his face ash-grey. 'And it's not looking good.'

Chapter 37

The silence in the Incident Room was palpable. It hung in the air, casting a cloud over everyone and everything.

Logan stood facing the Big Board. Or, more accurately, *not* facing the rest of the team. The CID guys had been brought in, and even Jinkies was hanging around near the back of the room, back straight, buttons polished.

The others—Ben, Caitlyn, and Tyler—stood in a huddle near Hamza's desk, as if drawing comfort from it. Sinead hung back from the others, trying not to look as awkward and self-conscious as she felt.

It was DI Forde who eventually spoke. The words came slowly and tentatively, like he was taking his time to choose just the right ones.

'It wasn't your fault, Jack,' he said. 'You weren't to know.'

'Bollocks it wasn't,' Tyler spat. His pale blue shirt had been purpled by blood, and all the nooks and crannies of his hands were caked with the stuff.

'DC Neish!' Ben snapped.

'Well, you said it yourself. Ham shouldn't have been up there on his own,' Tyler continued. 'He should never have gone up there without support.'

'That's enough, Tyler,' Ben warned. 'I won't tell you again.'

Up front, Logan turned to face them all. 'He's right. Leave him, Ben. He's right. This should never have happened. I didn't think it could be connected to the live case. I thought it was historic. Not...'

He sighed and looked up at the ceiling tiles, gathering his thoughts.

'I made a bad call. Hamza never should've been up there on his own.' He looked across their faces. 'I'm sorry.'

At the back of the room, Jinkies cleared his throat. 'Can I ask? What's DC Khaled's condition?'

'They're airlifting him to Glasgow Royal, sir,' DI Forde explained. 'Haven't got the facilities here. His condition's critical, but they've got him stable enough to move to ICU down the road.'

'Family?' Jinkies asked.

'Wife and a little one, sir,' Tyler said. The words were meant for Logan as much as for the Chief Inspector.

'Bugger.' Pickering stood up. 'I'll arrange transport for them. Blue light them down there, if needs be.'

'Thank you, Hugh,' said Logan.

'Least we can do,' said Jinkies, more than a little reproachfully. He gave a nod to the room. 'Good luck.'

The door squeaked as he left to get the transportation sorted.

'There are two ways we can play this,' said Logan. 'We can all, myself included, stand around here blaming me for this. Or, we can catch this bastard, get Connor home, and make him pay for what he did to Hamza. What's it to be?'

'There's not even a question there, Jack,' said DI Forde. He looked to the rest of the team. 'Is there?'

Everyone was in agreement, although some more enthusiastically than others. Logan gave a clap of his hands.

The *bang* they made was a starting pistol designed to propel everyone into motion.

Caitlyn and Ben returned to their desks. The CID boys sat up straighter. Constable Bell, who wasn't entirely sure what she was supposed to be doing, took out her notebook. She wasn't sure why she took out her notebook, exactly—it was a brand new one, with only a few scribbled remarks from the discussion with Bamber earlier on the first page—but it was better that than just standing there doing nothing at all.

'I think the boy was there.'

Tyler's words stopped everyone in their tracks.

'What?' Logan asked.

'I'm not sure. Hamza was going in and out,' Tyler said. His eyes were glassy as he replayed the memory in his head. 'I think he said he saw Connor. In the house.'

Logan leaned against the edge of the desk. 'Connor? He saw Connor? Alive?'

'Alive, I think. Pretty sure he was trying to save him when he... you know.'

'Jesus,' Logan muttered. He turned to Ben. 'Have we organised—'

'Tyler called it in on the way down the road,' said Ben, interrupting. 'Got uniforms sealing the place off. Crime scene boys are already there, combing over everything.'

'And?'

'Nothing. If Connor was there, he's not now.'

'Right. Aye. Suppose it was too much to hope for,' Logan said. He nodded at Tyler. 'Good work, son.'

DC Neish flashed a sarcastic smile. 'Gee. Thanks, boss.'

'Tyler...' Ben warned.

'It's fine,' Logan told him. He beckoned the young DC closer. 'Come here.'

Tyler hesitated.

'Hurry up. Come here,' Logan said.

All eyes watched as Tyler approached the DCI. He stopped a couple of feet away, eyeing the bigger man warily.

'You want to hit me?' Logan asked.

Tyler said nothing.

'Do you? Because you can. I'll give you one free shot. One-time offer. No consequences, no repercussions. One free smack in the mouth, punch in the guts, or whatever you prefer,' Logan said. 'Ideally, not the balls, but whatever you think'll help.'

Tyler's gaze flicked to DI Forde. Ben offered him nothing in response.

'Come on, son. Get it over with,' Logan told him. 'The sooner you get it out of your system, the sooner we can get back to work.'

He jutted his jaw out, offering it as a target. 'So, hurry up. Hit me.'

'I don't want to hit you,' Tyler said.

'No? Last chance.'

Tyler shook his head. One of Logan's meat slab hands fell on his shoulder.

'I made the wrong call, son. That's on me,' the DCI told him. 'We can talk about it later. But for now, how about we stop with the squabbling and catch this prick?'

There was a nod from Tyler, a straightening of his back, a firming-up of the lines of his face.

'Yes, boss,' he said. 'I'm all for that.'

'All right, then,' Logan said. 'Go grab a fresh shirt, take a minute to get yourself cleaned up, then get back here.'

Tyler didn't argue. As he headed for the door, Logan called over to DS Boyle and DC Innes from CID. 'Get anywhere with Mr Bamber?'

'Not really,' said Boyle. 'The most he's been able to tell us about the person who gave him the teddy was that it was, "some guy", which doesn't really narrow it down.'

'Narrows it to half the population,' DS McQuarrie pointed out.

'Well, aye, there's that,' agreed Boyle. 'We're bringing in a sketch artist to see if we can get some sort of picture.'

'How long will that take? Do they have to come down the road from Inverness, too?'

'Normally, sir, aye. But, we've asked one of the art teachers from the high school to come in and have a bash while we wait. He used to be Bamber's teacher for a while. Reckons he might be able to get something out of him.'

'Good. OK. Keep on that, give me a shout when you have something more,' Logan told them. 'Can you also coordinate with the Scene of Crime team up at the house? Anything that comes in, no matter what it is, I want to see it. Even if it's their lunch order, I want to see it.'

'Got it, sir,' said Boyle. He and DC Innes got to their feet. 'We'll be in the office next door. We're already set up, no sense moving.'

'Aye. Time is against us, lads,' Logan reminded them. 'Best case scenario, Connor has maybe twelve hours left. Worst case...? Well, let's not dwell on the worst case. Twelve hours. Keep that in mind. And, let's not forget, that this is no longer just about Connor Reid. We're also investigating the attempted murder of one of our colleagues. One of us.'

'Yes, sir.'

'We're on it, sir.'

Even before the CID boys had reached the door, Logan had wheeled around to address DI Forde and DS McQuarrie. 'Right. What else? Anything on HOLMES yet?'

'Shit. Forgot to check, sir,' said Caitlyn. 'Sorry, just… with Hamza, and everything.'

'Don't apologise, Detective Sergeant, just look,' Logan instructed. 'Constable Bell, get onto the local paper, will you? They're running a story about a woman who keeps losing her cats. Try to find out where she lives, then get a description of the cats, see if any of them match ours?'

'You think the cat's connected, sir?' Sinead asked.

'Maybe. Petrie had a habit of torturing them. Dogs, too. Can't hurt to look into it.'

'Right,' said Sinead, just happy to finally have a purpose. She reached for her mobile, but Logan stopped her.

'Take a desk. Get set-up.'

Sinead looked from the DCI to the vacant desks, then back again. 'Uh, right. OK, sir. Thanks.'

'Don't thank me, just get it done,' Logan told her.

As she hurried off, Logan turned on his heels to face DI Forde.

'Why was Connor there, Ben?' he said, voicing his thoughts aloud. 'We didn't even know about the Petrie connection to the place until today. How did someone else? And why use there to hide him?'

'It's out of the way. No-one to see you coming and going,' said Ben.

'But there are loads of places like that,' Logan said, gesturing to the map on the Big Board. 'Why *that* house? It has to be the Petrie connection, but… I don't get it. The bear, the envelope, and now the house. It has to be

225

someone close to the case. Someone who's been involved from early on.'

'And someone savvy enough to be able to figure out the house thing before we did,' Ben added.

'No answer at the paper, sir,' Sinead called over from the desk she had installed herself at.

'Damn. There's a journalist.' Logan clicked his fingers a few times, searching for the name. 'Fisher. Tom Fisher. He might be out front. See if you can dredge him up.'

'Aw, shite,' Ben said, jumping to his feet.

'What now?'

'He's not out front. None of them are. They're at the hotel for the press conference. The Gozer wants you sitting in.'

'Bollocks. What time?' Logan asked, checking his watch.

'Twelve.'

'Twenty minutes. How far away is it?'

'Maybe five,' said Ben. He looked the DCI up and down. 'You going to smarten yourself up a bit?'

'For the press? What do *you* think?'

Ben managed a grim smile. 'Good man.'

'Right, fifteen minutes,' Logan boomed. He nodded an acknowledgement at Tyler as he returned to the room, fastening the top button of a fresh shirt. 'How far can we get in the next quarter of an hour? What else have we got?'

'Something I forgot to mention, boss,' Tyler began, pulling his tie over his head. 'There were bones in the house. In a cupboard at the top of the stairs.'

Logan stopped, turned on his heels. 'Bones?'

'Yeah. And not like a cat or a dog, or whatever. Bigger. Bloodstains on the floor, too. Old. Way back.'

Logan felt the room undulate around him. He leaned on the desk, steadying himself for a moment.

Dylan Muir.

Finally.

'We'll let the crime scene lot worry about that for now,' Logan said, dragging his thoughts back to the present. 'Let's concern ourselves with the living for the moment.'

'Update in, sir,' said Caitlyn, looking up from her screen. 'DNA results back from the teddy bear. As suspected, nothing connecting it with Ed Walker. They've got a match for Forbes Bamber, but we already knew he made the delivery.'

'Anyone else?' Logan asked.

Caitlyn's gaze returned to the screen. She stared at it for a while, her mouth moving silently, like she was trying to figure out how to describe what she was seeing.

'Detective Sergeant?' Logan prompted.

'Aye, sir. Sorry. Three other samples. One of them hasn't yet been identified.'

'And the other two?'

'Owen Petrie, sir,' Caitlyn replied. 'And Matthew Dennison.'

She raised her gaze until it met Logan's. He stared back at her, too stunned to speak.

'Petrie's third victim.'

Chapter 38

He could hear them. Moving. Talking. Laughing. Out there, beyond the door, beyond his little cube of darkness and fear.

Beyond his prison.

He was hungry and thirsty, his stomach cramping, his lips cracked and dry. They felt raw against the rough material of the gag, like it was sandpapering them down, whittling them out of existence.

The boy had put the cat in with him a few hours ago, set it on his lap, watched and laughed as he'd sobbed into the mouth covering.

When the door had closed, he'd tried to shake the cat off him, but the ropes were too tight, and his legs were asleep. There was nothing he could do but sit there with it on him, feeling what was left of its life soak into his trouser-legs, whimpering whenever it twitched and spasmed.

Once, it had mewed angrily, its front claws scratching at his legs. He'd screamed and screamed and screamed, but nobody had come. Nobody had heard.

Or nobody had cared.

After a while, the cat stopped fighting. It stopped breathing shortly after. He'd heard the life leave it in a throaty gasp, and had cried for a while. Tears of relief, and of helplessness, and of hot, burning shame.

And of fear, of course. The ever-growing sense of dread that told him no one was coming. No one was going to save him.

He would die here, alone and afraid, like the cat on his lap.

The voices became louder. Closer. His breath wheezed through his nose, adrenaline flooding him, preparing him for what might come next. For what they might do.

There was a knock on the cupboard door. Sharp, but jolly.

'Everything all right in there?'

The man's voice. That hoarse, scratchy rasp.

'You decent?'

The door opened. Two faces looked in at him. Both were smiling. Happy. Excited.

Eager.

Tears came then. He thought he'd run out of them hours ago, but they flowed freely, caressing the lines of his cheeks before soaking into the gag.

'Look who I found,' said the boy. He held up a threadbare grey teddy bear, then moved its head as if making it speak.

'Hello, Matthew,' the boy said in a high-pitched baby-voice. 'Haven't you been naughty, naughty?'

And there, with the man and the boy leering in at him, Matthew Dennison knew that the end was near.

Chapter 39

'Thank you for coming. We're going to keep this brief. I have a short update to provide you with, then I'll take one or two questions alongside DCI Logan, who is heading up the investigation.'

Logan nodded, just briefly, at the sound of his name. Instinct, nothing more.

Physically, he was present. Physically, he was sitting beside the Gozer at a long table in a hotel not far from where he'd nabbed Ed Walker, gazing out at a sea of faces, microphones, and cameras.

Physically, he was right there in the room.

Mentally, though, Logan was elsewhere. His mind had been a whirlwind since Caitlyn had dropped the DNA bombshell, thoughts crashing together as he struggled to come up with an explanation.

It didn't make sense. None of it made sense.

The teddy bear that had been left at the Reids' house carried the DNA of Owen Petrie, a man who had been in near solitary confinement for the best part of a decade.

Worse, it carried the DNA of Matthew Dennison, a boy who had been murdered all the way back in 2005, and whose remains had been buried four years later in a small private ceremony that Logan had been invited to but had the good grace not to attend.

DS McQuarrie was getting in touch with Matthew's parents to see if the teddy bear looked familiar. Logan suspected that it would turn out to have belonged to the boy.

Which meant… what? How had someone come into possession of it? Why here? Why now?

What did any of it mean?

He kept an ear open, listening as the Gozer rattled off the usual stuff. *Family devastated. Support of the community. A number of promising leads.*

Logan sat up straighter at the mention of DC Khaled's name, watched the vultures scrambling to write down all the lurid details.

He recognised a few of the faces, but most were new. The old print guard had been getting gradually pushed out for a while now, their ranks thinning year-on-year. Logan had no sympathy for them, but if there was one thing he hated more than old school print journalists was new school digital ones. At least a handful of the journos in the room were from online-only outlets.

Fucking *bloggers.*

'And now, we'll take a few questions,' said the Gozer. 'Although, you'll appreciate we don't have a lot of time.'

A dozen or more hands raised. Detective Superintendent Mackenzie looked around for a friendly face, then settled on a woman near the front. 'Yes.'

'Can you confirm if the abduction is related to the Owen Petrie 'Mister Whisper' investigation from a decade ago?' she asked. 'And, if so, what's the connection?'

Logan waited for the Gozer to respond, then realised that the Detective Superintendent was looking to him for answers.

'Oh.' Logan sat forward. 'We don't believe there's a direct connection at the moment, as such.'

'But there are similarities?' the female journalist pressed.

Logan nodded. 'We think we're looking at a copycat situation. It's ten years since Petrie's arrest. Twenty since he abducted his first victim. Fourteen since he killed Matthew Dennison, his last victim. Or the last one that we know of. We think someone is trying to capitalize on Petrie's—and I hesitate to use this word—"fame".'

'Why would they do that?'

Logan scratched his chin. 'Why do any of them do any of it? Notoriety? To get their kicks?'

'We wouldn't like to speculate at this time,' said the Gozer, shooting Logan a warning look. 'Next question.'

The hands went back up again. The Gozer considered the alternatives, but it was Logan who singled one out. Tom Fisher, the local boy. Might as well give him a second chance to shine.

'Yes?'

Fisher looked taken aback at having been picked. 'Um...'

His eyes went to his notes.

'Did you have a question?' Logan pressed, sensing the impatience and growing resentment from the other journalists.

'Uh, yes. Yes. I did. I just... Yes.'

Fisher cleared his throat. His cheeks were reddening before Logan's eyes, like someone had just slapped him on both sides of his face.

'It was... I was just going to ask, is it possible that you got the wrong man? Owen Petrie, I mean? Is it possible that he wasn't guilty of what he was guilty of?' Fisher shook his head, annoyed at himself. 'Of what he was accused of, I mean? Could it have been someone else?'

'No,' said Logan, dismissing the question with a shake of the head and a scowl.

'Right. It's just… with the…' Fisher swallowed, wilting under Logan's gaze. 'How can you be sure?'

'Because the court found him guilty,' said the Gozer, spotting the warning signs in Logan's body language and interrupting before the situation could escalate. 'Because he confessed to all three murders, and because we were able to gather overwhelming evidence that proved his guilt beyond any measure of reasonable doubt.'

'Right. Right. Cool,' said Fisher. His blush deepened. 'I mean, not "cool", but… Thank you. Thanks. That was my only question. Thanks.'

More hands shot up. Logan watched Tom Fisher scribbling down the answer the Gozer had given in his notepad. Or, attempting to, anyway. He was having problems getting his pen to write by the looks of things, and kept shaking it every few seconds to get the ink flowing.

Fair play to the kid, though. The question had taken Logan by surprise. He'd have expected that sort of thing from Ken Henderson, but not from a snottery-nosed wee…

Logan's eyes flicked across the faces of the reporters, searching for Henderson but failing to find him. He wasn't there. Henderson wasn't at the conference.

Arguably the one man on Earth who had invested as much of his career into the Petrie case as Logan had, *wasn't there*.

'DCI Logan?'

Logan became aware of everyone in the room watching him, waiting for an answer to a question he hadn't heard.

'Huh?'

'Do you want to field that one?' the Gozer pressed.

Logan blinked. The legs of his chair scraped across the vinyl flooring as he pushed it back. He stood up, leaned on the table, and glowered out at the media.

'Henderson,' he said. 'Has anyone seen Ken Henderson?'

Chapter 40

Logan rapped his knuckles against the Big Board.

'Where's my picture of Henderson? Come on, come on, people.'

'Coming, sir,' said DS McQuarrie, grabbing a sheet of A4 from the printer the moment the machine spat it out. 'It's a blow-up from the web, so not great but—'

'It'll do,' said Logan, glancing at it then motioning for her to put it on the board. He shot looks at Ben, Tyler, and Sinead, making sure they were paying attention.

'Kenneth Henderson, fifty-eight, freelance journalist and all-round pain in the arse. Made his name reporting on the Petrie case, and dined out on it for years after. Knows almost as much about the investigation as I do. I've now been told that he's even interviewed Petrie a couple of times in the past few years for follow-up stories, although they never saw the light of day.'

'Petrie could've told him about the house,' suggested Ben.

'And the envelopes,' added Tyler from his desk.

'Aye, it's a theory,' Logan agreed. 'We said it had to be someone involved in the original investigation. Someone close. They didn't get much closer than Henderson. Our priority now is finding him. Tyler, find out what car he's driving, get everyone on the look-out for it. Circulate a digital copy of his picture, too. And get word down the road to Glasgow. Check out his old haunts. I want the bastard sweating in an interview room within the hour.'

'On it, boss.'

Ben ran a hand through his thinning hair, teasing what was left of it around his fingers. 'You really think he'd do something like this? Henderson?' the DI asked. 'I mean, he's an arsehole, no doubt about that, but this… and with Hamza…? That's way beyond arsehole territory.'

'I don't know. I honestly don't,' Logan admitted. 'By all accounts, he's had it rough, lately. Job's not as safe as it once was. He needs a scoop, and what better than the Ghost of Mister Whisper? He's built a career on Petrie's story. Maybe he thought another chapter would help put him back on top.'

'Seems a stretch,' said Ben.

'It is. I'm not saying he did it, I'm saying we need to talk to him. Any time anything happens with the Petrie case, Henderson is right there, front and centre,' Logan said. 'But not today. Today, right after one of our officers was attacked, he's nowhere to be seen. I want to know why.'

Caitlyn's phone rang. She hurried back to her desk and picked up the receiver.

'Detective Sergeant McQuarrie,' she said, then she tucked the handset between her ear and her shoulder, and started making notes.

Tyler popped up from behind his screen. 'Henderson's driving a red Vauxhall Mokka, boss. 2014 plate. Putting a shout out for it now.'

'Good,' Logan said, then, '*shite*.'

'Boss?' Tyler asked.

'No, not you. I forgot I meant to talk to Tom Fisher and ask him about the cat story. Sinead, can you chase up the paper again? Find out where that woman lives.'

Sinead nodded and picked up her phone.

'We have anything back on the cat I brought in?' Logan asked.

'Aye, didn't you get the note?' Ben answered. 'Moira got the local vet to take a look. Injuries were inflicted deliberately, he reckons.'

Logan had been expecting that answer, but hoping for a different one. He groaned, rubbing his temples to nurse the headache that was building behind his eyes.

'God. OK. Right.'

'What's with the cat anyway, boss?' asked Tyler.

'Petrie used to... I don't know. Torture them, I suppose,' Logan explained. 'Cut them open, break their bones. The usual mental bastard script.'

He leaned on his desk, taking some of the weight off his feet. His eyes went to the battered cardboard folder he'd left there earlier, and his mind went back a decade or more.

'When we initially tracked Petrie down, we... there was a cupboard in his flat, and it was...'

Logan sucked in his bottom lip, then spat it out again. 'I opened it, and there was just... death. Just all this death that came tumbling out onto the carpet at my feet.'

'Death?' Tyler looked around at the others. 'I don't follow.'

'There was an old poem I heard once. Or, I don't know, a song, maybe. It had this line in it. '*A litter of bones strewed the mighty bestiarium.*' That's what popped into my head when I opened the door. Can't even remember where I heard it.'

He stared blankly at the folder on the table, as if seeing through it.

'A *litter of bones*. Cats. Dogs.'

He swallowed.

'Children.'

Logan gave himself a shake and straightened. 'We thought they were all in there. The boys, I mean. I thought we'd found them all. If I'd known we hadn't, I wouldn't...'

He course-corrected.

'I would have made more of an effort to catch Petrie. Before he fell.'

He contemplated the folder for a while longer, then snatched it up with both hands. 'Let's get this stuff up on the board,' he said, flicking the folder open. 'Henderson's our first priority, but let's see if we can make some connections. If it was him, how did he get that teddy bear? How did he find out about the house and the text on the envelope? Was it Petrie? If so, we need to know when they spoke, what was said, and what else Henderson knows.'

There was a clack as DS McQuarrie put down the phone. 'Report from the crime scene, sir. The bones in the cupboard at the house?'

'Yes?' said Logan, then he held his breath.

'Not Dylan Muir's. Not even human, sir. Sheep.'

Logan's heart plunged down into his stomach. 'Sheep?'

'Aye, sir. A lot of the bones had been broken. Deliberately, they think.'

'Damn it!' Logan kicked his chair, sending it clattering across the floor. 'I thought we'd found him. I thought we'd got him.'

'It's unfortunate, Jack, but not our priority,' Ben reminded him. 'This isn't that case, you said so yourself.

Dylan might still be there, but for now we need to focus on Connor.'

'Aye. Aye, you're right,' Logan agreed. 'What about the sketch artist? Any luck with the junkie, do we know?'

'Not that I know of, but I can check,' said Ben, heading for the door.

'Show Bamber a picture of Henderson. See if that jogs his memory.'

'Good idea,' said Ben. 'You're no' just a pretty face.'

Caitlyn cleared her throat. 'There's something else, sir. Update on HOLMES. The DNA on the teddy? The one they couldn't identify? They've got a match.'

'Henderson?' Logan guessed.

'No, sir,' Caitlyn replied. She looked at her screen again, checking the information for the fourth or fifth time.

'It's Dylan's, sir. It's Dylan Muir's.'

Logan staggered, like he'd been physically struck. The room spun. First one way, then the other, the walls blurring as his brain tried to process this new revelation.

Tried, but failed.

How could Dylan Muir's genetic material be on Matthew Dennison's teddy bear? The boys had been taken six years apart. There had been traces of Dylan's DNA in Petrie's flat, but not in the cupboard. Not on Matthew Dennison's remains.

He steadied himself against the Big Board, pulling himself together.

There were dozens of ways the bear could've been cross-contaminated, he told himself. Hundreds. Maybe Petrie had stored it alongside something of Dylan's. Kept it in his schoolbag, perhaps, which had never been recovered. Stuffed it in one of the boy's shoes.

There were explanations. Lots of explanations. *Plausible* explanations.

And yet, the room was still spinning, Logan's heart was still racing, and nausea was churning through his insides.

He'd had a suspicion before. No, not a suspicion, a concern. A *dread*. A nagging fear that ate away at him some nights when he lay awake, and wormed its way into his nightmares while he slept. He had always dismissed it, pushed it away, beaten it down. It didn't make sense. He *refused to let it* make sense.

And yet, it did. Here, now, it was perhaps the only thing that did, and the realisation of that fact knocked the air from Logan's lungs and threatened to bring him to his knees.

Someone connected to the original case.

Someone close *to it.*

Closer, even, than himself.

'The sketch artist,' Logan said, closing his eyes to block out the whirling, twirling walls. 'Tell him to forget Bamber.'

'Oh. Right. Want me to send him home?' Ben asked. He was standing over by the door, the update from Caitlyn having stopped him in his tracks.

Logan shook his head. 'Get him in here. I need him to try draw someone else.'

'Who?' asked Ben.

Reaching into the folder, Logan took out a photo of smiling, three-year-old Dylan Muir, his hand buried in a bag of *Monster Munch*. 'Him. I want him to draw him,' he said.

'But twenty years older.'

Chapter 41

The clock ticked, the hands simultaneously counting forwards and counting down. Logan tried not to look at it, to focus instead on the scratching of the pencil on the paper, the look of concentration on the artist's face as he carried out his task.

How long did Connor have left now? A few hours, at best. At worst, he'd been dead from the moment Hamza had discovered him in that house. Teams were sweeping the forest surrounding the building. Nothing, so far, but there was a lot of ground to cover.

'How's it going now?' Logan asked for the third or fourth time.

The artist was an older guy. Thin, prissy, face like a bulldog licking piss off a nettle. He sat with his legs crossed, his pad resting on a knee, half a dozen pencils tucked into the top pocket of his shirt.

'Getting there,' he said.

He'd been *getting there* for the past twenty minutes now. Logan had taken a look over his shoulder a couple of times, but *there* hadn't looked like it was going to be anywhere useful.

Ben had warned him he was expecting too much. The guy wasn't a trained sketch artist, he was a high school art teacher. Sure, he could probably pull together something half-decent from a detailed description, but asking him to accurately predict what a three-year-old would look like as an adult was a big leap from there.

Logan looked around the Incident Room at the others. Aside from Ben, who was reading the Petrie case file at his desk, the others were all on phone calls. There had still been no sign of Ken Henderson or his car. Tyler was talking to the CCTV boys to see if it had been picked up heading back down the road to Glasgow, but cameras were few and far between along the route, and the line of enquiry was looking increasingly like another dead end.

Sinead was still trying to get through to the newspaper. She'd found a couple of numbers for the publisher who owned the paper, and was working her way down from there until she reached the local editor.

Caitlyn, meanwhile, was back onto the lab. Logan wanted to know if they could tell how recent the sample of Dylan Muir's DNA had been, or take a stab at how old he'd been when he'd come into contact with the teddy bear.

She was looking pretty animated, and her voice was stern, so Logan guessed he wasn't going to get the information anytime soon.

'Getting there. Almost done,' said the artist, correctly predicting Logan's question before he could ask it.

Across the room, Sinead stood up, the phone still cradled to her ear. 'Thank you. No... That's... Yes, thank you. You've been very helpful,' she said into the receiver, her eyes meeting Logan's.

'Well?' he asked, before she'd even had a chance to hang up. 'You find out where the cat lady lives?'

'No, sir,' Sinead said. 'I spoke to the editor. Got her mobile from her boss. They're not running any cat story this week.'

'I don't care when they're going to run it, I just need to know where the woman lives.'

'No, I mean, there is no cat story, sir. She knew nothing about it,' Sinead said. 'And she doesn't know anything about a Tom Fisher, either. He doesn't work there. Never has.'

'Ta–daa!'

The artist turned the pad. Logan knew what was going to be on it before he saw it.

'Shite!' Logan spat. He raced out of the room, skidded along the corridor, then launched himself through the reception area and out to the front of the station.

Cameras flashed. Microphones were switched on. A sea of faces turned his way.

'Where is he? Where's Tom Fisher?' he demanded, suddenly wishing he'd brought the pad. 'The kid at the press conference. The one who asked if Petrie might not be guilty. Where is he?'

There was some confused murmuring. A few of the journalists glanced around, but most had started to fire questions at him.

'Why do you want to know?'

'Is he involved?'

'Is Connor Reid still alive?'

Logan growled. 'Ah, get it up ye,' he told them, then he turned and thundered back inside.

Moira buzzed him in without a word, the expression on his face making it very clear that he was not in the mood for a debate.

He was barking orders before he'd even entered the office. 'Ben, Caitlyn, coordinate from here. Find me everything you can on Tom Fisher, starting with his address. Tyler, Sinead, you're with me.'

Everyone jumped to it. The art teacher got up from his chair, looking uncertain.

'Someone mentioned I'd get forty quid,' he said.

Logan's eyebrows practically knotted themselves together. 'What?'

'For the…' He gave a little wave of his sketchpad. 'For the drawing.'

'Oh, for fu—' Logan spat. 'Ben, give him forty quid, then get rid of him. Keep that drawing.'

Grumbling, DI Forde reached for his wallet. Grabbing his coat, Logan turned and stalked back towards the exit, beckoning Tyler and Sinead with one finger.

'Right. You two, get a shifty on.'

'Where we going, boss?' Tyler asked, falling into step behind the DCI.

Logan raised his phone, the map screen open, a red flag standing proud in the centre.

'There,' he said. 'Wherever the hell that is, we're going there.'

Chapter 42

Logan sat behind the wheel of his Ford Focus, watching Tyler pinch-zoom in on the map screen of the DCI's phone. He had parked up just along the road from a little Co-op supermarket, across from a building that, Sinead had told him, had been one of the small local polis stations until the new soulless monstrosity had been built on the outskirts of town.

'So, if the kid is right, he found the cat up there,' Tyler said, pointing ahead to where a row of green wheelie bins stood with their backs to the metal mesh of a fence.

'That seem right?' Logan asked, glancing in his rear-view mirror.

'That's the way he'd walk to school, aye,' Sinead agreed. 'I drop him at the road end here, and he walks the rest of the way himself.'

'Right. Tyler, you're with me. Sinead, wait here, up front. I'll leave you the keys. If Fisher's around, I don't want him seeing the uniform and getting spooked.'

'You mean Dylan, boss,' said Tyler.

'I mean Fisher. He might not even know that he ever was Dylan Muir,' Logan said. 'What do you remember from when you were three?'

Tyler nodded. 'Aye. Suppose you're right.'

'I'm always right, son,' Logan told him. He caught the look on the younger officer's face, and thought of DC

Khaled lying in the ICU at Glasgow Royal. 'Well, most of the time. Now, come on. Let's see what we can see. Sinead, up front, but don't get out of the car in case he spots you.'

'What am I meant to do, clamber through?'

'Bingo,' Logan told her. 'I'll leave the keys in the ignition. We've got radios. If he shows face, call us. Don't engage unless you absolutely have to.'

He and DC Neish both opened their doors and stepped out onto the pavement. The sun had tucked in behind a growing bank of grey cloud, and Tyler shivered in the cool March breeze.

'Chilly, innit?'

Logan glanced both ways along the street, then stalked across it. 'Hadn't noticed.'

─

There was nothing on the ground that corresponded with the flag Harris had placed on the map. Logan had been hoping for... something. A clump of fur and a blood trail, ideally, leading directly to someone's front door, although he knew he wouldn't get that lucky. He never got *that* lucky.

So, he hadn't been expecting to find anything that conclusive, but he'd hoped for something. A suggestion of something, even. A hint that they were on the right lines here, and that this wasn't just a waste of what little time Connor Reid might have left.

Tyler gagged as he poked around in the last of the bins. 'Fucking hell,' he grimaced. 'Why do all bins smell like that? Doesn't matter what they've had in them, they've all got that same smell.'

'Aye,' Logan agreed, not really listening.

The houses around were all two-storey terraces, with short paths leading to numbered doors. They were not dissimilar to Sinead's house, or the Reids' home. A little older, maybe, the Highland weather having tired the construction out a little more, but more or less the same.

'Should we start knocking on doors, boss?' Tyler asked. 'See if anyone's seen him around?'

'Not yet,' Logan said. 'We'll do another once up and down of the street, see if we can find where the cat was left. Or, if we're lucky, where it crawled to. It hasn't rained this morning, and it was bleeding pretty badly, so there should be… in fact…'

He looked back down the street in the direction of the Focus. 'Ask Sinead to give her brother a ring. Try to get him to pinpoint where he found it, or at least narrow it down. If there's still nothing, then we'll start the door-knocking.'

'Right, boss,' Tyler said, setting off in the direction of the car.

He'd only gone half a dozen steps when he stopped and looked down at the vehicle beside him. At first, Logan thought he was checking his reflection in the window, but then he stepped back, frowning.

Logan saw it a moment later.

'Red Vauxhall Mokka,' he said.

'2014 plate,' Tyler added, checking out the front of the vehicle.

'That's Ken Henderson's car,' Logan said. His voice was low. Gruff. 'Come on,' he said, walking off.

Tyler looked from the car to the house it was parked outside. 'What?' he asked, then he hurried after the DCI.

'Stop looking back at the house,' Logan warned him. 'Once we're around the corner, phone in to the station. Find out who owns that house. There's plenty of parking along this street. Henderson could've parked anywhere, but he's right outside that gate.'

They took a right at the end of the block, turning into an alleyway that ran between one end terrace and the next.

'Get us back-up. Tell them to stay out of sight, and no sirens. Last thing we need to do is spook him.'

Logan stopped and took the radio from his inside pocket. Beside him, Tyler got dialling on his phone.

'Sinead. You see the red Mokka parked along the street near where we were standing? Keep lookout on that house. Let me know if there's movement, no matter how small.'

'Will do, sir,' came the reply. 'Is that Henderson's car?'

'Aye. It is. So, eyes peeled, constable,' he told her. 'Shout if there's anything.'

Logan and Tyler both finished their conversations at the same time.

'Caitlyn's on it,' Tyler said. 'DS McQuarrie, I mean.'

He leaned out and looked along the front of the row of houses. 'So... it's Henderson, then?' he said. 'Not Dylan Muir, or Tom Fisher, or whatever we're calling him.'

Logan gave a shake of his head. 'No, it's Fisher. Dylan.'

Saying the name in that context hurt him, made him flinch.

'But I think Henderson might be egging him on. I think that Petrie told him Dylan was alive during one of his visits, and spilled the beans on where to find him. Henderson wouldn't have the balls to kidnap a kid, but he's enough of a weasel to convince some poor, mixed-up bastard to do it for him.'

Logan took a few steps towards the back of the block and peered over the top of the high fence, counting the gardens until he found the back of the house Henderson's car was parked outside.

'I don't like the man, but I doubt he thought it'd go this far. He's a publicity-hungry, parasitic bastard, but he's no' a killer.'

'So, Fisher attacked Hamza?'

'I reckon so, aye.'

'And Fisher's in that house?'

'I think it's a safe bet.'

'Then what are we waiting for?' Tyler asked.

'We've got back-up on the way,' Logan told him. 'We should wait for them to get here.'

'And in the meantime what, boss? What happens to the kid, if he's in there with them? You said yourself, we're fighting the clock here.'

'I'm not going to let what happened to Hamza happen to anyone else,' Logan said.

'Hamza was blindsided. We're going in eyes open.'

Logan sucked air in through his teeth, looked the DC up and down, then gave a nod. 'Aye. Right. You take the back, I'll go in the front. Wait for my signal.'

Tyler bounced from foot to foot, becoming animated. 'All right! Nice one. Let's do it. What will the signal be?'

Logan took a pair of blue gloves from his pocket and slipped them on. The latex *creaked* as he flexed his fingers in and out.

'It'll be a big crash,' he told the junior officer. 'And quite a lot of shouting.'

Chapter 43

The door was sturdier than it looked and took three good kicks before it surrendered. It swung inwards, banged against the wall of the hallway, then bounced back again.

Logan shouldered it aside and stormed in, fists raised.

'Fisher? I know you're in here!'

The smell hit him mid-sentence, knocking him back half a step and a whole decade.

Rot.

Decay.

Things long dead.

No. *No*. Not again.

Please God, not again.

Blood spotted the walls in the hallway. A slug trail of the stuff was smeared across the laminate flooring, leading from the living room on the left to what looked to be the kitchen up ahead.

Logan followed the trail, picking his route so as not to contaminate the scene any more than was absolutely necessary.

He didn't know what he'd find at the other end of that streak. Didn't want to know, but had to.

Stopping at the door, he took half a second to compose himself, then leaned through into the kitchen.

Henderson was on the floor. Face down, eyes open but seeing nothing. His skin was chalk-white, aside from a caved-in area in the side of his forehead. His life was a puddle on the floor beneath him. No point checking for a pulse. A day ago, maybe, but not now.

There was a thud against the back door. Then another. Logan heard DC Neish mutter on the other side of it, then turned the key and opened the door just as Tyler let fly at it with another kick.

'Shit!' the DC ejected, stumbling into the kitchen. He slipped on the blood, waved his arms frantically as he tried to find his balance, then caught Logan's offered arm and steadied himself.

'Thanks, boss,' he gasped. His eyes went to the floor. 'Is that Henderson?'

'What's left of him, aye,' Logan confirmed.

'Any sign of Fisher?'

'Not yet. I haven't—'

There was a squeak from beyond another door in the kitchen. A faint cheep, like the wailing of an injured bird. Soft, but unmistakeable.

Motioning for Tyler to open the door, Logan positioned himself in front of it, feet ready to move, hands ready to grab.

With a sideways look to Tyler, he nodded.

The door was pulled open, sharp and suddenly.

A boy was revealed, all sobs and snot, bound and gagged and terrified.

But alive.

Connor.

From out in the hallway there came a thump. Footsteps. The front door slamming hard.

'Boss!'

'Stay with the boy!' Logan bellowed.

He dodged past Henderson's body, skidded through the blood, all thoughts of preserving the crime scene now playing second fiddle to catching the bastard responsible.

Logan made it into the garden in time to see the red Mokka roaring away from the end of the gate. He caught a glimpse of Tom Fisher behind the wheel, but then the car was speeding off down the street and hanging a left at the end.

The Focus screeched to a stop in the middle of the road ahead of him. Logan vaulted the gate and hurried around to the passenger side. Sinead had already thrown the door open, and floored the accelerator before Logan could pull it closed again, rendering his shouts of, 'Go, go, go!' completely redundant.

Flicking a switch on the dash, Sinead fired up the car's lights and sirens while Logan got on the radio. 'All units, all units, we are in pursuit of a red Vauxhall Mokka, registration KT12 XOH, currently headed…'

'South-East.'

'South-East, along…'

'Kilmallie Road.'

'Kilmallie Road. We're the ones with the flashy blue lights going *nee-naw, nee-naw*. You can't miss us,' he said, then he scrabbled for his seatbelt as Sinead skidded off the side-street and onto the main road, drawing a prolonged honk from an oncoming Co-op delivery truck.

'Christ, and you said my driving was bad,' Logan muttered. 'We got Connor.'

'You got Connor?'

'I think he's all right.'

Sinead's head snapped around, eyes wide. 'He's all right?'

'Is there an echo in here?' Logan grunted. He stabbed a finger ahead. 'Watch the bloody road!'

Sinead faced front, catching sight of the back of the Mokka just as it powered around a bend.

'What's up ahead?' Logan asked. 'Can he get out?'

'They know he's coming,' Sinead said. 'They'll block the road at the Farmfoods junction. It's his only way out.'

Logan punched the roof in triumph. 'Yes!' he cheered. 'Catch up with him, though. Get right up his arse, I'm not having him slip through our fingers.'

Sinead started to respond, then stopped in a gargle of panic. The car decelerated in a sudden lurch, tyres smoking, brakes howling in protest. Logan swore loudly and creatively as he was slammed forward, the seatbelt tightening across his chest.

'What are you doing?' he wheezed.

'He's there. He's there,' Sinead cried, unbuckling her belt and scrambling out of the car.

Logan followed her gaze until he found the Mokka. It was halfway through a fence, driver's door open, engine running, abandoned in the small front garden of a house.

No. Not just any house, Logan realised.

Sinead's block.

The neighbour's garden.

Harris.

Chapter 44

Sinead was younger, fitter, and had a head start. Logan did his best to catch her, but she was through the hole in the garden fence and up the path before he'd hit top speed. The house's front door stood open. Shouts and screams came from inside the house, all of it escalating when Sinead charged inside, baton extended.

Logan's chest was heaving with the effort when he barrelled inside behind her, almost knocking her off her feet.

Tom Fisher—Dylan Muir—stood in the centre of the living room, a hand clamped down over Harris's head, the retractable blade of a packing knife pressed against his throat.

Maureen, the woman Logan had seen on the door-step earlier, knelt on the floor next to an old man—her husband, presumably—shielding him with her body. A deep gash ran across the side of his face, splitting his cheek from his ear to his nose.

'Let him go!' Sinead barked. 'I swear to God, let him go.'

'S-Sinead?' Harris whimpered, then he gasped when Fisher tightened his grip, jerking the boy back by the hair.

'Shut up. All of you, shut the fuck up,' Fisher hissed. His eyes were wild, the knife trembling in his grip. He was out of control, or on the brink of becoming so, at least. 'Anyone tries anything, and I cut this kid a new mouth!'

Logan raised a hand in a calming gesture and positioned himself between Sinead and her brother. Down on the floor, Maureen quietly comforted her husband and pressed a handkerchief against his wound.

'All right, all right. Let's all stay calm, OK?' Logan said. 'You're fine, Tom. You're fine. Just relax.'

'I'm relaxed! *I'm perfectly fucking relaxed!*' Fisher practically screamed. He glared at Logan, eyes blazing. 'You want me to kill this kid? I'll kill him. I'll do it. I'll do it. Is that what you want?'

'I don't want that, Tom, no,' Logan said. 'I don't want anyone to die. Not him, not you, and certainly not me.'

Fisher scowled, looking the detective up and down. 'You think you're clever, don't you? You think you're so smart. But you didn't see me, did you? None of you saw me. Watching. Listening. That's how I knew when to get the kid. Connor.'

He shook Harris. 'And this one. He took one of my cats, so I followed him. And I watched.'

'I don't think I'm clever, Tom, no. Far from it,' Logan said. 'If I was clever, I'd be the one holding the knife, not you.'

'Exactly. So back off! You hear me? Back off!'

'I'm backing off, Tom. Look? Here's me backing off,' Logan said, raising both hands and shuffling back a few paces.

Sinead side-stepped out of the DCI's path, and then took another shuffled sideways step that brought her out of Fisher's immediate line of sight.

'The thing is, it's not me you have to worry about,' Logan said. 'It's the marksmen.'

'What?!'

'Windows, Tom,' Logan said, gesturing to the panes of glass at either end of the room. 'Direct line of sight, wherever you go. If they think you're going to hurt the boy, then they'll take you out. They have to. They don't have a choice.'

Fisher's gaze went first to the window behind Logan, then turned to look at the other window a few feet away at his back.

Sinead shuffled a step closer, staying wide.

'Bullshit. There's no-one there,' Fisher spat. 'You're lying!'

'I'm not lying, Tom. I wish I was, believe me,' Logan told him. 'Like I said, the last thing I want is anyone dying today, but I'm afraid that decision is no longer in my hands, son.'

Logan indicated the window with a thumb. 'It's not even in theirs. It's in yours. You've got the power here, Tom. You're the one making the decisions.'

'Fucking right, I am! Fucking right, I've got the power!' Fisher barked.

'I'm glad you understand that, Tom. And I'm sure you appreciate the responsibility that goes along with it.'

Fisher's face contorted, his eyes narrowing. 'What?'

'Well, decisions have consequences,' Logan told him. 'And, unless you're careful, one of those consequences is going to involve you getting shot through the head by a polis sniper.'

Logan raised his hands again, fingers splayed, palms forward. 'And, like I say, I don't want that. I promise you, I will do everything I can to avoid that outcome. But you have to help me, Tom. You've got to give me a hand here.'

Down on the floor, Maureen began to cry. 'Just let him go. Let him go!'

'Shut up!' Fisher seethed, tightening his grip on Harris's hair. 'I told you, everyone *shut up*!'

'This situation isn't as bad as you think it is, Tom,' Logan told him. 'Connor's unharmed. DC Khaled—the detective you stabbed—he's alive.'

'He shouldn't have been there! He shouldn't have come snooping around!'

'Aye, I'm pretty sure he regrets that now,' Logan agreed. 'But the point is, they're both going to live. They're both going to be OK.'

For a second or two, Fisher almost looked like he might buy it, but then his face darkened and his voice took on a desperate, frantic edge.

'What about Henderson? Henderson's not going to be fine, is he?'

'No, but he was probably asking for it,' Logan told him. 'I've known him for years. It's a miracle I never killed him myself.'

Harris squealed as Fisher pressed the knife more firmly against his skin. 'You're *joking*. Stop joking! You think this is *funny*?'

'No, Tom, I—'

'You think it'll be funny when I split this kid's throat open? Will you joke about that, too? Eh? Will you?'

'Relax, Tom. Relax. I was just—'

'*Stop telling me to fucking relax!*' Fisher howled. He thrust the knife forward, waving it in Logan's face. 'Now fuck off before I—'

The baton caught him on the wrist. Fast. Hard. Sudden.

The room was filled with the sound of breaking bone, although this was almost immediately drowned out by Fisher's screams. The knife landed on the floor at Logan's feet. A sudden shove on the back sent Harris staggering forwards.

Sinead dived and caught him before he could fall, blocking Logan as he tried to grab for Fisher. He missed, tripped, stumbled. Fisher was already racing for the door, his shattered wrist held close to his chest, sobs of agony bursting as bubbles on his lips.

'Stay here. Watch them,' Logan instructed.

He was out the door a handful of seconds behind Fisher, along the path in time to see the lad racing along the pavement and tumbling awkwardly over a fence that divided it from a narrow strip of overgrown wasteland.

Fisher wailed with the pain the landing brought, but it drove him on, launching him to his feet and propelling him through the undergrowth.

Logan ducked through the fence like a wrestler entering the ring. He didn't have to catch Fisher, just keep him in sight. He could hear sirens somewhere close by. The place was going to be swarming with uniforms any minute.

There was nowhere left for Fisher to run.

Chapter 45

'The dogs will be coming in a minute, Tom,' Logan announced, picking his way through the jaggy bushes and nettles that turned the waste ground into a maze of low-level suffering. 'No point running. Not now.'

Fisher stumbled up an incline, then stopped at the top. He turned back to Logan, swaying unsteadily, his arm clutched to his chest.

'That *bitch*,' Fisher spat. 'She broke my wrist. She broke my fucking wrist!'

'You didn't give her a lot of choice in the matter,' Logan told him. He stopped halfway up the slope and looked Fisher up and down.

It was there, right enough, around the eyes. The similarity. The resemblance to the boy in those photographs. The boy he'd never found.

The victim he couldn't save.

'Come in quietly, Tom. With me. We can talk,' Logan told him. 'Given the circumstances… We can talk.'

'What *circumstances*?' Fisher said, spitting the word out as if it left a bad taste in his mouth. 'I know who you are. I know what you did.'

He caught the look on Logan's face and grinned. 'Yeah! Didn't know that, did you? I know what you did to my dad. You messed him up. You locked him away.'

'Your *dad*?' Logan spluttered. 'Who, Petrie? Petrie isn't your dad, son.'

'What? Yes, he is!'

'No. No, I'm sorry, Tom. That's not true.'

'*Yes, he is!* He's my dad, and you set him up. You threw him off that roof! You took him away!'

'That's what this is about, isn't it?' Logan said, inching closer. 'You thought that you could make us doubt the conviction. If Mister Whisper was still out there, then we'd have to let Petrie go.'

'Well, you would!' Fisher spat. 'You'd have to. Henderson told me!'

'No, son. That's not how it works,' Logan said. 'Did Henderson put you up to this? Was that it? Did he tell you we'd let Petrie go if you kidnapped Connor and sent the bear?'

A jolt of pain shot through Fisher's arm, making him gasp. He glanced behind him, then danced on the spot, nursing his wrist.

'He was going to turn me in. After I stabbed the policeman. He said it'd gone too far,' Fisher said. 'I couldn't let him tell you. I couldn't let him tell anyone.'

'So you killed him,' Logan said.

'I had to! I didn't have any choice. I just wanted everything to go back to the way it was. I just wanted my dad back!'

'Whatever Owen Petrie made you believe, he is not your dad, son. I've met your dad. He's a good man. He's nothing like Petrie.'

'Stop saying that! He's my dad! He's my dad and you took him from me! You took everything from me!'

The way he said it – the twisted snarl, the clenched fists, the shriek of desperation – brought the terrible reality of the situation home for Logan.

'Jesus. You've been alone this whole time,' he realised. 'Since we caught him. You've been on your own.'

Fisher—Dylan—said nothing. He just stood there, staring defiantly as he gulped back tears.

'I'm so sorry, son. I tried to find you. For years. I really did, you have no idea,' Logan said, his voice thin and croaky. 'But I was looking in all the wrong places.'

The ground rumbled faintly. Fisher glanced behind him for a moment, then back to Logan. 'You're lying. You locked up my dad, and now you want to lock me up, too.'

'You need help, son. Specialist help. You've been lost too long.'

Logan held a hand out, bridging the gulf between them. 'Come on with me, Dylan. Come on home.'

Fisher blinked. Once. Twice. A series of expressions crossed his face. Surprise. Confusion.

'Dylan? Who's…?' he began. 'What are you…? What do you…?'

Then his expression became something else. Realisation. Acceptance, maybe.

His eyes went wide. The rest of his face went slack.

He gave a half-hearted snort. The ground rumbled, louder this time.

Logan worked out, too late, what it was.

'Shit, shit, no!' he bellowed, powering up the incline.

'Dylan,' Fisher said, rolling the word around inside his mouth.

And then he stepped backwards beyond Logan's reach, fell onto the train tracks on the other side of the incline, directly into the path of the 11:41 to Glasgow.

And was lost to the oncoming thunder.

–

DCI Jack Logan and DI Ben Forde sat in the front seats of Logan's Ford Focus, watching Duncan and Catriona Reid take their boy home. The family stopped at the gate, as Logan had advised, to let the press photographers fire off a few hundred snaps in the space of three seconds, and to utter a few rehearsed soundbites.

'We're just grateful to have him home.'

'We thank the police and the community for all their hard work.'

'I'm going to have ice cream!'

That done, Constable Sinead Bell escorted the family up the path, while four other uniformed officers moved in to encourage the press to be on their way.

'You did good, Jack,' Ben said.

Logan didn't respond. Not at first. He kept his eyes fixed ahead as a few spots of rain flecked the windscreen. The sky was once more heavy and fat with dark clouds, and they were doing more to chase off the media vultures than the polis.

'Storm's coming,' said Logan, looking up.

'There's always a new storm on its way up here,' Ben told him. He shrugged. 'We get through them. They all pass, sooner or later.'

They watched Sinead and the Reids disappear inside the house. The liaison was going to hang around for the rest of the day to offer them any immediate support they might need. Connor had been checked over at the hospital, but he was going to need a lot of help going forward. Professional help.

Logan hadn't been able to stress that to the family enough.

'Christ. We should probably let Ed Walker go,' Logan said, his eyes going to the house next door to the Reids.

'God. Aye. I'd forgotten we still had him,' Ben said. 'What about your head?'

Logan reached up and felt the sharp ends of the sutures with the tips of his fingers. 'It's fine.'

'He tried to ruin your youthful good looks.'

Logan chuckled drily. 'Take more than a clout to the head to mess up this mush.'

'No charges, then?' Ben asked.

'No charges.'

They sat in silence a while longer. The press were all getting into their cars and vans. One by one, they were pulling away, leaving the Reids to get on with their lives.

'So, Henderson, then?' said Ben.

'Aye,' Logan confirmed, his contempt evident in just that single word.

'But, I mean… for a *story*? I don't get it. Why would Petrie tell him about Dylan? And, if he did, why didn't Henderson just run with that? He could've found the missing kid. Been a hero.'

'Christ knows,' Logan sighed. 'Maybe Petrie did tell him, or maybe he just figured it out himself, somehow. He's always maintained we didn't do things by the book with the original case. Maybe he thought he could prove he's been right all these years. Get one over on me, or something.'

Logan shrugged. 'Maybe Petrie put him up to it. Or manipulated him into putting Dylan up to it, anyway. Maybe it was all an attempt to cast more doubt on his conviction. He can be a persuasive bastard when he wants to be.'

Ben looked sceptical.

'He's no' the cabbage he makes out he is,' Logan insisted.

Ben tactfully steered the conversation in a different direction. 'You think Henderson would have let Fisher kill Connor?' Ben asked.

Logan blew out his cheeks. 'I don't know. I mean, he was an arsehole to the core, but I'm still not convinced he was a murderer.'

'Guess we'll never know,' Ben said.

Logan nodded. 'Aye. Guess not.'

The front door to the house opened. Sinead emerged and stood on the step, chatting to someone inside. She was all smiles and animated gestures, so Logan guessed it was one of the Reids. Catriona, probably.

'She worked out well,' Ben said. 'You've still got a knack for spotting the good ones.'

'Not always,' said Logan, shooting Ben a disparaging look.

'Funny,' said DI Forde.

Sinead said her farewells and turned away from the house as the door closed.

'Dylan Muir's parents,' he said, still facing front. 'They never find out.'

Ben turned to him. 'You're not serious?'

'I am. Dylan helped kill those two boys. And then… all this. With Connor. Henderson. And Hamza.'

He met Ben's gaze. 'They can't find out. It'd kill them.'

'But isn't it better they know? Isn't it better they get some sort of closure?'

'Not this. Not like this,' Logan said. 'This wouldn't be closure. This would be the end of them.'

'Aye. I mean…' Ben began, but words failed him and he stopped there.

'As far as they know, we're still looking for their boy,' Logan told him.

He turned the key in the ignition as Sinead closed in on the car.

'And we'll never stop.'

Chapter 46

There was a going-away party for Logan in the station canteen. It wasn't a particularly grand affair—DS McQuarrie bought a pack of cakes from the *Farmfoods* up the road, and DC Neish put the kettle on—but it was the thought that counted.

The conversation started slowly, and mostly centered on the case. Gradually, things picked up. They discussed DC Hamza's serious-but-stable condition, the fact that Ben had never got the double chips he'd asked for, and then Sinead had demonstrated, via the medium of mime, what Logan's high-speed driving skills were like.

By the time they were onto Tyler's inability to kick in a door, they were laughing like old friends. But by then, the cherry bakewells had been eaten, and the tea had been drunk, and it was time for the party to come to an end.

Logan wasn't big on goodbyes at the best of times, so he kept things short and sweet. Or sweet by his standards, at least.

'I'll be honest, when I first met you, I wanted to beat the shite out of you,' Logan told DC Neish. 'Nothing personal, mind. It was just the hair. And a bit the face. Mostly the hair, though.'

Tyler grinned and ran his fingers through his immovable locks. He'd reapplied whatever chemical concoction

266

held it in place, and it immediately returned to its original position when he took his hand away.

'You're just jealous, boss,' the DC said.

'Aye. Probably,' Logan admitted. He shook Tyler's hand. 'Good work, son. Pleasure working with you.'

'You, too.'

'Well, "pleasure" is maybe stretching it...' Logan added.

Tyler laughed and stepped away as DS McQuarrie approached. Logan spotted Tyler sidling closer to Sinead, considered putting a stop to it, then decided not to bother just this once.

'Sir,' said Caitlyn, shaking his hand. 'It was good working with you. You have some... interesting methods. I reckon I've learned a thing or two.'

'Oh, God. No, forget anything you've learned from me,' Logan told her. 'Seriously, keep doing it your way. I'm the last person you should be getting inspiration from.'

Caitlyn smiled. 'Yeah. I was just being polite, sir. I'm not going to do any of that.'

Logan wiped a hand across his brow. 'Phew. Had me worried for a minute there.'

And then, it was DI Forde's turn. Neither man said much. They didn't have to. There was a handshake that became a shoulder-pat, then a hug.

'Tell Alice I said hello,' Logan said.

'I will.'

'Does she still hate me, by the way?'

'With the fire of a thousand suns.'

'Jesus, still?'

Ben shrugged. 'You killed Harry.'

'By accident,' Logan stressed.

'We both know it wasn't an accident, Jack,' Ben scolded. 'Anyway, even if it had been, it doesn't matter. You still killed him.'

Both men realised then that the others were staring at them in confusion.

'Harry Pricklepants,' Ben said, as if that explained everything.

'It was this ugly bastard of an ornament,' Logan clarified. 'Little hedgehog with trousers on. It was a mercy killing, if anything.'

The sense of relief from the others was palpable.

'Tell her I said hello, anyway,' Logan told Ben.

DI Forde nodded. 'I'll pass on your best.'

'Mind if I walk you out, sir?' Sinead asked when Logan turned to talk to her.

'Aye, escort this man off the premises, Constable,' DI Forde instructed. He lifted a napkin from the table, revealing the cherry bakewell he'd been keeping hidden, then peeled it out of its little foil case.

'And see that he doesn't come back.'

–

'How's Harris?' Logan asked, as they crossed the car park, headed for Logan's car.

'He's all right. Surprisingly,' Sinead said. 'Our aunt and uncle came down from Nairn. They're going to stay a few days. Jinkies... I mean, Chief Inspector Pickering has said I can take a few days off to get him sorted.'

'Take him up on that,' Logan advised.

'I will, sir. I just... I wanted to be there this afternoon to get Connor home. I wanted to, I don't know, see it through.'

'Aye. I get that,' Logan told her.

They reached the car and stopped by Logan's door. The rain had come down in sheets for half an hour, but now the blanket of cloud had become thin and patchy, allowing glimpses of the blue sky beyond.

The storm was over. For now, at least.

'I wanted to say "thank you", sir,' Sinead said. 'For getting me involved. And for everything with Harris. You didn't have to do either.'

'Well, I kind of do have to help kids who're being held at knifepoint,' Logan pointed out. 'It's pretty much in the job description.'

Sinead smiled and nodded. 'Oh. Is it? I should probably read that at some point.'

Logan wrinkled his nose. 'I wouldn't bother. It's a bit dry, and you can see the ending coming a mile off.'

'Besides,' he added. 'You don't need it. Just keep doing what you're doing. You've got this.'

'Thanks,' Sinead said, blushing slightly. 'So, I suppose it's back to directing traffic and stopping the high school kids drinking down the riverbank at lunchtime,' she said. She smiled dreamily. 'Can't wait.'

'Aye. Well, I wouldn't get too used to it,' Logan told her.

He offered a hand for her to shake, but she stepped in and hugged him, instead. He patted her back a little awkwardly, then she pulled away and stepped back, making room for him to open his door.

'Safe journey, sir.'

'Thanks, Sinead. Tell Harris I'll send him tickets to my next ballet performance. Then we'll see who's laughing.'

'I will, sir.'

Logan opened the car door, shrugged off his coat, then tossed it onto the passenger seat. He was about to get in when Sinead spoke again.

'You should call her, sir.'

Logan paused, one foot in the footwell.

'Your daughter, I mean. You should call her.'

For a moment, Logan looked lost in thought.

'Aye,' he said, climbing into the car. 'Maybe.'

And then, he pulled the door closed, fired up the engine, and the Focus swept out of the car park to begin the long journey south.

–

DC Hamza Khaled regarded the bag of grapes with an expression that was giving very little away.

'Did you check if they're halal, sir?'

Logan's eyes widened. 'What? Shite. No, I thought—'

'I'm kidding,' Hamza said. He grimaced as he shuffled himself up the bed a couple of inches. It was the best he could do for now, but it was a start. 'Sit down, sit down.'

Logan shook his head. 'I'm not stopping. I've got an appointment. Just wanted to stop by and say hello. Make sure they were treating you all right.'

'It's mental, sir,' said Hamza, dropping his voice to a whisper. 'They're treating me like a proper hero. I mean, check it out. Private room. Some of the nurses have even been asking for autographs and selfies. Whatever you do, don't tell them all I did was get myself stabbed.'

'You did a lot more than that, Hamza,' Logan told him. 'A lot more.'

'Says the man who brought Connor home.'

Logan shook his head. 'Team effort. All the way.'

They chatted for a while. About the case. About the attack. About DC Neish's hair.

Logan apologised. Hamza waved it away.

And then, Hamza's wife popped her head impatiently around the door, and it was time for Logan to go.

'I'll check back in tomorrow,' the DCI said. 'Assuming I can fight my way through the mob of fans out front.'

'Aye, good luck with that,' Hamza told him.

He met Logan's eye, and while they said nothing, something passed between them. Some understanding. Some bond.

'So, that's it then, sir? Case closed, all done?'

Logan drew himself up to his full height. 'No' yet, son,' he intoned. 'There's one last thing to take care of.'

Chapter 47

The city had felt more claustrophobic than he remembered as he'd made his way through it, the M8 busier and more choked with traffic as he'd crawled along it, heading east.

His conversation with the receptionist had been brief, but friendly enough. She hadn't asked any questions as he'd signed the book. They knew him well here. Well enough.

'Any joy?' he asked, indicating the open newspaper on her desk. A couple of the jobs had been ringed in black pen. She smiled nervously as she flicked the page.

'I was just having a look,' she said.

'Don't blame you,' Logan replied, finishing his signature with a flourish. He picked up his own newspaper which he'd brought in, then tucked it under his arm. 'Good luck.'

Petrie was sitting in his usual chair, back to the window, glassy doll-eyes fixed on nothing in particular. Logan approached without a word, then stood looming over him, the two men separated only by the little rolling table where Petrie ate his meals.

Still saying nothing, Logan unfolded the newspaper. It was a copy of that day's *Herald*. He could've picked any one of the Scottish dailies, but had selected this one for the impact its combo of headline and image would make.

He placed the newspaper down, turned to give Petrie the best possible view of the front page. Logan watched him, waiting for the moment when the fog behind Petrie's eyes would briefly clear, revealing the monster that lurked within.

When it happened, Petrie's throat tightened, ejecting an involuntary grunt. His eyes met those of a young man in his early twenties. A pencil drawing, but a damn accurate one. Well worth the forty quid.

KIDNAPPER DIES IN TRAIN SUICIDE was the headline. Logan had liked the simplicity of it. No messing. No wordplay. Just the facts, blunt and raw and brutal.

Logan watched as Petrie tried to stop his shoulders shaking. Almost admired the bastard's attempts to hold himself together.

The door opened at his back. Dr Ramesh's voice was one long sigh of exasperation.

'Detective Chief Inspector Logan. I thought I'd told you not to turn up here? I thought I'd explained you couldn't keep doing this?'

'Don't worry, Doctor,' said Logan. 'I'm done here.'

He allowed himself another moment to enjoy Petrie's suffering.

'I'm done.'

And then, he turned to the door, strode out of the hospital, and headed back towards the city he called home.

Read on for an excerpt from

Thicker Than Water

the gripping second instalment in the DCI Logan series
by JD Kirk.

Chapter 1

They were going to get in trouble. She was certain of it.

She was sure she could feel her parents' eyes on her as she slid clumsily down the embankment. Sure her dad would shout after her as she sprackled through the heather. Sure she would hear the rustling of the tent being unzipped, and see the beam of a head torch sweeping across the campsite towards her as she stumbled the final few rocky steps to where the water met the land.

But, she didn't. Instead, she stood there shivering at the shore of the loch, listening to the gentle lapping of the waves and the faster crashing of her own heart.

Nathan was a pace or two ahead of her, the moonlight bathing him as he hopped on one leg and wrestled off a shoe.

'We're not actually doing this, are we?' Lolly asked. They were a good hundred yards from the campsite, tucked out of sight, but the fear of getting caught turned the question into a whispered giggle.

She'd only known Nathan for a day and a half, but he'd quickly turned a tedious family camping holiday in Scotland into much less of a soul-crushing ordeal. He was two years older than her—almost in Sixth Form—and she had immediately taken a shine to him.

He was funnier than the boys back home. Smarter, too. He'd been able to tell her all kinds of stuff about the history of the area. Yes, her dad had told her almost exactly the same information during the drive up, but the difference was that Nathan had explained it in a way that didn't make her want to self-harm. He managed to make it *interesting*.

Mind you, she would quite happily listen to him reading the entire GCSE Maths curriculum, she thought.

He was from just outside Oxford, less than a hundred miles away from where she lived. They'd already made plans to meet up back home the night before, arranging the details via Snapchat. Lolly had lain awake in her sleeping bag for hours, listening to her parents snoring through the dividing canvas wall as she and Nathan swapped messages and photos.

His GIF game was top-notch, and when he'd sent a version of the 'distracted boyfriend' meme to her with one of her own photos superimposed over the face of the attractive passing woman, she'd felt her heart skip half a dozen beats.

It had been momentarily concerning, in fact, before she realised that she wasn't about to go into cardiac arrest and that instead this—*this*—was what love must feel like.

'Yes, we are. But it's freezing!' Nathan yelped, placing a bare foot in the water then immediately yanking it back out again. He kicked off his other shoe and tugged on the end of his sock. 'Come on, hurry up before I get frostbite!'

'You're not exactly making it sound appealing,' Lolly told him, but she pressed the toe of a trainer against the heel of the other shoe and prised it off.

The rocks were smooth and rounded, and she was able to stand on them in her bare feet without too much discomfort. Nathan already had his T-shirt off, and she spent a moment just staring at his exposed top-half, partly in admiration but mostly in shock.

Was this actually happening? She glanced nervously back in the direction of the campsite, still expecting to see that lighthouse-beam of her dad's head torch sweeping out over the water. When she didn't, she wasn't sure if she felt relief or disappointment.

Nathan covered his nipples with two fingers of each hand and fluttered his long eyelashes. Lolly laughed despite her nerves. Or perhaps precisely because of them.

'Don't laugh! You'll make me all self-conscious,' he told her.

She stifled the giggles, and he saw the look of uncertainty that moved in to replace the smile on her face.

'You OK?' he asked, dropping his hands to his sides. He reached down for the T-shirt he'd discarded on the rocks. 'Want me to put this back on?'

Lolly took a moment, then gave a shake of her head. Her fingers went to the buttons of her shirt and she fumbled with them, her hands shaking through cold and nerves and… something else. Anticipation, maybe. She couldn't give a name to it, but she liked it, she thought.

Mostly.

Her skin goose pimpled along her arms as she folded them across her chest and wished that she'd brought a nicer bra with them on holiday, or that she filled better the one she had on.

Nathan didn't seem to mind, though. She heard his breath catch in his throat and hoped that he wouldn't notice her blushing in the darkness.

'Wow,' was all he said, then he set to work unfastening his jeans and wrestling his way out of them.

Once he had struggled his way free, he tossed the jeans down next to his T-shirt and held his arms out, presenting himself like a gameshow prize.

'Ta-daa!'

He grinned at her, showing none of the embarrassment or self-consciousness that Lolly felt. His underwear was tight enough to reveal a bulge that turned Lolly's anticipation into something more apprehensive.

Was she really going to do this?

Nathan noticed where her gaze was pointed and shifted awkwardly. 'It's cold out here, all right?' he said, still smiling. 'That's my excuse, and I'm sticking to it.'

He flicked his gaze to her lower half. 'Your turn,' he said, indicating her cut-off cargo pants.

She kept her arms folded, hugging herself in an attempt to stop the shaking. Her mouth felt dry. She felt like she should say something, tell him this was a mistake, but the words wouldn't come.

What was wrong with her? She liked him. *Really* liked him. And he liked her. So, it was fine, wasn't it? This was how it was supposed to happen. Better here with him, than back home at some party with someone she had no interest in six months from now.

Right?

He stepped in close, derailing her train of thought. The heat of him warmed her. Melted her.

'Hey, it's OK, it's OK,' he soothed, placing his hands on her shoulders. He looked so calm, so serene in the moonlight. Angelic, almost. His skin, unlike her own, was smooth and near-flawless. She felt an urge to run her hand across it, to check if it was real.

'It's just swimming, that's all,' he assured her.

Lolly's voice came as a series of unsteady breaths. 'Is it?'

'If that's what you want, then yeah,' Nathan promised. 'I'm not going to do anything that makes you uncomfortable, OK?'

Lolly swallowed. Nodded.

'OK, then. Good.' He leaned a little closer until she could feel his breath on her skin. 'Trust me, all right?'

She shivered as his fingertips trailed delicately down her arms. Almost spasmed as they tickled down her ribcage, his palms brushing the sides of her covered breasts.

He kissed her. His lips were soft, but the shock of them suddenly pressing against her own hit her like a sledgehammer. She ejected an 'Umf!' of surprise right into his mouth, which made him draw back, a puzzled expression furrowing his brow.

'Sorry,' she whispered, flushed with embarrassment. 'I was just… You just… I wasn't expecting…'

She tensed and closed her eyes as he kissed her again. This time, to her relief, she was able to avoid making any involuntary sounds of surprise, even when she felt his tongue pushing its way into her mouth.

His tongue. His tongue was in her mouth.

On purpose.

Was this nice? She wasn't sure. Probably. It wasn't *not* nice, exactly. Strange, definitely. It wriggled around like a worm in there, brushing against her own.

She wished she'd brushed her teeth before coming out.

She was so focused on the tongue-waggling, and so worried about her dental hygiene, that she didn't notice him working the buttons of her shorts until they dropped down around her ankles.

He was kissing her neck now, less tenderly than he'd kissed her lips. She felt his hand on her bum, kneading one buttock through the thin cotton of her underwear.

Another hand pushed one side of her bra up, briefly exposing her breast before his fingers clamped over it, concealing it again to everything but his touch. He grunted and pressed himself against her, the bulge in his boxers making its presence felt.

'Wait,' Lolly said. 'Stop.'

He paused just long enough to whisper an, 'it's fine,' in her ear before he brought his hand around from her bum and moved it between them. She felt it press against her belly, felt the fingers slide down inside her underwear, stalking down through her pubic hair.

'No, I said *stop*,' she objected, more forcefully than she'd intended. It got the message across, though.

She pushed back from him and saw a flash of frustration screwing up his face. It lasted only a moment, before he masked it behind something kinder and gentler.

'What's wrong?' he asked. 'What's the matter?'

Lolly repositioned her bra and pulled up her shorts.

'What are you doing? Come on,' Nathan said. 'It's just a bit of fun.'

'I don't want to,' Lolly said, not meeting his eye. 'Sorry.'

'What? Why not? I go home tomorrow,' Nathan told her, struggling to hide the impatience in his voice. 'This is our only chance.'

Picking up her shirt, Lolly pushed an arm through the sleeve. 'We can meet up back home. Get to know each other a bit before... before we... you know. Before we do anything.'

'For fuck's sake. What are you, *twelve*?' Nathan spat, and the tone of it hit her like a slap to the face. 'We live a hundred miles apart. We're not going to meet up. This is it.'

'But, I thought we said...'

'Jesus Christ, you actually thought we were going to... what? Become boyfriend and girlfriend? Have a *long-distance relationship*?' Nathan said. The scorn in his voice made Lolly's cheeks sting with shame. 'I hate to break it to you, but that's not going to happen. This is it. This is our only chance. It's now or never.'

Lolly swallowed down her embarrassment and began buttoning her shirt. To her surprise, her hands didn't shake this time. Not one bit.

'Never, then,' she told him.

The firmness in her voice surprised her. From the look on Nathan's face, it surprised him, too.

'Hey, wait. Come on,' he said, his voice softening again as he moved to close the gap between them.

'I swear to God, come near me and I'll cave your head in with a rock,' Lolly warned.

'OK, OK! Jesus,' he said, raising his hands in surrender. 'I'm sorry. Honest. I got carried away. I overstepped the mark. It's just…' He motioned to her. 'I mean, look at you. You're beautiful.'

Lolly said nothing. The breeze coming in across the water toyed with her hair.

'Of course we'll meet up back home. I can get the train over,' Nathan told her. 'We can get to know each other, like you said. Or you can come to me. I'll introduce you to my mates. They're all dicks, though. I feel I should warn you.'

'What, like you?'

'Worse than me,' Nathan said. 'If you can imagine such a thing.'

Lolly sighed. She should be walking away by now, she knew, and yet her feet hadn't found their way back into her trainers.

'Just come swimming. That's all. Just swimming,' Nathan pleaded.

'No thanks,' she said, although not with the same conviction as just a few moments before.

Nathan backed into the water. He was all smiles again, back on the charm offensive. 'But what if Nessie gets me?' he asked. 'You're not going to let me face a big scary monster alone, are you?'

Annoyingly, Lolly felt herself smirk as Nathan kicked back through the waves, his eyes and mouth widening into three circles of surprise.

'Shit! It's cold! How can it be this c-cold?'

'It's Scotland.'

'But it's July!' Nathan said, slapping at his bare arms.

'But it's *Scotland*,' Lolly reiterated.

'I know, but s-still,' Nathan continued through chattering teeth. The water sloshed around him as he forced himself back a few more icy-cold steps. 'You'd think that it'd at least be a *little bit*—'

He went down suddenly, arms flailing, face twisting in panic. There was a yelp, then a splash.

And then silence.

And then nothing.

'Very funny,' Lolly said, watching the spot where he'd gone under.

Ripples expanded lazily across the loch's surface, moonlight dancing across each undulating peak as they steadied back into stillness.

'Nathan?' she said, as loudly as she dared. 'Nathan, this isn't funny.'

She took a step closer to the water, then cried out in shock when he exploded up from below, eyes wide, breath coming in fast, frantic gasps. He grabbed for her. At first, she thought he was trying to pull her in with him, but then she saw the fear on his face and the panic in his movements.

'What? What's the matter?' Lolly yelped, her voice becoming shriller as Nathan's terror awoke the same response in her. 'What is it? What's wrong?'

Slipping and stumbling, Nathan dragged himself clear of the water, clawing his way up onto the rocks on his hands and knees, coughing and wheezing. Lolly saw a dark shape following, sliding out of the water right behind him. He kicked out at it, squealing now like an injured animal, but a long blue tendril was tangled around his foot, attaching him to the shapeless mass.

No, not shapeless. Not exactly.

As the dark water fell away and the moonlight played across the thing, Lolly saw a hand, fingers curling upwards like the legs of a dead spider.

She saw an arm, cold and blue.

She saw a face. Eyeless, yet somehow staring at her from within the folds of a bright green tarpaulin shroud. Begging. Pleading.

Accusing.

With the dark water lapping around her feet, and the cool night air swirling around the rest of her, Lolly screamed and screamed and *screamed*.

Q&A with JD Kirk

What do you love about the crime genre? Why do you write crime fiction?

I hadn't read many crime novels until I started writing them. I'm not drawn to any particular genre as much as I am to characters, whether individually, or in a group. When I had the initial idea for the first DCI Logan book, I didn't think I'd ever get around to writing it, because crime wasn't my thing. As my subconscious worked away on it, though, I began to develop this cast of characters who would be involved in the investigation, and it was that lot of misfits that I fell in love with more than the crime genre itself.

That said, I've now read plenty of crime novels, and the ones I really enjoy are in line with my own – a dysfunctional 'family' that is slung together in a quest for justice. I think that description fits a lot of books in a lot of genres, but it's very common in crime fiction, particularly police procedurals like the ones I write.

Your novels have such a fantastic balance of gritty crime and humour. Do you think that's important for a crime novel?

I think it all depends on the reader. Personally, I struggle to read anything that doesn't have at least a suggestion of humour in there. I think it's rare for life to be unrelentingly grim without the odd funny moment. Even when things are at their bleakest, we often use humour as a coping mechanism. My dad, sister, and I have never laughed together as much as we did at my mum's funeral, for example (sorry, Mum!) From talking to front line emergency services workers, many of them have said that without a sense of humour, they couldn't cope with the things they have to deal with, so I felt it was important to reflect that in the DCI Logan series.

A Litter of Bones has some brilliant, vivid scenes. Do you have a favourite scene in the novel?

The first scene – where the dad returns from looking for his dog in the trees and finds his son is missing – will always be a big favourite of mine, as it was based on something that happened with my daughter and I, and ultimately led to the creation of the whole series. However, I also love DCI Logan's first time in the Highlands, when a sheep wanders into the crime scene, and he realises he's not in the big city anymore!

You are a very prolific writer! How do you come up with so many ideas? Where does your inspiration come from?

I've written well over 200 books across a range of genres, under a dozen or more pen names, and ideas are constantly pinging around inside my head.

I sometimes describe my brain as being like a room with a dozen different radios all playing different things. Sometimes, something one of the voices says will prompt me to come up with the germ of an idea, then I'll ask questions about the idea until I have a fully fledged story outline.

I explained this to my neurodiverse daughter and she said, 'You have ADHD.' So, maybe that's something to do with it.

There are so many fantastic characters in the DCI Logan series. Do you have a favourite character to write?

This feels a bit like I'm being asked to pick my favourite child! I love writing all of them, but if I had to narrow it down, I'd say it's between the loveable, upbeat, and sometimes accident-prone DC Tyler Neish, and the foul-mouthed whirling dervish of anger and violence that is Robert Hoon.

Or maybe Bob's sister, Berta. Or Shona, the pathologist, or Heather, or Ace, or... Oh, I don't know! I love them all, and you can't make me choose!

Do you love crime fiction and are always on the lookout for brilliant authors?

Canelo Crime is home to some of the most exciting novels around. Thousands of readers are already enjoying our compulsive stories. Are you ready to find your new favourite writer?

Find out more and sign up to our newsletter at canelocrime.com